# SAGAS &
# SEA SMOKE

## SUSAN NICOL

**◆ FriesenPress**

Suite 300 - 990 Fort St
Victoria, BC, V8V 3K2
Canada

www.friesenpress.com

. Excerpts from the Saga of the Greenlanders adapted from various translations, including:

- *The Norse Discovery of America*, A.M. Reeves, N.L. Beamish and R.B. Anderson (London: Norroena Society, 1907).

- *The Vinland Sagas: The Norse Discovery of America*, Magnus Magnusson, and Hermann Pálsson (ed. and trans.) (Harmondsworth: Penguin, 1968).

- *Saga of the Greenlanders*. At notendur.hi.is/haukurth/utgafa/ greenlanders.html. (Accessed June 7, 2018).

*Relativity* limerick, A.H. Reginald Buller (Punch, December 1923).

ISBN
978-1-5255-3158-3 (Hardcover)
978-1-5255-3159-0 (Paperback)
978-1-5255-3160-6 (eBook)

*1. FICTION, HISTORICAL*

Distributed to the trade by The Ingram Book Company

# Acknowledgments

With grateful thanks for the guidance and counsel of my college writing instructor, the late architect/musician/film and TV producer Neil Harris; for the wisdom of my beta readers and alpha advisors, historian Erik Thomson, writer/arts facilitator Patricia Greenwell, journo/communications strategist Amanda Lefley, and artist/world traveller Marion Mearon; and for the exceptional astuteness of my husband, Dennis Mearon, in *not* offering counsel (other than to take a break occasionally). Your collective insight is deeply appreciated.

# CHAPTER ONE
## Voyage of Discovery

*Then Bjarni Herjolfsson said, "This voyage of ours will be considered foolhardy, for not one of us has ever sailed the Greenland Sea." However, they put to sea as soon as they were ready and sailed for three days, until the land disappeared below the horizon. Then, the fair wind died down, and they were beset by fogs and north winds until they lost all track of their course. This went on for many days, and then the sun came out again, so they could get their bearings. They hoisted sail and sailed all day before they sighted land. They wondered what country this might be, but it was Bjarni's opinion that it could not be Greenland. They asked him, was he going to land, but he said, "It is my advice that we only skirt the shore." As they did so, they found that the land was not mountainous (like Greenland), but covered with small wooded knolls.*

*—Saga of the Greenlanders*

The Greenland saga—in its Old Icelandic vernacular and her amma's soft staccato voice—echoed in her memory as Audrey Vincent squinted through the oily window of the tour boat's cabin. She yearned to see clearly the wooded knolls described by Bjarni Herjolfsson after Atlantic gales blew his *knarr*-style Viking cargo ship far south of his mountainous Greenland destination.

Audrey stretched the cuff of her hoodie over the heel of her left hand and wiped the grime from the glass. She pushed the other cuff above her watch and noted the time it took to reach each promontory and every bay of the conifer-clad coastline. Her work had begun.

It was much later in the day when she saw it: a jutting cape rising high out of the sea, just as the saga described it, with a cove to shelter a ship and plenty of timber to build a home. She grabbed her rubber-clad phone and took photographs. Then she turned to the two men locked in a conversation about hockey not ten feet away—her companion, Luc Laliberte, and his newfound friend, Brian Rickman, the boat's captain. It was clear she would not easily catch the attention of either. By the time she turned back to the window, the cape had vanished. After closing her eyes to recall the image more vividly, she tapped every detail into the note section of her phone.

Eventually, the Newfoundland coast morphed into mostly rock with empty bog beyond. Audrey bowed her hooded head slightly so as not to make eye contact with the men, crossed the boat's tiny cabin to her coffee cup, and faded past the still oblivious sports fans. Then she padded up a few short steps and confidently strode the open deck to the bow.

It was eerily still, as it must have been that day over one thousand years ago when the winds halted and Herjolfsson and his crew likely became the first Europeans to scan the shores of North America. She could hear wooden oars dipping rhythmically into glassy water.

The sun was on the verge of setting. She could see the land well enough, but not all the surrounding sea. It was open in spots, revealing a marvellously mirrored surface, but the view was largely veiled with a dense brume, more ancient than the sea itself. It wafted over the water and dangerously shrouded its source—mountains of blue-white glacier ice that slid past like ghostly ships of the gods.

Audrey knew the icebergs were present even when she couldn't see them; she could hear them groan and shudder, and could feel their frigid fearfulness in her soul. She snapped more shots with her phone. It was so quiet she could hear the clicking sound effects over the clanging heartbeat of the tour boat's motor.

"*Aud!*" Luc shouted. Audrey jumped, spilling some of her coffee. She licked it off her hand as she turned to see Luc's gleeful grin and the light beaming from the upraised phone in his hand. He had obviously intended to startle her. "What are you doing out here?" He chuckled. "It's colder than Hades!"

Luc's playfulness was out of character. Her former schoolmate was always intently focused on his studies in journalism or on odd jobs to pay for them.

Now he appeared carefree, revelling in the early days of this adventure. It would be the closest he had come to a vacation since he was twelve years old. She winced only slightly at his use of the name abbreviation she so despised. Being called "odd" by schoolchildren still haunted her.

"You mean Ragnarok," she replied.

"What's that?" he said, as he swept her up in a rare moment of unchecked affection and plunked her back on the deck.

"Ragnarok," she repeated. "Hades was the Greek concept of hell. Ragnarok was the Norse apocalypse—endless winter."

"Sounds like the Vikings discovered Manitoba first, not Newfoundland," Luc quipped. "You know, Captain Brian was sure quick to talk hockey when he found out we're from Winnipeg. He goes to all the IceCaps games in St. John's. The IceCaps are the Jets' farm club."

Audrey adopted a suitably vacant stare. "This must be how you feel when I make obscure historical references."

Luc's half grin reappeared, etching the dimple on his left cheek even deeper into his face. Then he pointed to the crest on his hockey jersey. "You know about the Winnipeg Jets, the National Hockey League team that returned home two seasons ago after a fifteen-year absence?"

"Yes, but you lost me with the cappuccino."

Luc laughed. "IceCaps is the name the Jets gave their farm club—" Luc caught himself, paused, and then explained further, "their *minor league player development team*—when they moved it to Newfoundland. It used to be called the Manitoba Moose, but Newfoundlanders told them not to use the name 'Moose'. Turns out, moose overrun this island and cause all kinds of accidents. So, they called the team the St. John's IceCaps instead, after icebergs. Damn, Audrey. I could've sworn I saw you with a Canadian passport at the airport."

"*Now* I understand why guys find sports so fascinating," Audrey deadpanned.

Luc sighed, then unexpectedly inhaled an icy shot of salt air. His shoulders jumped to his ears reflexively, and he jammed his bare hands into his jeans. "Crap, it *is* freezing out here. That damp cold is a thing!"

Audrey sipped her coffee once again and instinctively turned northeast, looking across the sea to Norway, the original home of her fabled ancestor, Eirik the Red. Luc took the cup from her hands, placed it on the deck, wrapped his hands around her waist, and marched her to the very edge of the bow.

"Let's do the '*I'm Flying*' scene from *Titanic*!" he exclaimed, as he suspended her beyond the bow rails.

She was frightened at first, but then relieved when she felt his clamp-like grip—enough to raise her arms like wings and briefly close her eyes. She felt as if she had transformed into a living figurehead, the elaborate carving used to adorn the prows of ships since ancient Egyptian times.

"You know those are actual icebergs out there, eh?" she said, as she lowered her arms and lifted her eyelids again. "The *Titanic* sank just four hundred miles south of Newfoundland." She smirked when she felt him freeze with the sudden realization. An iceberg moaned and emerged from the fog on cue. "Welcome to Iceberg Alley."

"Goddamn you kids and that goddamned movie. Get the hell back in here!" roared Captain Brian through the speakers on the cabin. "Flatlanders! No rogue wave of wheat will ever sweep you to yer death, but a real one can knock you off yer pins soon enough. And we're about to dock, so grab yer gear and get ready."

Luc took Audrey's hand and started back, chastened. On the way, Audrey gazed seaward one more time, then froze to the deck. He gave her hand a tug, then turned to see why she hadn't moved. Her other hand pointed to a suspended veil of fog. "*Fire!*" she screamed.

Captain Brian steadied the boat and dashed to the deck. He glared first at Audrey and then at the line of her outstretched arm. He saw the evaporation fog in the distance and the glow of the setting sun on the craggy ice behind it.

"That be sea smoke! A fog cloud from a berg."

"I see a *húsasnotra*! The *knarr* is on fire!" The terror on her face was real as she watched the magnificent dragon figurehead catch alight, with its shrouded cargo smouldering its way into Valhalla.

Audrey turned to Luc and Captain Brian, her eyes pleading for action. They stared back at her, mouths agape. She glanced back at the burning ship, but this time saw only fog and a shimmering shard of ice. She was abundantly thankful when she realized she had shouted the last statement in Icelandic.

"Don't you think it's awfully close?" she pretended to ask again with alarm, this time in English. Then she bent down, scooped up her coffee cup, and slipped between the speechless men.

*** 

Audrey was rolling her highly functional, high-end luggage away from the pier with one hand and adroitly texting messages with the other while Luc was still tipping Captain Brian for a safe and entertaining voyage.

"You needs to watch out for that one," Captain Brian said, as he nodded his carrot top toward Audrey. "She's not all there, is she?"

Luc bristled at first, but then he saw Audrey continue to walk, head down, into the traffic at the end of the parking lot.

"I will, and thanks again," he said, quickly grabbing his duct-taped hockey bag to chase after her.

"Audrey!" Luc shouted. She stopped, turned, and waved her phone as if it held treasure. A two-ton delivery truck whizzed inches past her carry-on, which had been converted into a backpack.

Luc laboured across the lot, overstuffed hockey bag in one hand and the ragged backpack he didn't have time to don in the other.

"I'm getting all my emails now. There must be good cell coverage here!" Audrey exclaimed. "I've got one from Dr. Olsen. She wants me to contact her as soon as I get to the Views of Vinland Hotel. But first, I must find a washroom. Watch my bags for me?"

Luc caught his breath as Audrey headed toward a convenience store. Memories of last summer flooded back. He tried to shake his feelings of foreboding as he fumbled for his own phone.

When Audrey returned, she was still exuberant. She had changed clothes and brushed her hair, which flowed like milk chocolate over her shoulders. Her eyes, which seemed to change colour depending on how she was feeling and what she was wearing, now appeared a deep blue, matching the denim jacket that replaced her hoodie. They also glinted with flecks of gold like the cartouche that always hung from the chain around her neck.

The only other time Luc had ever seen her this joyful was at the beginning of last summer's dig. He became aware of the real reason he was here. He felt compelled to be her guardian.

"I speak several languages and still couldn't understand their Newfoundland dialect." Audrey laughed as she gestured toward the store. "I had a heck of a time trying to get information."

"It's called Newfinese. I had a tough time with Aunt Peggy too," Luc said, shaking his phone as if she were inside. "I *think* she said she'd be here soon. I'm sure glad she sent Captain Brian to pick us up. It would've taken more than twelve hours of driving a rental over to Deer Lake and up the Viking Trail to get here from St. John's."

"That ferry ride was long enough, but it was awesome to see the coastline from the sea, just as the Norse would've done," Audrey beamed. "Now I understand why they call Newfoundland 'the Rock.'"

"It's not really a ferry, Audrey. It's a tour boat—for sightseeing. Captain Brian was just repositioning it here from St. John's for the season. He doesn't normally make that trip, even though he's promised to take us back in September, so don't be mentioning him to the UNESCO crowd," Luc warned.

"How much do I owe you?"

"Don't worry about it. Aunt Peggy paid him up front. Part of the keep I'm earning by doing odd jobs at her B&B." Luc grinned playfully. "And I'm sure I can find a way for you to make it up to me."

Audrey smiled wryly. "I don't think I'm ready for this barter economy. I'll calculate the cost myself and buy you dinner and drinks till we're even."

Luc smirked as he took panoramic shots of the jumbled mix of neutral-coloured and white-siding buildings clustered around the cove. So, this was St. Anthony. He wasn't sure he was ready for this peculiar place, either. His nose was still adjusting to the damp tang of fish and seaweed. While Audrey had been a world traveller since birth, this was the farthest he had ever been from home.

"Why aren't you staying with the other Young Canada Works students?" Audrey asked, as if she could read his mind. "It doesn't sound like you and your aunt are very close."

"She's my great-aunt. With the YCW program, you have to pay for your own accommodations. It made sense for me to stay with her in St. Lunaire-Griquet. It's not that far from L'Anse aux Meadows, and she isn't charging me anything. Besides," he teased, "it will be easier for me to keep my eye on you if I'm on my own."

"Wait, what? You patronizing jerk! I'm quite capable of taking care of myself."

"That so?" Luc asked. "Where's your backpack?"

Audrey's hands flew to her shoulder blades. Then she sprinted back to the convenience store in a blur of brown hair and blue denim.

When she returned, backpack in hand, she kept her head down, checking each compartment for every item. Just then, Captain Brian reappeared. He had reversed his yellow rain jacket to its soft-shelled beige interior for wearing in town.

"So's yer Aunt Peggy coming?" he asked.

Luc nodded as Audrey, with her head almost buried in her backpack, chastised him once again. "You bastard! How long were going to wait to tell me?"

Captain Brian laughed. "And you swears yer not a couple!"

At the sound of the captain's voice, Audrey snapped her head up. Her peaches and cream complexion turned watermelon red. "Oh, hello. Didn't see you there. Obviously. But since you are, I have a question. How fast were we travelling on the way here?"

"Sorry, what's that you say?" Captain Brian stumbled.

"How fast were we travelling along the coast? I marked the time between certain landmarks, but I need the velocities to calculate distances. Knots will do."

The captain gave Luc an "Is she for real?" look. Luc replied in the affirmative with pursed lips and a barely perceptible nod. The captain accepted the pad and pencil Audrey gave him, wrote down the speeds as well as he could remember them, and warily passed the pad back.

"Those numbers are a tad past what most would recommend, so I wouldn't be advertising the fact," he said. Again, with only a raised eyebrow, he silently asked Luc if she could be trusted. Luc raised his chin slightly, then lowered it along with his eyelids.

"Aye, well, here's me card then," Captain Brian said, and handed it to Audrey. "In case you two part company before it's time to return in

September." Then he touched the grimy end of his cap and strode with a rolling gait to the nearest pub.

Audrey gathered up her suitcases and backpack. "I studied body language in psych, you know. You both think I'm an idiot."

"So says the girl with a Rhodes Scholarship," Luc replied. "When it comes to the days of yore, Aud, you're a genius; it's just that your here-and-now needs a little work."

"I don't need a babysitter."

"What happened on deck, Audrey?"

"Is that why you came? You think I'll have another episode! Did my parents put you up to this?"

"I told you, Parks Canada only notified me last week that I got this job. It was like winning the lottery. I only had a 300-in-90,000 chance of landing one anywhere in the country, never mind here. Besides," he said, his tone becoming conciliatory, "I scored a national journalism award by breaking the story on your last discovery. I plan to nail an international award with your next one."

Tears of fear welled in her eyes. "One-in-three hundred," she said.

Luc looked at her, mystified.

"If there were three hundred jobs available and ninety-thousand applicants, you had a one-in-three hundred chance of landing a Young Canada Works position. To truly assess the odds of getting the specific job you wanted out of the options available, you need to factor in the other variables. You're a carded Métis. Most sites in the country need Indigenous interpreters. You have experience doing exactly that. You have an arts degree. You're bilingual—"

With his head thrown back in awe, Luc interrupted her. "Okay, okay, I get it. I'm a lucky asshole."

Audrey tried to wipe her eyes surreptitiously with the corner of her jacket cuff. "Actually, I was trying to point out that the odds weren't as high as you think."

"I'm not a lucky asshole?" He smirked.

"You got the job because you're highly qualified for it. Let's just enjoy the experiences we'll have this summer and forget about the past, okay?"

"So says the archeologist."

It was Audrey's turn to snicker. "An archeology joke. Not bad. Let me rephrase. We shouldn't spoil the present by worrying about something that might not even happen in the future."

"Sorry. You know my motto," Luc mocked. "Life's a bitch and then you die."

Audrey added, "And then some random archeologist digs you up and sticks you in a museum."

The pair passed the time alternately discussing their itineraries and updating their social media profiles. Luc was about to make another phone call when an ancient Dodge pickup truck with rounded fenders and a missing grill rolled up to the parking lot. He noted with amusement the flat red barn paint and mismatched hubcaps. Aunt Peggy, wearing an enormous straw hat and an equally wide-brimmed smile, leaned sideways to peer through the passenger window.

"Forgive me, luv, but I have to ask. Are you Luc Laliberte? It's been a bloody age since I saw you last!"

"You haven't changed a bit, Aunt Peggy," Luc lied, as he lifted their luggage into the truck box.

"And you must be Audrey."

Audrey smiled. "Yes, ma'am, I am."

"Ma'am? Oh, you've done well for yourself, Luc! A lady for the lad. Well, hurry up and get in. We're going to be late."

Luc opened the door for Audrey, who gave her luggage, with her precious laptop inside, a worried glance through the back window.

"What are we going to be late for, Aunt Peg?" he asked.

"We're heading to the Legion for a Scoff and Scuff."

Luc flashed Audrey a rakish smile.

"I didn't think they started till mid-June," said Audrey, who, as always, had done her homework.

"Parks Canada just booked the Legion to put on a special Scoff and Scuff for all the scientists and government mucky-mucks coming into L'Anse aux Meadows. I suspect that includes *you,* luv," Aunt Peggy said as she patted Audrey's arm. "I have to work the damn thing. I'm sneaking you in, Luc, so I don't have to feed you later. Okay by you?"

"I'm just about gut-foundered," Luc replied in what he hoped was the local dialect for 'I'm hungry.'

"Well, aren't you the smart-arse, Mr. Wikipedia? Don't get too comfortable, the Legion's just up here on East Street."

Audrey was enthralled by the rugged and ready edges to the town, as if the well-kept and often new houses were plunked down in the rolling wilderness with little opportunity to do much more than cut the bit of grass in front.

St. Anthony reminded Luc of northern Manitoba towns. Nothing fancy. Few flower beds or fences. But he did note a surprising lack of stucco.

The Royal Canadian Legion building took them both aback. It was in a predominantly residential area, although there was no apparent evidence in St. Anthony of a zoning plan. Aunt Peggy suddenly revved her truck up a rise of cement that had been poured right over a sidewalk. The parking lot was nearly full beside a nondescript, elongated structure covered in white and baby blue siding. The foundation was painted a bright royal blue. A small sign at foot level near the entrance advertised, "Newfie SCOFF, Wednesday at 4 p.m."

Aunt Peggy found an open parking spot and neatly backed her truck against a steep grassy embankment. It had steps cut into it that led to a fenced area above with flagpoles, a cenotaph, and woods beyond.

Luc and Aunt Peggy exited quickly and headed for the building. Audrey hung back, eyeing her luggage in the open truck box.

"Don't worry about yer bags, luv, they're safe enough in these parts. Unless a bloody moose falls over the fence, and that wouldn't be the first time. Me doors are wonky, so I can't lock them up in the cab anyways. The bags, that is, not the moose."

Audrey followed slowly at first, fingers flying on her phone. Then she raced up to join them before they entered the building.

"It's okay," she whispered to Luc. "Dr. Olsen's already here."

"Good," said Luc, "because I'd be going in anyway. I'm hungry enough to eat a moose. I hope there's one on the menu."

Once inside, Luc's grin grew all the wider. The interior looked like any Legion hall he had ever frequented in Manitoba's Interlake region. Plain, but welcoming. Utilitarian, but adaptable. Pictures of Queen Elizabeth and Prince Philip and an electronic bingo board mounted on the wall. However, the military rifle with a fixed bayonet hanging over the wood-panelled bar was a decidedly different decoration.

"Where do I buy drink tickets, Aunt Peg?" Luc inquired eagerly.

Aunt Peggy leaned over and whispered to Luc just loud enough for Audrey to hear as well. "First, b'y, don't ever call me Peg again or I'll stick one up yer arse. I was teased to death as a kid, and I've no desire to relive those times again."

Audrey stuck a knuckle in her mouth and bit down hard to stop from laughing.

"Second, there's no tickets tonight, it's an open bar. And wipe that smile of joy off yer mug because you'll not be shaming me by getting half-cut here. Those are real mucky-mucks at the head table; you can tell because those tablecloths are linen, not plastic. The bugger's that's got hair is the mayor of St. Anthony, the bugger that's losing his is the premier of Newfoundland and Labrador, and the woman with the poufy hair is a cabinet minister of something or other from Ottawa. You two can drink a beer, wine with dinner, and yer Screech, but that's it, wha? Am I clear? Now excuse me, there's cod to cook, it's Fish and Brewis tonight."

Luc turned to Audrey. "I need my DSLR and a fresh shirt."

Audrey turned to Luc. "I need a blazer and dress pants."

Both raced back to the truck.

"Your bag's on the driver's side," Luc called out as he ripped off his Jets jersey on a dead run.

Audrey, also on the run, glanced over and was struck by the breadth of his shoulders and definition of his abs.

Luc reached the truck box first, leapt over the side in one bound, and unzipped his hockey bag. The jersey went in, a white shirt came out, and he donned it unbuttoned. While he was rooting for his camera, Audrey reached the truck and adroitly jumped into the back. She swapped her denim jacket for a black blazer, found matching dress pants, and stretched her tank top over her derriere while deftly dropping her jeans. She would have managed to pull up the dress pants without exposing any underwear if there hadn't been an enormous face staring at her from above. She screamed and fell backwards over her suitcase.

Luc looked up, also screamed, and fell backwards over his hockey bag. The pair lay there for a few moments transfixed by the big brown eyes of a moose hanging its head over the fence directly above the truck.

Without taking his eyes off the animal, Luc slowly reached with one hand for his camera. He wished it were a rifle. Audrey reached for her phone. For several moments, they quietly snapped photos until the moose became bored, turned back toward the wood, and slowly loped away.

It took a while for the pair to stop laughing.

"We better get back in there," Luc said eventually. "If anyone saw us right now, they'd think we've been making out." As Audrey scrambled on her hands and knees to find her pants, Luc quickly brought the DSLR to his eyes and silently shot a memorable image of her well-rounded, thong-exposed buttocks.

Once back inside the Legion, Luc secured a beer and a prime spot at the front of the hall by claiming to be media. He had shrewdly retained a press pass from an internship with APTN—the Aboriginal Peoples Television Network. Audrey recognized Dr. Anna Olsen at the head table and managed to introduce herself before the formalities began.

Dr. Olsen was a relative of Anne Stine Ingstad, the Norwegian archeologist who, along with her explorer husband Helge Ingstad, discovered the Norse buildings at L'Anse aux Meadows in 1960. In 1978, after the area was identified as the only verified Norse encampment in North America (established about five hundred years before Columbus set sail), it was declared to be the planet's very first UNESCO World Heritage Site. Olsen had always wanted to examine it further, but after each previous excavation, the site had been reburied to protect it. It had taken her over a year to acquire the approvals and funding for another dig.

Audrey was surprised at her elegance. Her fair hair was tightly drawn back into a sleek chignon, her makeup was impeccable, and her fingernails, although free from polish, were meticulously shaped and buffed. She wore a designer-label tweed jacket and skirt with classic heels. A gold cartouche lay among the pearls around her neck.

Audrey was also surprised at how warmly Dr. Olsen greeted her. It was as if she were acknowledging a kindred spirit.

"I am so pleased you were able to respond to the sudden change of plans," Dr. Olsen said in a Norwegian accent with vaguely British overtones. "Originally, this was to be a fun welcoming party for young people later in the evening. I thought we would have plenty of time to meet at the Views of Vinland Hotel first, but the press secretaries for all three levels of government found out about it. They decided it would make a good photo opportunity. Naturally, I have been tied up ever since."

Dr. Olsen led her to the front of a nearby table.

"Audrey, allow me to introduce you to a new colleague. This is Alexis McQueen from Trent University. She is a protégée of your parents. She volunteered to email you about this event. Alexis will be your roommate for the next two weeks while the UNESCO personnel are here for the launch of the dig. Apparently, accommodations in the area are at a premium."

The two young women stared at each other in barely masked alarm; Alexis, because she purposely did *not* let Audrey know of the change in plans, and Audrey, because she had specifically requested a private room because of her very private issues.

They greeted each other woodenly.

"Excuse me, it looks like the formalities are about to begin," said Dr. Olsen. "I'll let you two become better acquainted."

Alexis' keen eyes quickly spotted the cartouches worn by Dr. Olsen, her hero, and Audrey Vincent, her new rival. They indicated both women had visited Egypt, at least once. She watched in envy as the oblong pendant with Audrey's name in hieroglyphics swung from her neck as she took her seat. She did note that Audrey's cartouche and chain looked older than Dr. Olsen's. Much older.

Audrey was astonished at Alexis' appearance. She looked like a pop star at a posh nightclub instead of a rookie archeologist in a small-town Legion hall. Her breast-length blond hair was meticulously spun into matching rows of curls. Her lips were emblazoned in a fashionable shade of red. She was wearing false eyelashes, and her metallic silver dress barely covered her lap. Her paper serviette was longer.

Then there was the matter of the missing email.

"Sorry, I didn't get your message." Audrey apologized in a very Canadian manner for something she was not responsible for, although in this case, she hoped the double entendre would be clear. She *was* sorry she didn't get the email because she was unable to prepare properly for the event.

"You didn't? We're in such a remote area, the cell coverage must be bad. And yet, here you are. How fortunate." Audrey noted that the pitch of Alexis' voice was just a little too high, indicating tense vocal chords. And while her smile was model perfect, the lack of muscle movement around her eyes betrayed her disingenuousness.

It was one of those crossroads incidents in a human relationship. Audrey could have faked a smile in return, dismissed the matter, and started afresh with this new acquaintance. But she was too fatigued to bother. Instead, she remained stony faced and stared down Alexis' wolf blue eyes, clearly demonstrating that she knew she was lying. There was no going back.

Thankfully, the formalities began shortly thereafter. In a feat that could only be accomplished in Newfoundland, the speeches from Aunt Peggy's "mucky-mucks" proved highly entertaining. Students and experienced archeologists from across Canada and around the globe laughed heartily. Some until they cried.

Then the Fish and Brewis was produced. Alexis poked at it as if its various components were still alive. "I don't understand why you'd mix cod and crackers together," she said.

"Brewis isn't so much a cracker than it is a large biscuit," Audrey corrected. "It's rehydrated hardtack. And those cubes you're examining are scruncheons. Fried pork back fat."

"Well, that sounds *so* much better," Alexis responded sarcastically. She noted Audrey's upright posture and how elegantly she handled the cutlery, as if she'd been educated in an upscale finishing school as opposed to the hard-scrabble, inner-city schools Alexis had attended. Charitable bursaries had covered the cost of Alexis' graduate degree in anthropology from Trent. *Shit, she even looks like Kate Middleton*, Alexis fumed silently.

Audrey was thankful for the arrival of the Quebecois undergrad and the British professor who asked to assume the seats beside them. Until they spoke.

"Oh my god, you are Manitoba Jones!" Gabrielle Bédard gushed, as she recognized Audrey on sight. While Audrey's face remained immobile, her eyelids fell shut. She was mortified by the nickname Luc had given her when he publicized her achievement from her fieldwork studies. Gabrielle continued to rave. "I read about your discovery at The Forks Historic Site in Winnipeg. A cache of three-thousand-year-old trading goods! That must have been so exciting!"

"News of the find even reached Britain," added Dr. Clive Osborne, a professor at a British centre for Viking studies. "Although we know you as Audrey Vincent."

Audrey managed an embarrassed smile. It was the first time anyone had identified her by her own reputation. This was the kind of notoriety her professors-turned-television-celebrity-parents regularly received, not her.

"I don't know what to say. Thank you, I suppose? I'm still not sure why I was centred out or given that silly moniker. I was part of a very large team that uncovered over four hundred thousand artifacts."

"But wasn't it you who looked outside the search grid and found the cache?" Dr. Osborne asked.

The conversation had strayed into a very uncomfortable area.

"The Forks site is huge. The fieldwork had to concentrate on the area slated for construction of the Canadian Museum for Human Rights. I happened to stumble across an intact ceramic vessel by the Red River during a work break. Oh look, here comes the Figgy Duff!"

As everyone else consumed steamed pudding and coffee, Alexis was being consumed by jealousy, so much so, her eyes even watered. The sickening feeling of inadequacy she felt as a child resumed its gnawing habitation in her gut. At first, she blamed it on the Fish and Brewis, but when she heard the praise bestowed on Audrey by complete strangers, she recognized it for what it was. This same feeling once drove her to attack schoolmates physically when she couldn't beat them in the classroom or on the sports field. That, in turn, led to years of counselling.

Alexis rose unsteadily on her stilettos to make her way to the restroom. Then she spotted an opportunity to prove her superiority in at least one arena. Her wolf eyes sparkled at the sight of the handsome young man striding up to her table.

His blue-black hair was captured in a man bun at the back of his head and he sported a stylishly rogue day's growth of beard. Alexis flashed the sexiest smile she had ever practiced in a mirror selfie. And then—disaster! He didn't even cast an errant look her way. He walked right past her and stretched out his hand to Audrey.

Reticently, Audrey placed her hand in his and rose from the table.

"Excuse me," Luc said to her dinner companions. "I hope you don't mind me borrowing Audrey for a little while."

"Gabrielle, Professor Osborne, Alexis: this is Luc," Audrey announced. "I'll be right back—I hope."

From that moment, Alexis determined her mission this summer was to take everything she could from this well-born, well-connected, and well-respected young woman: her job, her reputation, and her good-looking boyfriend. Knowing how to destroy people was the one skill she knew she possessed in full measure.

Luc wrapped Audrey's arm around his in an overtly chivalrous gesture. It made Audrey nervous. It made Luc feel secure that she couldn't bolt when she saw what lay ahead.

Stepping in front of the head table, the emcee, now wearing bright yellow mariner rainwear, gestured for volunteers to bring buckets of salt water, rubber boots, and bright yellow Sou'wester hats.

"Now we come to the most important part of the evening when all you come-from-aways get a chance to be screeched-in as honorary residents of Newfoundland and Labrador," the emcee proclaimed with practiced bravado. "Before we ask for volunteers from the audience, I call on the Canadian Minister of Heritage and Official Languages and Dr. Olsen of the UNESCO World Heritage Centre to join us out front here." Then he gestured to the Newfoundland dignitaries at the head table. "I know the rest of you are Newfoundlanders already from how much free wine you drank at dinner."

The audience laughed again. Audrey began to pull away, but Luc reminded her about their pledge to enjoy all present opportunities to their fullest. She acquiesced when it looked like he was leading her to the area in front, but to the far end of the head table. At the last minute, he stepped back and deferred to the minister of heritage rounding the table from the left side, then cleverly positioned Audrey beside her. Dr. Olsen, arriving from the right side, joined Audrey to her immediate left.

Luc stepped back and smiled, thinking how pleased his public relations instructor would be at such a clever manoeuvre. Then he picked up his camera and lenses from the media table and began to focus on the trio. As other archeologists and volunteers filed in beside them, Audrey, who was now the centre of attention, was ready to strangle Luc.

The emcee ordered the initiates to don a Sou'wester hat and a rubber boot, then to place that boot in a bucket of saltwater. They were then handed a piece of paper to recite after he asked, "Do you want to become a proper Newfoundlander?"

The initiates wildly shouted, "Yes, b'y!" and the chant that followed managed to sound quite lyrical.

"From the waters of the Avalon, to the shores of Labrador,
We've always stuck together with a rant and with a roar,
To those who've never been, soon they'll understand,
From coast to coast, we raise a toast,
We love thee Newfoundland."

The audience cheered and began to clap. The emcee feigned distain. "Wait a minute, this is not over, not by a long shot. That only proves they can read, which in these parts is no proof they really 'long here." Laughter ensued.

The emcee's assistants began to hand out pieces of what looked like raw meat to the initiates, accompanied by shot glasses full of dark rum called Screech. Maybe it was the warmth of the crowded room, the strength of the Canadian table wine, or the heat of her embarrassment, but Audrey's view of the proceedings gave way to a much colder vision. Instead of a cherub-like emcee in a funny hat, she saw grizzled men on a grey shore, digging up a rotting sack of putrid fish that they cut up with an elaborately hilted knife for the young men who knelt before them.

"All right," the emcee continued. "Now you must eat a genuine piece of Newfoundland steak, which you'll notice looks and smells a lot like baloney. That's because, for the longest time, we Newfoundlanders paid dearly for the baloney, but the lobster was free. Just an idea of what a strange and wonderful place this really is."

He interrupted himself. "Na na na, you saves that till last," he exclaimed, racing to prevent an initiate from sampling the rum first. "You needs follow the directions here or we needs to ship you back, that's all there's to it."

In Audrey's vision, a woman in a hooded cloak recited an incantation and waved a silver wand that looked like an elongated eggbeater while the boys were served cubes of the reeking shark meat on the ceremonial knife blade. The initiates forced the *Hakarl* down their gullets and fought back their vomit while the grizzled men sternly observed. Ironically, the meat wasn't poisonous, not in its putrefied state. Fresh Greenland shark, on the other hand, would have been fatal.

Luc noticed that Audrey seemed to be daydreaming, but he was distracted by the moans of Lonny MacLeod, the reporter from the St. Anthony *Northern Pen* newspaper.

"Ah na! Ah na! This is terrible. You bastard piece of garbage!" The reporter swore and moaned again.

Luc turned away from his viewfinder to see what had irritated his dinner companion from the media table.

"The focus buggered up as well as the flash; I can't take a single shot," the reporter lamented, almost ready to cry. "Me editor will have me balls for bookends with all these heavyweights here. This story's to go straight to St. John's." He tried not to beg, but a pleading tone still crept into his voice.

"I hate to ask, we're a small-town paper with no money to pay you, but do you t'ink you could send us some of yer shots for me story, especially of the three ladies upfront in the screech-in? We'll be giving you the photo credit, to be sure."

Luc empathized with his predicament. He also realized that photo credit in a story going to local, provincial, and possibly national news outlets suited his purposes anyway. He would make sure that Audrey was the star. "Sure," he said, "no problem at all."

The emcee began again. "Now look at the bottom of your paper so you can correctly answer this all-important question: ARE – YE – A – SCREECHER?"

The response was raucous and almost unrecognizable. "Deed I is, me ol' cock! And long may yer big jib draw!"

The crowd cheered vociferously.

"Just so you know, it means, 'Yes, I am, my old friend, and may your sails always catch wind.' Na na na na na." The emcee interrupted himself again and raced back toward the same young man. "Not yet, not yet!"

Audrey saw the boys in her vision struggle to keep their composure until the hooded woman offered each a draught of caraway-flavoured alcohol. The boys grabbed the leather flask and drank to save their lives. The grizzled men laughed. Dr. Olsen leaned toward Audrey and whispered, "This is remarkably like the Norse initiation ceremony." Audrey was jolted into the present. "I was thinking the same thing," she replied. "I participated in something like it at the Lofotr Viking Museum in Norway."

"Is this Screech liquor easier to drink than Aquavit?" Dr. Olsen asked.

"No," Audrey said of the potent brew. At forty per cent alcohol by volume, it purportedly received its name from an American serviceman stationed in Newfoundland during World War II. Supposedly, he screeched when he took a large swig of it without fair warning. "It would make a Viking proud," she said, and smiled.

All three women readied their shots of Screech. Then volunteers produced a large frozen cod for them to kiss. As Audrey puckered up, Luc knew he had the image that would land on the front pages of all the right news sources.

When the next set of initiates took the place of the first, and after Audrey had said her goodbyes to the minister and Dr. Olsen, she hurried over to the media table.

"Luc, may I have a word?" she asked. Luc left his camera plugged into the *Northern Pen* reporter's laptop for the image download and picked up his beer bottle.

"Yes, Audrey of Newfoundland," he grinned. "How may I be of assistance?"

"Aren't you going to get screeched-in?"

"Don't know yet. This has turned into a working gig. The local reporter needs my shots. And I want to fire off queries to those archeology publications I contacted during The Forks dig. Maybe I can pick up a few cheques before my YCW job starts."

"I have a real problem and I need your help," she pleaded. "I was supposed to get a private room and now they're forcing me to share it with someone."

"Who's the lucky guy?"

Audrey was panic-stricken. "I'm serious, Luc. I can't share a room with anyone. I really can't."

Luc became serious too. "That does sound grim. What's the problem?"

Audrey leaned toward him and whispered. "I walk and talk in my sleep with people who aren't there."

Luc looked at her compassionately. "Audrey. *Ma chère*. You do that in the daytime."

Audrey gazed back in anguish. "And I'd rather that no one besides you knew that, Luc."

He straightened up when he fully realized the ramifications of what she was saying. "Who's your roommate?"

Audrey nodded toward Alexis walking slowly and deliberately back from the bar, balancing her fifth drink. "Alexis McQueen."

In the manner common to Manitobans used to drinking at the often-raucous fundraising events known in the province as socials, Luc held his beer bottle tight to his chest. "Whoa. How'd I miss that!" he whistled. "Okay, I'll take one for the team. I'll sleep with Alexis. You can bunk with Aunt Peggy."

When he did glance back at Audrey, she was glowering.

"Sorry. Is this the deal for the whole summer?" he asked.

"No, only until most of the UNESCO people leave and more rooms open up."

"So, all you need are short-term measures. Bring your purse over here." Luc bent down to his backpack, rummaged around, and then surreptitiously passed Audrey an old flask.

It was the heft of it that first caught her interest. Then she recognized the triple fleur-de-lis crest and the crown above it embossed into the sterling silver. She rubbed it with her thumb, as if to verify its authenticity.

"It's full of Screech," Luc whispered. "Drink as much as you can before bedtime and you should sleep through anything."

"*Mais zut*, Luc! This is the coat of arms of the last royal family of France. The Bourbons." Audrey didn't realize she had spoken in French. Luc responded in kind.

"My great-grandfather gave me that flask. Are you telling me he was a descendant of the king of France?"

"Or the flask was stolen from the Bourbon family. The Versailles was pillaged during the French Revolution."

"Do you think it's worth money?"

"Yes, if it's authentic."

"Here is my offer: you check out the flask for me, and I won't charge you for the Screech."

Audrey gave Luc a scornful look, knowing he had helped himself to the free Screech at the bar. And she wasn't sure the rum would work as a sedative.

"The Screech will do the trick," Luc reassured her, this time in English. "It'll also keep you regular."

With the "Scoff" (dinner) concluded, it was now time for the "Scuff" (dance). In regimented precision, senior legionnaires moved all the tables to the front of the long hall, clearing the hardwood dance floor near the back. Lights were lowered as a Celtic band in matching shirts, vests, and jeans set up their drums and tuned their fiddles where the head table once stood.

"I can't believe how much Canada looks, sounds, and even tastes like Britain," Professor Osborne proclaimed as he swirled his glass of stout, evidently pleased at the reach of the empire.

"That's likely because Newfoundland *was* a British dominion until 1949," replied Audrey, who had rejoined her tablemates. "The other provinces and territories have different histories and, therefore, different identities."

"Such as Quebec," sniffed Gabrielle Bédard, evidently not pleased at being included in the empire. "Our culture was established long before the British arrived."

"And who are the British but descendants of successive invaders themselves?" said Osborne. "I, myself, am a descendant of the Norse who took York from the Anglo-Saxons who took it from the Romans who took it from the Celts."

He then walked away, indignant at students edifying him. Audrey never understood conventions that prevented speaking plainly about facts. Her parents, while seekers of truth, had perfected the finer points of manners and deportment, easing their ascendency in social circles. They despaired of their daughter's disregard for position and protocol.

Alexis, on the other hand, was quite pleased by the encounter. She had begun to uncover weaknesses in her nemesis. She was also shrewd enough not to underestimate her strengths, which now included the doting Gabrielle Bédard. But she was soon distracted by a stream of male admirers, ranging from awkward archeology students to cocky locals, including the *Northern Pen* reporter.

Over the course of the evening, Alexis also noted that Luc spent a great deal of time on the dance floor. Like every other woman in the hall, she was amazed at what a skilled and obviously schooled dancer he was. He jigged with some, joined the line dancers, and even cajoled his great-aunt Peggy into a two-step.

When the band announced the last dance, Luc went straight to Audrey. When Alexis saw that they waltzed together with the practiced precision of a married couple, she dug her thumbnail repeatedly into the soft label of her beer bottle.

"Care to dance, Alexis?"

*Not this carrot top again,* Alexis thought, all the while hoping her eyes weren't rolling at the young man who appeared at her side. "Cody, right?" she asked aloud, with a superficial smile.

"Na, that's me brother." The freckle-faced redhead grinned as he grabbed her waist and began waltzing before they even reached the dance floor. "I'm Finn."

It finally dawned on her. "There's two of you?"

Finn laughed. "Uh huh. We're the Murphy twins. We work at Norstead Village."

Alexis briefly wondered if having sex with two men would be as appealing as the prospect of having sex with twins always seemed to men. She peered into Finn's guileless eyes and decided it wasn't.

"Our adventure is off to a great start, don't you think?" Luc asked Audrey, as he cradled her in the crook of his arm.

The past forty-eight hours replayed themselves in Audrey's mind. Joining Luc in the taxi and being handed a perfect non-fat extra dry cappuccino with just a dash of cinnamon. Watching him pass repeatedly through the Winnipeg airport metal detector until, barefoot and beltless, he tried in vain to hold up his hands and his jeans at the same time while the wand was passed over him. Reading the *Saga of Eirik the Red* and listening to Edvard Grieg's *Peer Gynt Suite* on the plane while Luc binge-watched documentaries. Browsing the designer shops at the Toronto airport while he chased a Grey Cup-winning football coach into the restroom, begging for an interview. Spending the evening walking around the eye-exploding, brilliantly coloured buildings of St. John's while balancing beer-battered fish and chips. Then waking up early, dragging their luggage to the docks, and hopping aboard Captain Brian's tour boat that transported them here.

As Audrey recalled the *"I'm Flying"* scene they re-enacted, the final notes of the waltz faded. "If the past two days were any indication, it's going to be a very memorable summer," she murmured. "I better get my things from Aunt Peggy's truck."

Dr. Olsen caught up with the pair in the parking lot. "There is no need to take the bus to the Views of Vinland Hotel," she told Audrey. "Please join me, my assistant, and a few others in my van. I can brief you on tomorrow's agenda. It was very nice to meet you, Luc. You are a very good dancer."

Luc lifted Audrey's luggage out of the pickup. Instinctively, they both glanced at the knoll, scanning for antlers.

"I'll text you when I receive my schedule," Audrey said nervously.

"Me too. Good night. And don't forget to drain the flask. I promise, you won't move a muscle till morning."

Audrey managed a smile, then rolled her luggage across the parking lot. Luc watched her disappear into the darkness and wished he could afford to stay with her. Yes, he thought. He was definitely here to watch over her.

On the ride to the hotel, Dr. Olsen reviewed everything about the mission that Audrey already knew. Then she told her team they could sleep for an extra hour and half before their first briefing breakfast at 9:30 a.m.

They wearily checked in after 1:00 a.m. Alexis and Audrey received the cardkeys to their room with its lone queen-size bed. As they entered, Audrey silently recited ancient mantras to ward off her demons. She offered to let Alexis use the bathroom first, but was quite surprised when her roommate simply stripped off her dress and fell into bed in her underwear and false lashes. So, Audrey washed up and changed into her pyjamas in the bathroom, where she consumed most of Luc's flask of Screech.

By the time she climbed into bed—after arranging her luggage as hazards beside it to hinder sleepwalking—she realized she was quite drunk. The room spun for a while. It seemed to help to leave a leg grounded on the floor. Eventually, she fell deeply asleep.

When the rhythm of Audrey's breathing changed, Alexis slipped out of bed and picked up her phone. She dropped to her hands and knees, creeping along the carpet, until she reached Audrey's luggage. Then she slowly opened the zippers and systematically went through each pocket and pouch, using the flashlight app on her phone to examine every item.

She tried booting up Audrey's phone and laptop, but both were password protected. She found Luc's near-empty flask, sniffed it, and smiled. Then she went back to her bed and allowed herself to fall deeply asleep as well.

# CHAPTER TWO
## Age of Adventure

*Eirik the Red lived at Brattahlid (in Greenland), where he was held in the highest regard and was deferred to by all. Eirik's children were Leif, Thorvald, Thorstein, and a daughter named Freydis. She was married to one Thorvard and lived with him at Gardar, which is now the Bishop's Seat. She was a proud and grasping woman, but Thorvard was a weakling. She was married to him chiefly because of his money. In those days, the people of Greenland were all pagan.*

—*Saga of the Greenlanders*

The first faint rays of dawn through the open curtains were all Audrey needed to awaken. Her head was heavy. Her mouth was parched. And, as Luc predicted, she needed to evacuate her bowels at once.

Even though she had purposely positioned her suitcases by the bed, she was surprised when she stumbled over one. It wasn't quite where she remembered placing it. Upon returning from the bathroom wearing a racing maillot, a Finnish head wrap, and a terry robe, she slipped her cardkey into a pocket and left to find the sauna.

Views of Vinland was a well-appointed boutique hotel that UNESCO had booked exclusively for the entire summer. Its rooms were named for Vikings who, according to the sagas, stayed for a time in the land they called Vinland: The Leif (after Eirik the Red's eldest son, Leif the Lucky), The Thorvald (after Eirik's second son), The Freydis (after Eirik's daughter), The Thorvard (after Freydis' husband), The Gudrid (after the widow of Eirik's youngest son, Thorstein), The Thorfinn (after Thorfinn Karlsefni, who later married Gudrid), The Snorri (after Gudrid and Thorfinn's son, purported to be the first European child born in North America), The Helgi, and The Finnbogi (named after merchant brothers who were killed by Thorvard after Freydis accused them of attacking her).

Upon returning from her soul-restoring session in the sauna, Audrey discovered she had spent the night in The Freydis. Her roommate was still snoring loudly as Audrey rolled on a wetsuit and squeaked into rubber shoes. She regretted her actions instantly and hurried back to the bathroom. Exiting a brief time later—after she was confident there would be no further reoccurrences and after she cranked open a window—Audrey threw a bath towel around her neck, left the hotel, and clambered down the path to Wheeler's Cove.

"Sweet jaysus in the garden, would you look at that!" shouted the cook to Louise Tucker, owner of the Views of Vinland Hotel. "Tell me that's not one of yours."

Louise hurried to the window overlooking the hotel's outdoor deck and the cove beyond. Not knowing where she was supposed to be looking, she scanned the rough terrain, still brown with dormant grass. "I don't see anything," she responded.

"There. In the cove. That little black head bobbing up and down. Lawd thundering, there's someone *swimming* in the cove, on the first of May. With frost on the ground and bergs in the bay."

"I heard the sauna going at six this morning. Maybe our Norwegian guest decided to follow it up with a cold dip. They've been known to jump into snow afterwards."

"There goes that theory," the cook replied, as Dr. Olsen entered the dining area and set up her laptop on a table.

Louise swung by with a pot of coffee. "How are you Dr. Olsen? I trust you slept well?"

"Yes, wonderfully well, thank you."

"Will your people be joining you soon? I've brought in help for your morning meetings: a top-shelf cook, Annie Coulson. If anyone wants to order food, we'll be ready."

"My assistant will be here shortly, but I doubt I will be seeing the others for another hour or so."

"Any swimmers in your party, do you know?"

Dr. Olsen looked up from her computer, baffled. "I really couldn't say. I didn't think you had a pool."

"We don't," Louise replied.

"By gawd, she's a girl, by the looks of it!" Annie proclaimed. "She's out of the water now and moving her legs, thank Christ. Will wonders never cease." She returned to the kitchen.

Both Louise and Dr. Olsen went to the prospect window in time to see Audrey run up the embankment from the cove and peel the hood off her wetsuit, allowing her hair to flow in rivulets around her shoulders. She looked up and waved, smiling broadly when she saw the women in the window.

"She must be tougher than she looks," Louise commented, before returning to her duties.

By the time Audrey had showered and changed, Dr. Olsen, her assistant Else Pedersen, Alexis, Gabrielle, and the other archeologists in the hotel were seated at the breakfast tables. The rest of the team, who were staying at nearby accommodations, stood around holding coffee cups and chatting. Audrey joined them at exactly 9:30 a.m.

Dr. Olsen couldn't hide her amusement as Audrey sat down at the nearby chair reserved for her. "How was your swim?" she asked.

Alexis, also seated at the table, almost spit out her coffee.

Audrey beamed. "Refreshing! It was like swimming in a giant margarita. I got out when I couldn't feel my limbs anymore."

"And you started your morning with a sauna?"

Audrey looked around, concerned. "I didn't disturb anyone, did I?"

"Only the cook," Dr. Olsen replied. "You definitely have Norse blood. Do you like scuba diving as well as swimming? It is a handy skill to have as an archeologist."

"I'm a distance swimmer, primarily, although I do have a C-card for that very reason."

"Ah, so that is how you met the physical requirements of the Rhodes Scholarship," Dr. Olsen surmised. "May I inquire as to the subject of your thesis?"

Alexis' head pivoted so quickly, her eyes hurt to refocus. *A Rhodes Scholar and a scuba diver?* she raged inwardly. *Holy fuck, she's Lara Croft!*

Audrey was shyly evasive. Her parents had taught her not to reveal plans to colleagues in this highly competitive field. Archeology was like sport, they said. Being first was everything.

"I'm still evaluating a couple of possibilities," she said. "Hopefully, I'll have two successful digs in my portfolio to give me fodder."

"Hopefully," Dr. Olsen repeated, as she delicately sliced her gravlax.

Audrey ordered fried eggs, dark molasses beans, bologna, and toutons—Newfoundland pancakes made by frying bread dough with pork fat. Alexis felt the dry toast churning in her still queasy stomach. The black coffee had done nothing to quell the pounding in her head, either.

*If it turns out she can hold her liquor better than I can, there'll be nothing left to live for*, Alexis seethed silently.

After the small talk and breakfast dishes were cleared out of the way, Dr. Olsen got down to business. Else Pederson produced a small box and a pair of latex gloves. The other archeologists crowded around her table.

"Before we begin this significant enterprise, I wish to show you the reason we're here," Dr. Olsen began as she slipped on the gloves. Else opened the box lined with wads of acid-free tissue. Dr. Olsen gingerly removed a rectangular piece of wood with geometric scratches on it.

Audrey stared at it, agog.

In a habit formed in early childhood, Alexis eagerly rushed to be the first with an answer, even to an unasked question. "It's a rune stick!" she offered.

"Yes," said Dr. Olsen. "And what does it say?"

Alexis desperately wanted to reply, but she was stumped. Her study of Norse runes had only begun when she first heard of this project. She could identify most of the symbols on the stick, but they didn't seem to make any sense.

Magnus Stefansson from Iceland leaned in, but scrunched up his face in puzzlement. Dr. Olsen stared at Audrey, who, she was told, could read runes before she could read English.

Audrey, in turn, stared at a gnarled pair of soil-blackened hands, etching out the geometric lines with the tip of a crude knife. The carver was hurried and secretive.

"It could be *jötunvillur*," Audrey almost whispered, still in her reverie.

"The Norse code?" Magnus asked with surprise.

Audrey surfaced, groggily, from her vision. "Not to be confused with Morse code, but, yes." In the awkward silence that followed, she made a mental note to avoid Luc's punny sense of humour in the future. "May I ask where it was found?"

"First things first," said Dr. Olsen. "Any idea what this Norse code says?"

Audrey struggled. "I think I see the name Eiriksson. And perhaps something about 'rest' or 'sleep'? I'm not sure. I would need more time to study it."

Dr. Olsen said, "Reading runes—never mind *jötunvillur*—is always open to interpretation. But experts at the University of Oslo believe it says something to the effect of, 'Below this stick rests the body of Thorvald Eiriksson.' It is thought to be a grave marker."

"How old is it?" Alexis asked, anxious to contribute something to the conversation, even if it were only questions, not answers.

"It has been carbon-dated to be about one thousand years old. It is of the right period," Dr. Olsen replied. She interpreted Audrey's unblinking stare to be an encouraging sign of her personal investment in the dig, so she answered her first question as well. "It was found by a tourist near the primary longhouse at L'Anse aux Meadows."

*That can't be right*, Audrey ruminated silently, but as her parents taught her, she kept her supposition to herself. She could hear her father's voice, "Don't reveal your theories to anyone until you've researched them thoroughly and can come as close as possible to proving them. If you're wrong, you'll be dismissed for being inaccurate or, at the very least, slipshod. If you're right, you will have handed your theories to someone else who can claim them as their own."

"With this small stick, I levered nearly two million dollars through my contacts at UNESCO and with contributions from the federal and provincial governments here," Dr. Olsen proclaimed, as she expertly positioned the artifact in its resting place and herself as supreme commander of the dig.

"In 1960, my relatives, Anne and Helge Ingstad, established that the Norse were in North America five hundred years before Columbus by finding a bronze cloak pin buried in mounds that proved to be a Viking encampment.

"Now this rune stick has given us the opportunity to establish, beyond a doubt, those Norsemen included the children of Eirik the Red, and that Newfoundland is indeed Vinland, just as the *Icelandic Sagas* described it.

Furthermore, we have the chance to solve what may very well be the first murder mystery in North America!"

The group was transfixed. Dr. Olsen continued. "My challenge to you is this: We have less than five months to find what we can before the snow flies again. I am counting on you to ensure we conduct our search without compromising the site or any other artifacts it may contain.

"Naturally, junior members of our team will report to experienced field archeologists from Parks Canada, who have already set out the search parameters and will be monitoring the excavations. You, in turn, will help supervise a large group of volunteers. We must be disciplined, dedicated, and exceptionally thorough. Your orientation begins in exactly twenty minutes, when the bus arrives to take us L'Anse aux Meadows. To success!" she declared, raising a glass of Newfoundland glacier water in the air.

"To success!" her team replied, raising whatever cup they had handy.

As the group dispersed, Louise Tucker returned to the table to restock the condiments, including tiny jars of jam with handwritten labels. A jar with yellow contents caught Audrey's eye and she reached out to examine it.

"This bakeapple jam, where does it come from?" she asked Louise.

"It's local, my dear. In fact, Annie, our new cook, picks the berries herself and makes great batches at a time."

"Do you happen to know if it's called by any other name?"

Louise grinned. "Funny you should ask. Dr. Olsen calls it cloudberry jam. She says it also makes a great liqueur."

"It does indeed," Audrey replied.

She had just pocketed a jam jar when Dr. Olsen returned to the table, leaned forward, and whispered to her. "And from you, Ms. Vincent, I need one more thing. Your saliva."

Audrey was dumbstruck.

"I am asking everyone with Icelandic ancestry to contribute, since Iceland has a significant DNA database and three hundred years of genealogical data. Something we can use to help identify Thorvald's body when we find it."

\*\*\*

A sapphire sky bridged a caesious sea spattered with icebergs ranging from blinding white to striated cobalt. Audrey examined her bottle of glacier water from the Views of Vinland Hotel as the yellow school bus she was travelling in navigated the winding highway. Consuming something ten thousand years old seemed a proper toast to the archeological adventure ahead.

Although the landscape looked bleak, it was covered in vegetation, mostly stunted balsam and spruce trees the locals called tuckamore. Occasionally, this was broken by patches of marsh grass and rocky outcroppings blazing with orange moss.

Her phone buzzed. A text appeared from Luc: *U up yet?*

Audrey smiled, realizing he had only just arisen. She replied: *On bus to dig site.*

Luc: *Sleep well?*

Audrey: *Like a baby.*

Luc: *Woke up crying and wet the bed?*

Audrey laughed aloud, then clamped her hand over her mouth as other passengers turned her way: *Slept thru as far as I know.*

Luc: *Got ur sched?*

Audrey: *Not yet. When do u start?*

Luc: *YCW orientation in two weeks.*

Audrey: *Only two weeks to learn ur role?*

Luc: *Aunt Peg's got hi speed thank god.*

Audrey: *BTW what's her last name just in case.*

Luc: *Volkov.*

Audrey: *You're part Russian? Who knew?*

Luc: *Middle name is Stanislas. Tell no one.*

Audrey: *Promise.*

Luc: *Check today's St. John's Telegram. Breakie is ready. Bye.*

Audrey navigated to the website for St. John's major newspaper. An image of her kissing a cod while sandwiched between the federal heritage minister and Dr. Olsen filled the screen as the front-page story. Luc's photo credit appeared in the corner. Her jaw dropped and stomach flipped. It made her look like a glory seeker. She scanned the story in seconds. At least it didn't refer to her as Manitoba Jones.

She tossed her phone into her purse. Her parents were thrilled that Luc had orchestrated a certain degree of celebrity for her, since they so valued their own. However, Audrey would have preferred to work anonymously.

Just then, a middle-aged man in a brimmed canvas hat and multi-pock-eted vest stood up at the front of the bus to greet the passengers.

"To those of you who may have missed the Scoff and Scuff last night, first, let me extend my sympathies. You missed a helluva party."

Everyone laughed politely.

"Second, allow me to introduce myself. I'm Ryan Miller with Parks Canada, and I'll be the lead archeologist at L'Anse aux Meadows this summer."

Everyone clapped politely. Miller bent down to look out a window.

"Right about now you may be thinking I've got no business in this job because we missed the turnoff to the heritage site awhile back. But we're heading to Norstead Village first, which is about two klicks farther up the road.

"Norstead Village is a fair-sized recreation of an eleventh century Norse trading port. It's not open to the public yet, but we're getting a special sneak peek so you can get a feel for what L'Anse aux Meadows might've been like, but on a smaller scale, back in the day.

"As I'm sure you know, most of the original site at L.A.M. has been rebur-ied to preserve it, with the last excavation headed by Parks Canada archeolo-gist Birgitta Wallace in 2002. There are a couple of interpretative structures there that will be staffed by locals and some Young Canada Works students once it opens for the tourist season. But Norstead is a great place, especially for the undergrads among you, to get an idea of the lifestyle and artifacts we hope to uncover.

"Oh, one more thing. The residents of Norstead have volunteered to dress up in their finest Norse garb and explain their Viking occupations to you, as they will for the tourists come the first of June. I only ask that the Norse experts among you be courteous. Don't grill them too much, question their Newfoundland accents, or dispute anything they say. Most are not anthro-pologists; they're local interpreters who are part of a non-profit group that puts on a show for the tourists.

"Okay, it looks like we're here. You can leave your bags on the bus, folks. And tipping the driver isn't necessary."

The young archeologists stepped outside, squinted into the sun, and turned their collars to the icy wind blowing unimpeded from the Arctic

Circle. Its salty breath stung, sending many scrambling back into the bus for more clothes.

The sod-covered structures ahead reminded Audrey of buildings on the Suomenlinna fortress island near Helsinki, Finland, as well as the "soddy" homes created by settlers on the Canadian prairies. In the first instance, the sod provided a type of camouflage for the buildings when viewed from the sea. In the second, it offered an abundant source of insulation from the cold. She suspected both applications would be considerations in a North American Viking village.

But she was more interested in the sea beyond Norstead, wondering what it must have been like for men—and sometimes women—to cross the North Atlantic in shallow boats for weeks at a time with minimal provisions.

"*Allô, Audrey. Comment ça va?*" Gabrielle called out, as she sprinted along the boardwalk to greet her.

"*Ça va bien, merci,*" Audrey answered.

"I must ask a favour of you, since you are so fluent in French," Gabrielle asked, also in French. "I am having difficulty understanding the local accent. If I look at you with questioning eyes, would you mind translating for me?"

"Not at all. I'd be pleased to help."

"Your accent is very different than the accent that Luc possesses. I cannot believe he pronounces his name as *LA li bert' ee* instead of *La lib' air TAY*. Your accent is more Metropolitan."

"His accent is mostly Franco-manitobaine, with influence from Michif, the Métis language he also speaks. The pronunciation of his surname is Manitoba English. When I learned French, I did not learn any Canadian dialects at all. That never made sense to me."

"What does not make sense to me are the names in Newfoundland. Such as L'Anse aux Meadows—half French, half English. It is supposed to be L'Anse-aux-Méduses. L'Anse sounds more like the English word lance than *méduses* sounds like meadows, so why is the name not Lance of Meadows?"

"A mystery to be sure," Audrey replied, hiding her amusement.

"Your French is flawless. You know, when I was in high school, I spent a wonderful summer studying at the Université Paris-Sorbonne. I thought it might be helpful someday when making presentations to an international audience. And I wished to spend a summer in Paris." Gabrielle grinned.

"They are very strict about phonetics there, especially the pronunciation of certain words. These words tend to identify students of the Sorbonne."

Audrey lowered her head, slightly embarrassed at being called out. "You are correct, Gabrielle. My parents sent me to the Sorbonne for a time. They considered it a type of French finishing school."

"I have another question," Gabrielle said. "Are you and Luc a couple?"

Audrey hesitated, as she always did when asked. Then she shook her head. "We are good friends."

This time she added, "Since the first day of our first year at the University of Winnipeg. Luc was upset about his course load, and I was upset because I was too young to get into pubs during Homecoming Week. I helped him with his studies; he made me fake ID and protected me from the older guys for the next two years."

"Like a big brother."

"Something like that, yes. He was in a joint degree program in communications, so he has spent the last couple of years at Red River College. I have not seen him much." Her voice dropped. "Except for last summer when he covered the fieldwork at The Forks site for a local newspaper."

"So, it was he who gave you the nickname Manitoba Jones?"

Audrey winced and nodded.

"Big brothers can be a pain in the ass sometimes. I have four." Gabrielle laughed. "Would you mind if I were to date your big brother?"

Audrey was taken aback. "Ah, no. Not at all," she answered reflexively in English. "We better catch up to the rest of the group. We don't want to miss anything."

A grey-bearded man wearing a crimson cape and sporting a tousled mane of curly blond hair strode to the end of the boardwalk and introduced himself as the village chieftain and storyteller, or *skald*. He led the archeological team to the longhouse where men dressed in cloaks, knee-length trousers, and leather-bound boots sat with large tankards, ostensibly full of mead.

Tending to the fire were women dressed in cotton blouses and ankle-length dresses with narrow straps clasped by oval brooches. The archeologists looked at everything but the interpreters themselves when they spoke—their accoutrements, the furniture they sat on, and the implements they used.

Nevertheless, the role-players persevered valiantly with their scripts, even giving a couple of overly inquisitive undergrads a good-natured scare when they reached out to feel the fabric of their shirts.

Ryan Miller perked up at the sound of Audrey simultaneously translating the interpreters' words for the Francophones present.

The chieftain led the group back outside to a large woodpile stacked up against a rocky embankment. He introduced everyone to a couple of helmeted Vikings carrying round, vividly painted wooden shields. He pointed out that their helmets did not have horns—a common misconception in popular folklore.

The Vikings demonstrated the art of throwing a battle-axe by using the woodpile for target practice. Then they invited the archeologists to try it. Most threw the axe too delicately to travel far enough or revolve fast enough to embed itself into the wood. Audrey mustered enough speed, but missed the wood entirely. The blade broke off the axe when it crashed against the granite berm.

Her cohorts groaned loudly and booed, but another battle-axe was quickly produced. Alexis stepped up to the challenge and drove the blade of the axe so deeply into a log that the Vikings were still trying to remove it when the group moved to another door in the chieftain's hall.

They walked past furs and hides to a space where wool was coloured with natural dyes, spun into yarn, and knit using a technique called *nalbinding*. Using only one needle, the women fashioned scarves, mitts, and caps, including helmet-shaped toques that proved quite popular with the bareheaded men in the crowd. Other women were dipping beeswax candles and displaying amber, silver, and labradorite jewellery for sale.

"This labradorite ring looks just like yours, Audrey," Alexis called out, feigning friendship. Audrey was perplexed. She had yet to wear it.

While she was distracted, an older woman in period garb picked up her hand. She led her to a little table with a white cloth and dark stones, each marked with a rune. Audrey shivered.

"Allow me to tell yer fortune by casting yer runes," the woman said. A crowd gathered. The woman noticed Audrey's distress. "Don't worry, me darling, I knows me stuff," she whispered. "I reads tea leaves in St. Anthony during the winter."

The woman picked up the smooth stones and placed them in a leather pouch. "Hello, everyone. I am a rune teller, sometimes known as a *wyrd* sister. Wyrd comes from the Norse word *Urd,* which means destiny. Now, the Norse had a different way of viewing the passage of time. They didn't think it ran in a straight line from the past to the present to the future like we do. No, they believed that the Well of Destiny, called Urd, flows through a great ash tree, called Yggdrasil, that holds up the cosmos. The leaves of the ash tree then shed dewdrops that fall back into the well. Are you with me so far?"

Her audience chuckled.

"So, the well, which is the past, feeds the tree, which is the present. Then dewdrops, or the fallout, from the present return to the past, sometimes even changing it. The runes were a gift from the god Odin himself to help humanity make a better present by recreating the past."

The rune teller grinned mischievously as she added, "That's kind of like what we all do for a living." Then she spoke to Audrey. "So are you ready, me darling?"

Audrey nodded, although unsure if she actually was.

"Ask me a question that's close to yer heart. I'll toss the runes out of the bag, and they will give you the answer."

Audrey inhaled deeply. "Will we find the body of Thorvald Eiriksson?"

Everyone exhaled at the directness of her question. The rune teller stared into Audrey's multi-coloured eyes and seemed lost for a moment. Without blinking, she began a monotone chant, "Certain is that which is sought from runes that the gods so great have made and the master-poet painted." Then she cast the stones from the pouch onto the table linen.

After returning downturned stones to the pouch, the old woman touched each of the runes that were visible.

"First rune out of the bag is for elk, but in these parts, that probably means moose. Keep an eye out for them, all of you, they're a hazard, to be sure. Especially for you, me darling. The next rune is for ride or journey—could be the one yer already on, or another yer gonna take. That's where yer gonna find this," she said, picking up a stone marked with an angular B. "This is for romance, healing, and protection. I sees quite a few mind-runes or wisdom-runes here. You must be a pretty heavy t'inker."

The Francophones looked at each other, bewildered. The rune teller continued.

"You'll have a lot to t'ink about in the days ahead. That's probably why I sees a similar rune, but lacking an arm, here. "That's the rune for an ulcer. I sees water here, more than you bargained for, a boat ride gone bad maybe or an unplanned dunk in the sea. I hopes you can swim." She laughed.

"Now here you go," she continued. "This blank one is Odin's rune, for unlimited potential. And right beside it are the runes for man and victory. Looks like yer just the gal to find this fella yer looking for."

Everyone cheered. The woman kept her eyes on Audrey as she stood up and was replaced by a far more eager fortune seeker.

After a brief time, the chieftain led everyone to a timber and sod church with a Christian cross on its crude spire.

"By the turn of the eleventh century, the Norse were beginning to adopt Christianity," he told the group assembled inside. "The *Icelandic Sagas* say that Leif Eiriksson was a convert, charged by King Olaf Tryggvason of Norway to bring Christianity to Greenland. Leif's father, Eirik the Red, wasn't too keen on abandoning the old gods. But Leif's mother, Thjodhild, even had a church built that might've looked very much like this one. And speaking of building things, the next stop on our visit is the blacksmith's shop."

Alexis recognized the Norstead blacksmith to be one of the redheaded twins from the Scoff and Scuff. It was Cody Murphy who explained that the Norse likely chose L'Anse aux Meadows for a settlement because of its iron-rich bog and freshwater brook—two requirements for smelting iron. Then he demonstrated how he produced iron nails and hardware for both longhouses and ships. Again, the studious group watched closely as the malleable, red-hot iron was pounded into shape. One overzealous student had his eyebrows singed by the sparks.

"The hammer of Thor has smote thee!" Cody laughed.

The chieftain interrupted. "And now I'm going to show you the star attraction at Norstead. Follow me."

He led the team around the shore side of the village and inside a boat shed where he introduced Finn Murphy, Cody's twin, who played the role of a Norse shipmaster. Finn had to shout over the echoing buzz of excitement generated by the cargo ship under his care.

"This is the *Snorri,* a full-scale, seaworthy replica of a Viking *knarr* ship," he explained. "She was donated by the New Vinland Foundation. In 1998, eight men set sail in her to recreate Leif Eiriksson's 1,500-mile journey from Nuuk, Greenland, to L'Anse aux Meadows. She was the first authentic Viking ship to have completed the trip in six hundred years.

"The crew wanted to duplicate the experience as accurately as possible so they only used the sun and the stars to navigate. But in the Viking Age, that canvas sail would've been made of woven wool."

His words were wasted on most. They were busy examining the clinker-built keel and hemp lines with their hands as well as their eyes.

After a time, Ryan Miller knew the only way he could draw his charges away from the ship was to remind them how hungry they must be, and that lunch was waiting. He thanked all the interpreters who gathered to say farewell. His team gave them a hearty round of applause and then headed down the long boardwalk to the bus.

Audrey hung back a bit and scanned the shoreline once more. She even tried forcing herself to conjure up another *knarr* ship or a ghostly Norseman walking the village paths. She could not. All she saw were modern-day interpretive structures and Newfoundlanders in costume. She sighed in relief; maybe her demons were gone for good.

As she stepped onto the boardwalk to the parking lot, the old rune teller scurried to her side and held up two rune stones. "I didn't say anything at the reading, but these runes also turned up for you," she whispered. "They're ale runes. Someone may try to drug yer drink, me darling. It happened a lot back in the Viking Age. And I'm sorry to say, it's happening to young girls now too."

She pressed the stones into Audrey's hand. "Mark this one on yer coffee cup or water bottle. Paint this on a fingernail of yer drinking hand. They will protect you."

Audrey searched the rune teller's eyes to determine if this could be a prank. The woman seemed genuine.

*Well,* Audrey thought. *This is one way to make sure I get that ulcer.*

***

The bus didn't have to travel far to reach a restaurant called Thor's Place. Normally, it was closed until late May, but this year the proprietors opened early because of the excavations at the heritage site. Since Parks Canada was paying for the orientation lunch, the menu was set: fish chowder or Newfoundland pea soup with baking powder biscuits called 'doughboys' and molasses pudding.

When Audrey's coffee arrived, she stared at the steaming black liquid cautiously. She slipped a felt pen out of her purse when no one was looking and drew the rune protection symbol on the index fingers of each hand.

To her chagrin, Alexis joined her table along with Gabrielle, Magnus Stefansson, and Ryan Miller.

"That was an excellent introduction to the task at hand," Alexis gushed to Miller, who was checking his emails and the lunch tab at the same time.

"I'm glad you enjoyed it. The *Snorri* is a must-see, that's for sure," he said.

"Is it still seaworthy?" Magnus asked.

"It's been refitted and insured this year for special events," Miller replied. "It'll even take tourists whale watching. It doesn't give you much protection from the elements though, and some bailing is required. But it's quite the experience. I highly recommend it."

"When is the best time to see the whales?" asked Gabrielle.

"Anytime from now until September. I'm sure you'll get a chance to see them. Just remember to look up from the dirt once in a while and scan the horizon."

Everyone at the table was focused on his or her soup when Dr. Olsen and Professor Osborne walked in and joined them. Gabrielle, seated next to Audrey, groaned softly. The noise of conversation in the crowded restaurant was loud enough for the two young women to whisper to each other unheard, especially in French.

"Is something going on between you and the professor?" Audrey asked. She remembered they had entered the Scoff and Scuff together.

"He made a pass at me at the dance."

"That's terrible! You should report it."

"When I was in university, I worked all the time to pay for my education, serving drinks in bars and being forced by management to wear little dresses and big heels for tips. I dealt with much worse, believe me."

"I think he's one of the officials who'll be leaving soon anyway," Audrey answered.

Dr. Olsen stood up to speak. Dr. Miller clanged a spoon against his coffee mug to get everyone's attention.

"I hope all of you enjoyed your trip to Norstead Village." She smiled. "After this late lunch, we will be proceeding to the UNESCO World Heritage Site for the official opening of the excavation. The media is already there. Should any member of the media approach you for an interview, please direct them to Else Pedersen, my assistant and the media liaison for UNESCO, or to Dr. Miller of Parks Canada. Afterwards, you will be given an orientation of the site, your assignments, and your shifts for the work ahead. Tomorrow, we begin in earnest."

Her words sent the female members of the team scrambling to the restroom to primp for pending photo opportunities. Audrey dashed to the school bus instead.

On the way, she sent a text to Luc: *Press conference at dig site this aft.*

Luc replied: *Already here. Where r u?*

Audrey: *Restaurant called Thor's Place. Will be at site in ten.*

Luc: *See u then.*

From his seat at the restaurant, the driver opened the bus door remotely for Audrey. The door did not close behind her, but she paid no notice. She went to her seat and lifted her "Go Bag" from beneath it. The bag was a tip she had picked up from Luc. He was taught that journalists should keep two Go Bags packed at all times: one, a carry-on with essentials for a quick trip by plane on short notice; the other, a small tote with dress clothes in case it was necessary to appear on camera.

She slumped below window level to fix her hair, swap her hoodie for a fashionable hat and scarf, and change from jeans into dress pants. Barely zipped, Audrey popped up when she heard a creak on the floor. It was Professor Osborne, leering over her.

"Always pays to prepare for a press conference." He smirked. Audrey straightened up and glowered at him defiantly. He stared back for a while with an amused look on his face, knowing she wouldn't say anything—couldn't say anything—unless the exchange went further. Then he slowly returned to the front of the bus where he pretended to search for something.

For a moment, she considered trying to force the back doors open, but then she decided to walk up the aisle and wait for him to step aside. Osborne turned to face her and barely moved. She was forced to push her body past his. He reached for her breasts and whispered "Sshhh!" as his eyelids fluttered back in their sockets.

Audrey knew she should have been more upset at the assault than she was, but Osborne had grabbed nothing more than a handful of the down in her puffer jacket. The incident was disgusting, but at the same time, almost amusing.

She left the bus shaking, but quelled the urge to run to the restaurant. She strode back as calmly and confidently as she could manage. At the door was Dr. Olsen, glancing first at the bus, then at Audrey.

"Are you all right?" she asked. Audrey nodded. Then Dr. Olsen assumed her usual professional demeanour. "I saw the picture that your young man, Luc, took at the dinner last night. He is quite the photographer."

Audrey's distress was immediately replaced with apprehension. "The local reporter's camera seized up. He asked Luc for images to send to the St. Anthony *Northern Pen* and *The Telegram* in St. John's."

"I must make sure Else sends me those publications to read." Dr. Olsen smiled.

"I don't understand. Then, where did you see the photograph?"

"UNESCO headquarters in Paris sent me an email with links to *Archaeology Magazine, HeritageDaily, National Geographic*, and *Live Science*, among others. UNESCO is quite pleased with the coverage so far. For someone who was up dancing all night, your boyfriend was very busy. The bylines were his."

"Um, he's not my boyfriend," Audrey stammered, "and I have no control over what he—"

"He maintained my dignity and that of the heritage minister by showing a lovely young lady as the one kissing the cod," Dr. Olsen interjected. Then she became stern as Professor Osborne approached. "And sometimes it is good if people think you have a boyfriend nearby." Audrey turned to look at Osborne too.

"Ladies," he said curtly, without looking at either when forced between them to enter the restaurant.

\*\*\*

A clutch of dignitaries, senior field archeologists, Luc, and Lonny MacLeod, the reporter from the *Northern Pen*, were on the windswept bog when the bus pulled up. Audrey was never so pleased to see Luc's mischievous half grin. She stepped off the bus, walked up to him nonchalantly, and whispered, "Dr. Olsen wants to hire you as her press attaché."

Luc laughed. "That shot of you making out with the fish got pretty good coverage."

Audrey ignored the remark. "Did you hear anything about a rune stick?"

Luc was surprised at her divulging information. "It's mentioned in the news release. Is it here?"

"I don't know, but archeologists will want to see a close-up of it, that's for certain. I'll have to catch up with you later. I shouldn't be fraternizing with the media." Audrey peered over her shoulder. Osborne was observing them intently.

Given the near-freezing temperatures, the ceremonies commenced quickly. Luc took the standard shots of government, UNESCO, and Parks Canada officials delivering their speeches and looking somewhat ridiculous as the arctic breeze drove their hair straight up and their clothes sideways. Then there was the obligatory ribbon-cutting ceremony, only in this case, Anna Olsen and Ryan Miller hacked a ship's rope with a replica Viking Ulfberht sword.

Instead of watching the proceedings, Audrey chose to survey the sea and the sod-covered roofs of the interpretive buildings before her. It could have been the frigid wind that chilled her heart, but she feared it was something else.

While Luc pondered the sword shot, staged as it was, as a cover photo for his next story, he spied his gracefully beautiful friend in a bright rose cloche that popped against the blue-black clouds. The replica longhouse was perfectly framed behind her as she stared apprehensively off camera, as if waiting for the Vikings to return.

He knew she would hate him. He knew he would hate himself. But he also knew that he had to send that image along with his story to his media contacts.

Dr. Olsen guided the reporters and the dignitaries around the site now marked off with stakes and twine. Dr. Miller kept his team at bay until

Olsen's group disappeared down the boardwalk to the visitor centre. Then he launched his own tour and briefing.

Luc was chagrined that Lonny was following him around like a puppy. Lonny was grateful that Luc had provided images for the previous night's story, but now he was terrified this big city reporter might scoop him on his beat's most significant news story in decades.

By pretending to go to the restroom in the visitor centre, then hiding outside when Lonny entered it, Luc was able to double back and catch Dr. Olsen alone, after she had finished a private phone call. He asked about the rune stick. Olsen sent him with Else Pederson to take shots of it, before Lonny emerged, baffled, from the men's room.

Luc then ducked back into the restroom, posted the rune stick images on social media, and sent all the information he had gathered so far to his contacts. All he had to do now was follow up with a few interviews and write his story on the way home while Audrey drove. He knew he could complete all this before Lonny could return to the *Northern Pen*'s newsroom in St. Anthony. He was so pleased with his prowess, it never occurred to him that he would be making his first professional enemy.

Audrey was facing her own professional predicament after the archeologists were given their assignments. The Norse site included three complexes buried for preservation. Each complex featured dwellings and a workshop, likely for distinct types of craftsmen. It was believed that blacksmiths had lived in the complex closest to the freshwater brook. The three buildings in this complex were labelled A, B, and C. Building J, on the other side of the brook, once housed a furnace for smelting bog iron.

The complex with buildings D and E was likely home to carpenters because of the wood debris found in the area. Buildings F and G were in a complex that probably involved ship repair, given the number of broken rivets uncovered.

Audrey had been assigned to the excavations within Complex F-G, the largest complex in the site. This was considered a prime location since it contained the leader's hall, which was twice the size of Eirik the Red's home in Greenland and about the size of a chieftain's hall in Iceland. And the rune stick was found here. But she believed in the authenticity of the *Icelandic Sagas* that had so far proven valid, despite being written two hundred to three hundred years after the events they described. They claimed that Thorvald was buried at a cape farther south, along the eastern coast.

Given the notoriety she had garnered by overstepping the boundaries during The Forks dig, Audrey decided to stay within her assigned parameters, at least for the time being. Gabrielle would be working with her, and they both reported directly to Ryan Miller. Alexis was the supervisor of Complex D-E. Magnus Stefansson was the forensic anthropologist at an onsite mobile lab that would handle as much data and artifact processing as possible, eliminating the need to ship material to St. John's. Audrey tried to be content knowing many treasures and truths were still waiting to be discovered, and that time spent digging in the dirt here would not be in vain.

When the dignitaries returned from the visitor centre, it was evident they were done with the wind and the cold. They left as quickly as possible. Lonny beat them all to his car and sped to St. Anthony.

Luc walked up to Audrey as Ryan Miller was reminding his team about the next day's 8:00 a.m. briefing at the Views of Vinland Hotel. The archeologists then made a beeline for their bus as well.

"I found a place where I can afford to take you for a lobster dinner," Luc announced. "All you have to do is drive us there while I write my story. And I'll throw in lessons on how to shift a standard."

"No need," Audrey replied. "I can manage either a four-on-the-floor or a three-on-the-tree like your Aunt Peggy's."

Luc was astounded. "I learned because my family had nothing but beaters, but why did you need to?"

"Drivers at my parents' dig sites taught me how to drive jeeps and trucks as soon as my feet could reach the gas pedals. Mind you, most of the vehicles were right-hand drive."

Luc briefly wondered what Audrey's extraordinary childhood must have been like, but then quickly returned to the task at hand. Once inside the truck, he flipped open his laptop and showed Audrey the picture he took of her.

"I want you to use this on the blog post you're going to write tonight," he said, as a gentle reminder about maintaining her social media presence during the excavation.

Audrey was transfixed by the image. "You made me look good. Thank you," she responded. "But I also look scared."

"I'd use the word 'pensive', as if you could see Viking ships on the horizon," Luc said, as he emailed the image to her. He glanced back at Audrey when she didn't start the truck. "You didn't really see any, did you?"

"No," she responded, as she fired up the Dodge and effortlessly shifted it into gear.

"I took a shitload of shots today, Audrey. I have to send the best ones to my contacts."

She was ahead of him. "It will look like I'm encouraging you to make this whole dig about me."

"I'm sending a dozen images. The editors will choose the best—"

"Then you don't have to send this one!"

Luc looked down at his beat-up laptop in frustration. He had convinced himself that what he was doing was in her best interests as well as his.

"If you give me permission to use this image, I promise I won't take another shot of you for the rest of the month."

Audrey eyed him while smoothly shifting into second. "Nothing is going to happen on this dig for at least a month anyway. All we'll be doing is clearing away sand."

"A lot can happen in a month. What happened today, for example?" He was changing the subject to divert her concerns. As expected, he hated himself.

"Well, let's see. I deduced my roommate was poking around in my suitcases last night while I was sleeping. She commented on a ring I had packed away."

"Wha-a-at?" Luc was now fervently writing his story. Like most students, both Luc and Audrey could converse and compose simultaneously. "That reminds me, I have a two-six of Screech in the truck for you." He lifted his hand from the keyboard briefly to point to the 750 ml bottle of rum behind the seat. "That should hold you until you move out."

"You know I'm old enough to buy my own liquor now, eh? And you should get this clutch checked," she said, after shifting into third. "It slips."

"I thought so too. I'll mention it to Aunt Peggy."

"And that pompous Dr. Osborne made a pass at both Gabrielle and me. You should ask Gabrielle out. She's good-looking, smart, and she thinks you're hot."

Luc stopped typing. "Wait, what? Who made a pass at you?"

Audrey squelched a smile. She was beginning to wonder if Luc cared more about his career than her feelings. She now had her answer.

"That British professor with the UNESCO crew. He's a groper. I don't understand why men act like that: so predatory. As if women are slabs of meat to be grabbed and consumed."

"Not all men are like that, Audrey." Luc looked straight at her.

"You know, the 'not all men' phrase is often used to downplay the prevalence of attacks on women. But I understand what you mean." She smiled reluctantly. "Go ahead and send the shot, but promise not to take another one until June."

"How about Victoria Day?" he negotiated, hating himself even more.

The cares of the day vapourized as Audrey drove the main road that cut through the quaint village of St. Lunaire-Griquet, population 661, stretched along St. Lunaire Bay and Griquet Harbour. Luc was intrigued by how she examined every house and modest store in almost as much detail as he did as a writer.

"It reminds me a bit of Churchill," he observed. "They say polar bears even stroll through here sometimes."

Audrey braked suddenly and turned sharply into a private driveway. The manoeuvre made Luc hit the send button on his email before he was ready. *Oh well, guess that story is on its way,* he mused, as he looked up from his laptop. He saw a tidy home with a crudely made sign on the lawn about a used mountain bike for sale. Audrey leapt out of the Dodge and checked the quality of the bike while Luc had to explain to the homeowner why he was driving Peggy Volkov's truck. Luc shook his head as Audrey paid the asking price.

After securing her purchase in the truck bed with a rope and tarpaulin, Luc drove Audrey up to, and escorted her into, the cozy interior of The Cod and Claw. They were shown to a prime table with an idyllic view of the island-studded bay.

Audrey unfolded her linen napkin onto her lap and picked up the laminated menu. Her eyes widened. "You're right, these *are* amazing prices for lobster!"

"And I'd guess they're pretty fresh," Luc said, nodding toward the crates at the end of the dock.

Audrey peered through the window with child-like awe. "Fishing boats, coiled rope, lobster crates. It's like a scene out of a movie!"

Luc was over the moon at being able to provide a unique experience in her extraordinary life. He admired how she treasured the moment, despite having lived larger than most people could imagine.

"I'm supposed to be paying you back for the boat ride here," she said.

"No, this is definitely my treat," Luc answered.

She picked up the wine list. The waiter arrived on cue. "At least let me get the wine," she said, as she pointed to a lightly oaked Chardonnay. The waiter nodded and disappeared.

"How was your day?" she asked.

"Well, let's see," he began, mimicking her gently. "I wrote my stories until 3:00 a.m., slept in, ate an amazing breakfast... Do you know what toutons are?"

"Wha-a-at?" Audrey mimicked in return. "I had them too."

"I started replacing Aunt Peg's storm windows with screens. Who does that anymore?" Audrey shrugged.

"Then your boss's assistant called. Else Pederson. She told me about the news conference. I must have made the media list."

"You did, indeed. Dr. Olsen even mentioned what a great dancer you are."

"You don't think she's hitting on me, do you?" Luc joked.

"Ah, if only the overtures of men were as harmless," Audrey sighed.

Luc leaned forward. "Why didn't you Kung Fu kick that bastard the way you did my slobbering cousin Joe at that social I took you to? His balls didn't drop for a week!"

At that precise moment, the waiter reappeared. "By gawd, ma'am, I hopes you like the wine," he said pokerfaced, as he poured a tasting sample in her glass. Audrey buried her face in her shoulder. Luc roared and looked up at the waiter who kept his composure, except for twinkling eyes. *Damn, I love Newfoundlanders*, Luc thought.

Audrey, still unable to look up, slid the glass over to Luc who made a ridiculous pretense of sniffing and swirling the wine, having no idea what he was doing. Audrey peeked his way and buried her face again.

"Excellent," he proclaimed, and the waiter filled both glasses. "We'll have the lobster too, please. One each."

"Certainly, sir," said the waiter, who left with great propriety.

Luc lifted his glass and tilted it toward Audrey. "To the third day of our adventure!"

Audrey was finally able to compose herself. As she raised her glass, the angle of the sun's rays hitting the rim cast a halo around the room, around the table, and around Luc's laughing eyes. She suddenly had a 180-degree view from the waiter at the bar to the lobster crates on the dock. And, not for the first time in her life, time stood still.

# CHAPTER THREE
## Spoils of Conquest

*When they had finished building their houses, Leif said to his companions, "Now I am going to divide our company into two groups, for I want to get this country explored. Half the men will stay here at the camp, while the other half goes exploring. They shall not go so far that they cannot get back home by evening, and they shall stay together." So, for a time, they did this, and sometimes Leif went along with the exploring part and sometimes he stayed at home. Leif was a big, strapping fellow, handsome to look at, thoughtful, and temperate in all things.*

—Saga of the Greenlanders

The next day got off to a strange start. After boasting about having the sauna to herself the morning before, Audrey was joined in the cedar-lined room by Professor Osborne. He leered at her salaciously and disrobed, revealing a middle-aged paunch and a towel. He strode over to Audrey's bench opposite the door, sat down within arm's reach of her, and flipped open his towel.

He ogled her spandex-clad body and spread his legs farther apart to reveal his genitals fully. Audrey stared back, unafraid and unimpressed.

Then the very blond and extremely fit Magnus Stefansson walked in and greeted them cheerily. He also removed his robe, revealing a sculpted chest and chiseled abdomen above his towel. He sat on the bench to Osborne's left. He had been advised that North Americans did not appear nude in the sauna, but took his cue from Osborne and flipped open his towel as well.

Audrey also acknowledged Magnus, but struggled to appear as equally unaffected. He was significantly better endowed than Osborne, who was starting to draw his legs together again.

"Good morning, how are you?" Audrey asked in Icelandic.

Magnus beamed. "Very well, thank you! How is it you speak my language?"

"My amma's name is Signe Sigvaldason. She lives on Hecla Island in Manitoba. It was once an Icelandic colony."

"I have been there!" Magnus replied. "And to the town called Gimli. Is that where you live?"

"I live not far from there, in Winnipeg."

"This is wonderful!" Magnus was thrilled to meet an almost-compatriot. "No wonder you are so good at reading runes." Then he noticed Osborne's discomfort. "We should speak English."

The sauna door opened again and Gabrielle stepped inside, wearing a towel around her head and another around her body. Osborne's equipment was on full display in front of her. She froze.

"You should probably close the door. And your jaw," Audrey teased, in French.

Gabrielle abruptly did both as she lowered her eyes and darted to the empty bench on Audrey's right. When she dared to look up again, it was directly at Magnus's crotch.

"Eyes at eye level," Audrey cautioned in French before switching to English. "Magnus was just telling me this is not his first visit to Canada."

Magnus launched into an animated discussion about his earlier trip. Audrey was bemused by the dynamic in the room. She had relaxed in Turkish *hammams,* Russian *banyas,* Hungarian mineral springs, and Icelandic hotspots, all with various levels of public nudity. She was comfortable with it.

Not so Annie Coulson, who later dropped a carafe of coffee by the prospect window in the dining area when she saw Magnus Stefansson's white buttocks dive into Wheeler's Cove following Audrey in her wetsuit.

***

Later in the morning, Luc showed up at the dig site unannounced. Audrey was operating a ground-penetrating radar unit that looked like an oversized gas lawnmower without the tank or blades. The rubber wheels were taller and narrower, and a computer screen was positioned between the handlebars. She happened to glance up briefly and spotted Luc on the walkway with Dr. Olsen and Else Pedersen.

He didn't approach Audrey until it was clear she was taking a break. "I see they have you cutting the grass," he quipped.

"State-of-the-art ground-penetrating radar to learn what lies beneath. But I'll be cutting and rolling up sod for at least a week," she said, before taking a swig from her water bottle. Audrey had used Gabrielle's nail polish to paint the ale protection rune on her drinking utensils. At the very least, it was a means of identifying them.

"I talked Dr. Olsen into paying me to set up time-lapse video of the site excavation," Luc explained. "I got the idea from one of the documentaries I watched on the plane."

"So, you'll be here every day?"

"At least once a day until I start my job at the visitor centre. Then I can check on the video myself."

Audrey was perplexed. "You're working at the visitor centre? I thought you'd be playing a role at the interpretive buildings?"

"Most Young Canada Works students will be, but according to the archeologists, there's no evidence that Indigenous people were here at the same time as the Vikings."

"The sagas describe clashes between Indigenous peoples and the Norse quite vividly," Audrey said. "But they're considered fictionalized accounts. Archeologists are scientists. They'd need carbon-dated artifacts to prove it."

Luc shrugged. "So, once the doors open at the centre, I'll be joining some locals as a tourist guide and keeper of Indigenous artifacts that are pre- and post-Viking. In the meantime, I need to train someone to make sure my camera equipment is functioning. Audrey. Friend. Pal."

In her peripheral vision, she caught sight of Gabrielle approaching. "I've the perfect candidate for you." Audrey grinned, pleased she found a way to avoid the chore and introduce Luc to Gabrielle at the same time.

"You remember Gabrielle, don't you, Luc?"

"*Mais oui.*"

"Gabrielle, Luc needs a camera assistant for the next couple of weeks. I told him you'd be perfect for the job. Now, if you two will excuse me, I have more grass to cut."

Gabrielle smiled so appreciatively, Luc had no choice but to accept her.

***

The next two weeks settled into the rudiments of a routine. Luc's flask of Screech, administered nightly, kept Audrey from sleepwalking. She started each morning with a sauna and swim, and rode her newly purchased mountain bike to and from L'Anse aux Meadows. In the evenings, she joined co-workers practicing yoga, Tai Chi, or Pilates. The next generation of archeologists had been taught to extend their careers by keeping fit, countering endless hours of crouching, creeping, crawling, and climbing.

By mid-month, the time-lapse video equipment was functioning on a tower by the lab, the sod and most of the backfill had been painstakingly removed from the excavation site, Gabrielle and Luc were now a couple, Magnus and Audrey were now a couple, and Alexis was livid at being shut out of both the primary search zone and Luc's social life.

From Audrey's standpoint, it was time to celebrate. The last of the UNESCO officials, except for Dr. Olsen and Else Pederson, were leaving the Views of Vinland Hotel. That meant she was getting a room to herself—The Thorvald, named after the very Viking she was looking for. She could stop drinking daily doses of Screech and avoid a certain slide into either alcoholism or diabetes. She and Magnus would have a private place for their hookups instead of the bush on the far side of Wheeler's Cove. And last, but certainly not least, she would be rid of the lecherous Professor Osborne. Even Alexis's continued presence couldn't squelch her enthusiasm.

Luc suggested a night on the town at The Bait and Hook in St. Anthony, a popular haunt with his YCW colleagues. It was a peculiar place—part restaurant, part sports bar, part dance club—outrageously decorated with fairy lights and graffiti-style wall murals.

It wasn't the first time Luc and Audrey had double-dated, but for Luc, it was the most unsettling. In the past, Audrey had been underage, and her boyfriends were just that. He had felt more like a chaperone. But Magnus was two years older than him, and it was clear he and Audrey were lovers. And, although Gabrielle was beautiful and bright, Luc felt like he had been set up with a lonely cousin.

The foursome found a circular table in the bar with stools they could perch on. Luc ordered mussels, moose burgers, poutine, and a pitcher of beer, while the women strode confidently in their towering heels to the restroom.

They attracted the attention of every man at the bar: Gabrielle, dressed in Montreal Saint Catherine Street chic and Audrey, in London High Street glam. Luc and Magnus watched them disappear and looked at each other, acknowledging, without words, that they were both lucky men.

When the food arrived and Magnus sampled poutine for the first time, he scolded them all vociferously for not introducing him to the Canadian concoction sooner. When the beer arrived and everyone was carded, the server carefully scrutinized Audrey's driver's licence.

"G'wan! You just turned nineteen? Barely legal in Newfoundland, don't you know," she announced before heading back to the bar.

Magnus was nonplussed. "Nineteen? You are only nineteen?"

Luc grinned behind his beer glass. *That's it, squirm, you bastard*, he thought as he took a long, satisfying draught.

"The drinking age in Iceland is twenty," Magnus exclaimed. "You are not even old enough for me to take to a bar!" It was his turn to take a long draught of beer.

Audrey was embarrassed.

"I thought you were a grad student with a four-year Bachelor of Science degree," Magnus continued.

"I am," Audrey countered.

"I have my master's degree, so I can do the math. That means you started university when you were fifteen years old."

Audrey didn't blink. Gabrielle's jaw dropped the same way it did when she walked into the sauna and saw Professor Osborne nude.

"She's an idiot savant," Luc quipped.

Audrey's head swiveled at light speed so she could beam lasers at Luc. Then she ferociously kicked him in the shins with her chrome-toed booties.

Luc screamed like a girl and clutched his leg. As he bent over, he caught sight of her footwear. "What the fuck are those?" he shrieked, in an octave higher than normal.

Gabrielle and Magnus almost knocked heads as they instinctively peered under the table.

"You're wearing speed skates on dates now?" Luc hobbled off the barstool and limped around as if he'd just blocked a shot in hockey.

Simultaneously, Gabrielle and Magnus lifted their heads and looked at each other, stifling laughter. They glanced at Audrey, who was still glowering at Luc. She quickly shifted her searing gaze to Magnus, who straightened up at once and lifted his arms in surrender.

"I think they are beautiful shoes! I think nineteen is the perfect age! I think I am a very lucky man to be with someone so smart, so young, and so well dressed!" His fear wasn't entirely feigned.

Audrey's anger began to ebb.

Gabrielle slid off her barstool and tried to coax Luc onto the dance floor.

"Are you crazy?" he responded, still hopping on one leg. "I can't walk!"

Gabrielle whispered in his ear and then sexily led him away. His samba moves weren't quite up to par, but they still melted the heart of every woman who saw them.

"I am sorry I embarrassed you, Audrey. I should not have done that." Magnus apologized in Icelandic.

"It's okay," she replied, also in Icelandic.

"It is just that you caught me by surprise."

"I understand."

Magnus leaned forward to take her hands in his. He noticed how small they were. "I imagine you catch many men by surprise."

Eventually, Luc limped back to the table, giving Audrey's footwear a wide berth. As the evening wore on, he drank more and more, becoming increasingly morose. When he saw Audrey feeding Magnus nachos, he suggested to Gabrielle that they move closer to the monitors to watch the National Hockey League Stanley Cup playoffs.

When the server came to clear the table, Magnus left for the restroom, promising to bring Audrey back a cocktail. While he was gone, Luc returned.

"The Murphy twins are here. They've invited Gabby and me to a party. They'll drive us home after, so here are the keys to the truck." Luc extricated the keys from his pocket, then glanced up reluctantly. "In the morning, you and Magnus can put your bikes in the truck and drive it back whenever. No rush." Luc appeared watery-eyed and wistful.

"You okay?" Audrey asked.

He attempted a grin, but the dimple didn't appear. "Yeah, I'm good. Maybe a little more wasted than I thought."

"Well, don't pass out and leave Gabrielle at that party on her own."

The turnabout—Audrey as chaperone—hit hard. He nodded and exited quickly.

Audrey was checking her phone when a cosmopolitan appeared in front of her. Still reading her news alerts, she reached out for it and knocked it over. She looked up and saw her outstretched hand over the tipped glass. Her index finger, adorned with the ale protection rune, was pointing to a figure looming nearby: Professor Osborne.

"That was unfortunate. I meant it as a peace offering. Let me get you another," Osborne announced before heading to the bar.

Audrey was stunned for a moment. Then she leapt into action. She grabbed an alcohol-based wipe from her purse, cleaned the edge of her hand, and waved it wildly to air-dry it as she jumped off the stool. She used that hand to guide as much of the pink liquid back into the martini glass as she could. After wiping her hand and the table clean, she jumped back on her barstool and placed the glass on a stool beside her, below table level.

Professor Osborne soon returned with another cosmopolitan. "It's all cleaned up. That was quick." He stood there, waiting for Audrey to take a sip.

It was excruciating, but she managed to fake a smile. "Been here long?" she asked.

"I arrived a while ago. When I saw your boyfriend leave with another young lady, I thought I'd offer you a drink to cheer you up."

"Could you please excuse me for a moment, Professor? I do have to finish this message."

Audrey kept the smile stapled to her face as she sent Magnus a text: *Forget the drink. Go to restaurant, bring back two empty coffee cups with lids. Hurry!*

She wasted more time by flipping through other messages. Then she forced a laugh. "Today's world. We're always connected, wherever we may be."

"Yes. Even in this godforsaken part of it." He glanced down at the drink.

"When exactly do you leave for England?" Audrey asked.

"First thing Monday morning. No flights until then." One of his leering grins reappeared. "I have no idea how I'm going to keep myself amused in the meantime."

Audrey ground her teeth. She contemplated using her chrome-toed booties to damage his penis permanently. Magnus soon arrived, looking confused, but with the coffee cups, as directed.

"Hello, darling," she said, giving him a long, loving kiss. "You remember Professor Osborne, don't you, Magnus?"

"Yes, I do," he replied, extending his hand in greeting.

It was clear Osborne was unsure of what to do next. He looked at the cocktail in front of Audrey, and then meaningfully at Magnus. "Do have fun tonight, won't you?" he said, before he turned and left.

As soon as he was out of sight, Audrey grabbed a coffee cup, held it below table level and poured the hidden cosmopolitan into it. Glancing around cautiously, she swapped the empty martini glass for the full one. She poured that drink into the second cup and snapped on the lids.

"Are those what you Canadians call 'roadies?'" Magnus asked.

"No," said Audrey as she picked up a cup in each hand. "These are what we call 'roofies.'"

"I do not understand."

She switched to Icelandic. "Can you test for Rohypnol and GHB in that mobile lab of yours?"

Magnus's eyes widened. "He tried to drug you?"

"I won't know for sure until we test these."

"Yes, I can."

Audrey switched back to English. "Then we should pay our tab and head out."

Once in the truck, however, Audrey reached out to stop Magnus from turning the key in the ignition. She was staring at the neon sign for The Bait and Hook glowing over the door.

"We can't leave," she said. "The bastard's still in there, still fishing. Now that I've squirmed off the line, he'll try to hook someone else."

"We should call the police."

"I don't want to accuse him without proof. Let's stay here with the lights off until closing time. Make sure he comes out alone."

Barely an hour had passed before Audrey saw Osborne exit the building with a very intoxicated young woman. "Oh my god!" she exclaimed, as she jumped out of the truck cab and turned on her phone's video app. She approached him slowly, while holding up her phone and beaming its light into his face.

"Good evening, Professor Osborne," she called out loudly to ensure her voice would be recorded. Osborne had one arm around the woman's waist, while his other hand held her limp arm over his shoulder. Her head was slumped forward, hair draped over her eyes.

"Aren't you going to introduce me?" Audrey baited. The woman was mumbling inaudibly. "What's her name?"

"Well, I… I don't know," he stammered. "I was only trying to help this poor woman get home."

"That so? Where does she live, Professor Osborne?"

Osborne was now glancing around wild-eyed, like prey pinned by a predator.

"Where are you going to take her?" Audrey pressed.

It was evident that Osborne was thinking of dropping the woman and running.

"Does anyone know who this woman is?" Audrey called out to other patrons leaving the bar.

"Kinda looks like Jamie Sheppard," one girl said as she approached. She flipped up her hair. The woman's eyes rolled back in her head.

"By gawd, it is," exclaimed her boyfriend. "I've never seen Jamie so shitfaced!"

"Could you two be her wingmen tonight and get her home safely?" Audrey asked.

"Sure thing. Come along, luv," the girl replied as the pair lifted Jamie Sheppard off Osborne and shuffled her toward their car. Audrey kept the camera on Osborne.

"Well… uh," he stammered again, trying to regain his composure. "That's taken care of, then." He started walking toward his car.

"Explain it to me, Professor Osborne. How were you going to drive someone home when you don't know who she is or where she lives?"

Osborne stuck his outstretched palm toward the camera until he leapt into his rental car and sped off.

Audrey snapped off her video app and ran over to the couple stuffing Jamie Sheppard into their vehicle.

"You need to take her to the hospital. She may have been roofied."

"Son of a bitch!" snarled the boyfriend, who looked ready to chase after Osborne.

"Forget him. Just get her to the hospital safely and we'll report it to the police."

As she watched the car pull away, Audrey returned to Magnus in the truck. "At least the police station is only a couple of blocks up the street."

"This is getting serious, Audrey," Magnus replied. "I am only here on a work visa, remember? And I have been drinking."

"I understand. Just drop me off and drive a few blocks farther down the road. I'll meet up with you later."

Audrey walked up to the low-slung brown building with the Royal Canadian Mounted Police sign on one side and a communications tower on the other. As she entered, her heels echoed in the emptiness of the linoleum-lined hallway. After standing at what appeared to be a reception counter for quite some time, she looked for a bell or a button to alert someone to her presence. The wall to her right was short, so she leaned over sideways to peer around it. Her left leg, bare from her booties to the hem of her dress, rose as a counterweight.

"Well, this is new. Folks don't usually stroll in and volunteer for a sobriety test," a voice boomed from behind the counter.

Audrey almost fell off her booties. When she righted herself, she was standing in front of the tallest, most striking-looking man she had ever seen. Even in heels that added another three inches to her 5' 7" frame, she had to crane her neck to see his face. Instinctively, she tried looking over the reception desk.

"Na, I'm not standing on a box. Can I help you, miss?"

She tried to compress the story into a pertinent form in her mind while opening her oversized purse and extracting her phone and the coffee cups.

"You brought me coffee?" His sparkling blue eyes were not helping.

"My name is Audrey Vincent. I'm an archeologist with the new excavation at L'Anse aux Meadows."

"I'm Corporal Len Anderson. What can I do for you, Ms. Vincent?"

"Earlier this evening, at The Bait and Hook, I believe a fellow by the name of Professor Clive Osborne *might* have tried to drug me and a local girl by the name of Jamie Sheppard."

"That's a serious accusation, Ms. Vincent. Where's Jamie?"

"Patrons from the bar took her to the hospital. She was extremely inebriated. I told them to have her tested for flunitrazepam and gamma-hydroxybutyrate."

"I truly hope you didn't give the local kids those chemical names."

"No, I used the colloquial term 'roofie'. Earlier in the evening, the suspect, Professor Osborne, who recently groped me in a school bus, had been very eager for me to consume these two drinks he bought for me." She pointed to the coffee cups. "Exhibit A and Exhibit B. I didn't drink them, but rather put them in coffee cups for testing."

Corporal Anderson bit the small scar inside his lower lip, which helped him stay professional when he had the urge to smile inappropriately—or punch someone.

"I left the bar to test the samples myself, but then realized the suspect might move on to someone else. So, I waited outside until closing time. Then I recorded this."

While she played the video on her phone, she examined Anderson's perfectly symmetrical features. He was very practiced at not displaying emotion, but the muscles twitching at the back of his jaw betrayed him.

"Is that yer voice on the video?" he snapped.

"Yes, sir."

The office phone rang. It was clear that Anderson was the only member in the detachment. As he started back to answer it, he pointed to Audrey and barked, "That was very stupid, young lady! Very stupid, indeed. Now you stay put!"

Anderson terrified her. *My god, what have I done?* she thought.

He talked to someone on the phone and looked up at Audrey, who was quite competent at reading lips. "She's here right now. I'll deal with her. You get over to the hospital and take their statements."

*Statements! Should I have just left town?* Audrey wondered. Her apprehensiveness swelled.

Anderson hung up the phone and waved her around to a side door. He buzzed it open. She entered, and he directed her to a chair beside a desk.

"Corporal Anderson, what did I do wrong?" Audrey was on the verge of tears.

He relaxed a bit and sat down beside her. "Sexual assault is a very serious crime. Sexual predators are very serious criminals. You don't confront someone like that. You call the police. That's what we get paid to do."

"He's a professor. One of the top Viking experts in the world. I haven't even received my parchment yet. I had no proof. If I were wrong, my career would've been over before it began."

"Men like this go for jobs where they have access to young women and control over them."

"I know that. Osborne goes back to his English university full of young women on Monday morning. Will you get Jamie's tests results before then?"

Anderson straightened up in his chair, unused to being challenged.

"I could test these drinks tonight, and Jamie's urine if you wanted," Audrey continued. "You would have your proof *tonight*."

"There's no way I'm giving you access to a forensics lab."

"We have our own lab at the heritage site."

Anderson's eyes widened. "You have yer own lab?"

Audrey nodded. "For processing artifacts. Even human remains, if we find them." Then she took another chance. "You know Jamie Sheppard, don't you?"

He aimed a very authoritarian glare her way.

"I saw it in your face when you watched the video. You called her Jamie and me Ms. Vincent," she explained. "How could I have contacted you when nothing had happened yet? He bought me drinks. It could still turn out that those are just cosmos, and Jamie just overdid it."

"Even if yer tests were positive, they would not convict the man. They'd not be admissible in court."

"I thought they might give you probable cause. Something you could use to search his room, hold him here long enough until you find out if he's done this to anyone else. He's been here for two full weeks."

"Let me guess, you took a semester of criminal justice."

"Two."

The phone rang again. Anderson muttered something in Newfinese. "I want to see some ID, and I want to know where yer staying," he said, pointing to a pen and paper as he rose to answer it. This time he turned away when he spoke.

When he walked back to the desk, Audrey assessed his full figure. His pectoral muscles, biceps, and quadriceps stretched the material in his uniform to its limit. She estimated he was about 6' 9".

*Oh my god*, she thought. *Making love to a man like that regularly would be like owning a home gym.*

When Anderson returned to his seat, he picked up a pen and began to write in silence. Surreptitiously, Audrey tried to check him out further. Without looking up or at her, he merely held up his left hand and waved his wedding ring. Then he picked up her driver's licence.

"Yer only nineteen?" he exclaimed. "Yer barely legal in Newfoundland!"

"So I've been told." Audrey sighed.

"I have to go, so you have to go. But I want you back in here tomorrow." He looked at his watch. "Okay, make that later today. At 1500 hours. How are you getting to yer hotel?"

"I have friends in town," she lied. "I'll walk to their place."

"In that dress and those shoes?"

Audrey nodded sheepishly.

"The white-haired lad driving Peggy Volkov's truck is either a coward or he has outstanding warrants."

Audrey was perplexed until Anderson, still writing notes with his right hand, pointed over his shoulder with his left to a CCTV monitor in the corner of the office. The current view was of the front road and sidewalk to the attachment. *Does everyone in Newfoundland know Aunt Peggy's truck?* she wondered.

"He does *not* have outstanding warrants!" she replied, before realizing she just acknowledged the alternative. She reached for her phone on his desk.

"You can call him from our phone. That one stays here. It's evidence. The drinks you can take with you, if you want. The video on your phone is enough to for me to question yer professor. Is he staying at the Views of Vinland too?"

Audrey nodded.

"What's the password to your phone?"

Her mind raced to catalogue everything on the device. "Three one four one," she answered reluctantly.

"First four digits of pi," he replied. "Figures."

She raised an eyebrow in surprise.

"I'm not just another pretty face, you know," he countered with a hint of a grin.

***

On the road to L'Anse aux Meadows, Audrey and Magnus discussed the ramifications of what they were about to do. Magnus had cardkey access to the lab and the alarm system in case he had to work after hours, but the pair didn't want to be recorded by the site's security cameras, which would be activated at night by motion detectors.

Audrey used her eidetic memory to map the detectors' positions. There were fewer on the ocean side of the site. She remembered seeing a rowboat by the area where a giant statue of Leif Eiriksson was soon to be erected. The statue would commemorate the place where the Norseman first set foot in North America over a thousand years ago.

They drove to the harbour and found the rowboat near a concrete pad. Audrey grabbed a couple of overcoats and boots from the back of the truck. As they donned them, Magnus expressed his misgivings.

"Rowing a boat on the ocean at night with no lights is not safe. This is not a good idea."

"Some Viking you are," Audrey chided, as she threw on Aunt Peggy's slicker.

Thankfully, the moon was full and the ocean calm. Both Audrey and Magnus were excellent rowers, so they reached the rear of the site faster than expected. "I guess you really are a Viking," she recanted.

Once ashore, Audrey ordered, "Stay directly behind me." She adroitly led Magnus to the mobile trailer that housed the lab. He entered his security code and opened the door. Then he raced to conduct the tests on the contents of Audrey's coffee cups. His hands were trembling.

"I do not understand why we are taking this risk if the results are not admissible in court," Magnus said.

Audrey leaned against the table on which Magnus working. "If that Jamie girl was drugged, she may not remember a thing, not even Osborne's face.

But if the drinks he gave me were spiked with the same drug, with the same chemical composition as what she ingested, it could connect the dots back to him."

*This girl has a bigger set than I have*, he thought, as he glanced over in admiration. Audrey's face was now etched in terror as she gaped at the window behind him. He whirled around.

"Did you see something?"

"Not sure. Keep working," she directed, as she headed out the door.

She definitely saw someone peering through the window. The heavily bearded face was chilling: ash-grey, with large cheekbones and piercing eyes. She walked straight into the darkness and knew she would encounter him. Her veins had turned to liquid helium and her heart hurt as it flipped in her chest. In her head, she could hear a rhythmic sound growing ever louder, like that of an approaching train. These were all signs it was about to happen again.

Moonlight revealed the now-exposed outlines of the thousand-year-old encampment. *We have unearthed its ghosts*, she thought. Slowly, and with profound fear, she forced herself to face Building F and Hall 1 within it, including the private room of the camp's leader. And there he stood.

"Who are you? Why have you entered my camp?" the bearded man asked.

Audrey couldn't move.

"Do you understand my language?" His voice boomed.

"I understand," Audrey blurted in Old Icelandic. "My name is Aud."

The giant moved toward her with strides so huge and strong, he seemed to float over the bog. His blond hair and black cloak swirled around him.

"How did you come to be here?" he demanded.

Audrey's mind raced for a plausible explanation that a thousand-year-old Viking would accept. "We were shipwrecked," she answered. "I was washed ashore."

The man turned his head suspiciously. "With whom did you sail?"

"With Thorer of Norway and his wife Gudrid. Our ship was filled with lumber and trading goods."

"Your accent is strange."

"I have not spoken to anyone in a long time."

"You are alone? How did you survive?"

"By fishing, hunting, picking berries. The land is plentiful."

"Is it inhabited?"

"Yes. By a people the like of whom I have never seen. They rarely venture from the bush."

*"Skraeling."*

It was the name the Norse gave the Indigenous people of North America that some scholars have translated to mean "little men" and others "barbarian."

Audrey begrudgingly nodded.

"They have not carried you away?"

"I am a shieldmaiden. I frightened them off."

At that moment, an arctic hare dashed across the bog. Audrey hit the dirt and covered herself with Aunt Peggy's enormous slicker. A motion detector was triggered and a security camera flashed.

Leif Eiriksson roared with laughter. "Behold, the shieldmaiden!"

Audrey stood up carefully. Even if this were only a figment of her imagination, she would try to get information from it.

"Do you claim this land as yours?" she asked.

"This is my camp. This is my land."

"If I find the bodies of my kinsmen, may I bury them here?"

"I cannot allow it. I am a Christian now. Bodies must be buried in hallowed ground."

Magnus carefully opened the door of the lab and called out to Audrey. "Is anyone there?"

She glanced over her shoulder to address him. "No," she replied, and when she looked back, she discovered she had answered truthfully.

She retraced her route and re-entered the lab.

"I saw a flash. Did you trigger a motion detector?" Magnus asked.

"No. It was an animal. I hid. Have you finished?"

"Just printing off the results now." His face was grim. "There was enough Rohypnol in those drinks to incapacitate you for eight hours. The bastard!"

Audrey began to shiver uncontrollably at the horrifying thought of being raped by Osborne for hours with no way of fighting back. Magnus put his arms around her and kissed her clammy forehead. "You saved yourself. You saved that girl. Tomorrow, we will take these results to your Royally Mounted Canadians."

On the drive back to the Views of Vinland Hotel, Magnus began to worry. Audrey hadn't spoken since she saw the test results. When they had returned to the truck, she stood transfixed at the spot where Leif Eiriksson may have landed. After several minutes, she slipped into the chrome-adorned booties once more, placed her rose cloche on her head, and re-wrapped herself in her oversized shawl that flapped at her sides as she walked.

"Almost home," Magnus said, reaching for her hand, when he spotted the sign for the turn-off. Audrey came to life. Magnus caught the strobe effect of flashing blue and red lights across her face.

His head whipped forward. The lights emanated from a point about a mile past the turn-off.

"Keep going," Audrey ordered, trance-like.

"The last thing you need to see tonight is an accident," Magnus warned.

"I said keep going."

He obeyed. Road flares ignited in the darkness. An ambulance was parked sideways across the highway and a tow truck hovered nearby, like a raptor waiting to swoop in and pick up carrion.

As they approached, a member of the RCMP was walking down the row of cars in front of them, aiming his flashlight into the drivers' windows and briefly chatting with the occupants. When he reached Aunt Peggy's truck, his huge frame crossed in front of its headlights and arrived, instead, at the passenger window. It was Corporal Anderson.

"There's been an accident, as you can see," he said. "Someone you may know is involved."

Magnus peered at him anxiously, but Audrey was indifferent. He continued.

"At the end of that video you shot earlier this evening, Ms. Vincent, the professor drove away in a rented vehicle. Do you happen to remember the make and model?"

Audrey's green eyes closed briefly to replay the scene in detail. Then she met Anderson's gaze directly. "It was a grey Chevrolet Impala."

"Then it would appear the professor has been in a serious collision with a moose."

Without changing expression, she responded, "How's the moose?"

Even the battle-hardened Anderson had to whistle between his teeth. "Well, seems yer up for making an identification, then. He's conscious, but he won't tell us who he is. And his wallet was destroyed."

Magnus fumbled for his door handle. "Sir, I can identify him. My name is Magnus Stefansson. I know Professor Osborne, also."

"No problem," Audrey said. "I've got this."

As Anderson led her to the scene, he tried to prepare her. "There's a helluva lot of blood. They've put pressure pants on him because his legs were badly mangled. He'll probably be paralyzed, but the paramedics think he'll make it."

Osborne had been strapped to a spinal board, but was still struggling from the neck up. "Free me of these earthly bonds and let me fly, I beseech you!" he cried. In the blaze of headlights, he saw the dark outline of a graceful, helmeted figure descending toward him, her long hair wafting in the breeze and her wings fluttering rhythmically at her sides.

He blinked rapidly and tried to focus on her face.

"Oh, sweet Valkyrie, have you come for me?" he begged.

"What makes you think you're fit for Valhalla?" Audrey was more than keen to hone his morphine-fueled fantasies and twist them against him.

"I've been faithful to the sagas, a protector of Odin's treasure here in Midgard. You could dispatch me, if you chose."

"You are the most evil and vile of all men, a coward who needs to enfeeble women or they would sneer at you and reject you completely."

Osborne's head tried to fight against the strap. "No, no, no," he whined. The astonished paramedics reached out to stop him.

"You? Worthy of Valhalla? You're not even worthy of being Hel-bound! Instead I condemn you to live an eternity here in Midgard, unable to move, unable to die, cursed and despised by all!"

Osborne cried out and continued to wail in agony, not of the flesh this time, but of the soul. Audrey strode away in a ghostly aura of light. Anderson was incredulous.

"We just finished the tests on those drinks he gave me," she said, as he caught up to her. "They were laced with flunitrazepam. I'm sure you'll discover your friend, Jamie Sheppard, has the same drug in her system."

"Me cousin. Jamie Sheppard's me cousin."

"I can hand over the results right now, if you like."

"It can wait till this afternoon," said Anderson. "Osborne isn't going anywhere."

He walked her back to the truck and looked directly at Magnus. "Make sure she goes straight to her room and goes to bed, wha?"

Magnus nodded and restarted the truck. Corporal Anderson waved them out of the lineup with his flashlight so they could turn around and head back to the Views of Vinland Hotel.

***

Audrey returned to the RCMP detachment in St. Anthony about twelve hours later. This time, more members were present. Corporal Anderson took her statement. It was clear he hadn't slept.

He pushed papers over to Audrey to sign, glancing at the coffee cups and test results beside them. When her head was bowed, he was amazed by the Valkyrie from the night before who had reverted into a chastened schoolgirl. He was also amazed because her green eyes now appeared to be violet. He assumed she wore tinted contact lenses.

"Here's yer phone," he said, as he held it up. "We made a copy of the video, but it likely won't be needed now that Osborne's confessed."

He tried to give Audrey a reassuring smile, but he was overshadowed by the commotion behind him. The other members were hooting and pointing at the CCTV monitor. One reached for it and locked in the view.

Anderson stood up to see it more clearly. "Well, this is new," he said, as he planted his hands on his hips. Audrey strained over the desk to see it as well. Two men were engaged in a fistfight on the front lawn.

Without turning around, Anderson addressed Audrey. "Yer white-haired lad—Magnus was it?—has come to pick you up. I think I recognize the dark-haired lad with the topknot from pictures on yer phone. What's his name?"

"Luc Laliberte," she answered, as she rose to her feet. "Peggy Volkov's grand-nephew." She turned to leave the office.

"Na, na, na! You stay put! When two bull moose are butting heads, it doesn't help when the cause of the fight shows up."

He strode outside. The other members crowded around the CCTV monitor. Audrey eyed them coldly as she joined them. They dialed back their amusement only slightly.

"Don't worry, miss," a member smirked. "Lenny, er, Corporal Anderson's got this."

"Hey! Hey! Hey! *Hey! Hey!*" Corporal Anderson bellowed, as he marched up to the combatants now rolling around on the grass. He seized Luc by the shoulder and, with one hand, peeled him off Magnus, who used the opportunity to check his injured nose. When Magnus saw blood on his hands, he jumped up, swore in Icelandic, and swung hard at Luc. Anderson blocked the blow with his other hand. Muffled cheers issued from inside the detachment.

"Jaysus jumping Moses, what the hell's the matter with you two?" Anderson roared. "Can you not read this frigging sign? He bent forward, hands out and feet astride to keep them apart, then pointed to the RCMP crest on the sign near the sidewalk. Inside the detachment, Audrey tilted her head slightly to fully appreciate his flexed glutes.

"You're at a frigging RCMP detachment! And I'm the frigging horseman that's gonna lock up yer sorry arses if you don't stand down *now!*"

Luc was breathing hard and glaring at Magnus. There was blood all over his shirt and his knuckles, which were still clenched. At this point, Magnus was more concerned with his nose.

"Lawd thundering!" Anderson reached out and tweaked Magnus's nose to check it. Magnus screeched and grabbed it with both hands. Muffled groans issued from inside the building. "You be fine, b'y, it's not broke!" Anderson said. Luc sneered, the dimple in his cheek etched deeply.

"Luc! How'd you get here?" Anderson commanded, instantly removing the sneer off Luc's face.

"Ah, friends dropped me off," Luc stammered, wondering how this Mountie knew his name.

"Magnus! How'd you get here?"

Magnus held his nose with one hand, lifted keys out of a jeans pocket with the other, pointed to Luc and said, "I have his truck."

Anderson grabbed the keys. "Got another way back?"

"Audrey and I have bikes in the back."

"Go get them. *Now!*"

Magnus trotted off obediently.

"Where's Audrey?" Luc asked, pressing hard against Anderson's massive paw. "I have to see her."

"Na, you don't."

Luc's eyes flared as he challenged Anderson. "I'm driving her back," he snarled.

"Na, you're not. *I* am. And I'm phoning yer Aunt Peggy to say you better be back in twenty minutes or I'm coming with handcuffs. Here's yer keys. Now scoot!"

The two men glared at each other until Anderson's look changed from anger to respect. "Be sensible, b'y," he said under his breath. "I'll get her back safe." Luc finally backed down and snatched the keys. He pointed at Magnus defiantly as they passed each other on the lawn, then jumped into the truck and drove off.

Magnus handed Audrey's bike over to Anderson.

"Now, you scoot too, and stay away from that other bugger for the rest of the summer. Do you read me?"

Magnus wasn't entirely sure what he said, but he nodded.

Once both young men were gone, Anderson exhaled and dropped Audrey's bike on the lawn. Then he looked up at the CCTV camera and wearily gave his comrades the finger. Audrey appeared in the doorway and smiled shyly. "You handled that very well, Corporal. Now, how are you at solving cold cases? *Really* cold cases?"

\*\*\*

Corporal Anderson thanked the waitress for bringing two black coffees as soon as he and Audrey had squeaked into a red vinyl booth at the roadside cafe. He was still adding sugar and cream to his when Audrey finished hers.

"Would you happen to know where a gal could get a good non-fat extra dry cappuccino around here?" she asked.

"Na," he replied at once, still stirring. "By the way, me aunt and uncle want to thank you for what you did for Jamie. In Newfoundland, that usually involves large amounts of food. Be prepared." He finally took a sip of his fructose- and lactose-laden liquid. "So, tell me about this cold case of yours."

Audrey spun her tale in the lingo of a contemporary *skald*. "A long time ago, a really badass gang invaded the territory of another gang. The don of the badass gang sent his own sons to set up a base of operations in the new territory. Everything went well until the original gang whacked one of the sons."

Anderson grinned as he listened to Audrey's unique spin on the Norse incursion into North America.

"Where the badass gang came from, the custom was to bury their dead with their relatives or at sea. But the badass gang members didn't bring the body back with them. They said the son planned to stay in the new territory, so that's where they buried him. His brother flew into a rage and sent them back to get the body. But they soon returned saying they looked all over the place and couldn't find the grave. The brother sent different gang members back and they couldn't find the body, either. Eventually, the badass gang gave up the new territory because they were outnumbered and couldn't hold it.

"Much, much later, authorities investigated the activities of the badass gang while they were in the disputed territory. Two different teams of investigators dug up the gang's old headquarters and found no trace of a body. Each time, the area was backfilled with sand and sodded over to protect the crime scene.

"Then even later, a new clue turns up: an old marker that says, 'Below this stick rests the body of the don's son.' And the marker was found right where everyone had been looking. What's more, it's found sitting *on top* of the new sod."

The waitress returned to refill Audrey's coffee mug. Audrey savoured several sips while she waited for Anderson to digest her story. Then she asked, "So, what do *you* think? How would you investigate this murder? And how would you look for the body?"

"There's two ways to approach a cold case," said Anderson. "Start from the most recent tip and work backwards, or start over from the first clue and build a new case from there. If you have enough resources, create two teams and do both. See if they meet in the middle."

"We have two million dollars," Audrey said.

Anderson launched his recently sipped coffee across the table. If Audrey hadn't been so drained by the previous day's events, she would have laughed uproariously. Instead, she simply dabbed her blouse with a paper serviette.

"You have two million dollars for something that happened over a thousand years ago?"

"That's why we have all the toys: on-site lab, ground-penetrating radar, even augmented reality devices to plot the position of buildings and materials that no longer exist." She pinned herself against the wall in case of another explosion.

"You have ground-penetrating radar? I had a *warm* body to look for not long ago and couldn't get access to that."

"Well, if you get another one, give me a shout."

"That's unlikely," he said, as he leaned back in the booth. "I'm transferring out soon."

Audrey was shocked. "But you're *from* here."

"I love the Rock, but it's too hard investigating people you know—as suspects or victims."

"That's disappointing. I was looking forward to collaborating with you on this."

He held up his left hand and waved his ring finger again. Audrey managed an embarrassed smile. *It's like a Norse protection rune against silly young women,* she thought.

"I'm flattered, me dear, but I'm a happily married man with a daughter who, after yer escapades this weekend, I'm gonna lock up till she's thirty."

"That's a rather sexist comment, you know," Audrey remarked. "But I don't think you'll have to worry. With you as her father, no predator would dare go near her."

"There are a few things I plan to tell her, same as I'm telling you now. Number one: When it comes to yer work life, never believe you don't have options. You let that bastard Osborne harass you because you thought he could end yer career. Very few arseholes really have that much power. As soon as you calls them out, there's usually a line of people ready to back you up. If it turns out they do have juice, there's always another career. In fact, you'd make a damn fine horseman.

"Number two: When it comes to yer love life, *don't* give yerself too many options. We're always happier with just one person. We just are. Trick is picking the right one. Now take that Luc fella, for example. He was ready to go through me to make sure you were safe. Not too many men ever tried do that. Leastwise, not sober. He's certainly better than some wuss hiding down the street 'cause he's worried about the blowback.

"Number three: When it comes to solving crimes, in the past or the present, the same advice holds true. Follow the money. Now, it wouldn't be the first time something's popped up outta the bog; I had a whole body do that once. But I tend to agree with you, it's not likely trained investigators missed it twice.

"Two million dollars is a helluva motive. Find out who benefits from that and you just might find the person who planted that clue. He or she really does know where the body is buried."

Corporal Anderson plunked down a five-dollar bill on the table, stood up, and donned his RCMP cap. "Now, c'mon, me dear, I'm giving you a police escort to Vinland."

***

The next day, Audrey revisited the excavation after working hours. She had obtained a security passcode from Ryan Miller, explaining that she often chose to work late, which was certainly true. She walked to Complex F-G, sat in the area of Hall 1, which would have included Leif Eiriksson's room, and wondered if she could summon him back.

She closed her eyes and imagined what the room must have looked like one thousand years ago. She decorated it in furs and rough-hewn furniture, even placing an Ulfberht sword and painted shield against a wall. It didn't work. When she opened her eyes, all she saw was sand, grass, and sea.

Still exhausted from the drama of the weekend, she laid down on the sand, cushioning her head in her arms and lowering her eyelids. The sound of an approaching train returned as she started to fall asleep. Then she felt someone's warm breath on her cheek.

Forcing her eyes to open wide, a lucid dreaming technique she had learned as a child, she found herself face to face with Leif Eiriksson. Not only was she in his room, she was in his bed. And she was naked.

"So, you want to lay with me, shieldmaiden," Eiriksson whispered.

Audrey peered into his ice-blue eyes. His golden hair fell around his massive shoulders, but his beard obscured the beauty of his face. He drew a heavy sheepskin hide over her.

"I cannot touch you. I am married. It would be a sin," he said.

"But I am in your bed, unclothed."

"You need protection from the other men. This is the only place you will get it. I will lay a sword between us."

"It is difficult to be so close to you, to desire you, and not be able to touch you."

Eiriksson's husky voice replied, "My countrymen who have not accepted the new religion would think me mad right now. But Christianity is the path I have chosen."

"You could always confess your sin afterward and ask for forgiveness."

Eiriksson laughed heartily. "You are spirited. I think I will give you to my brother, Thorvald."

Audrey stiffened. "I am not a *thrall*. I am a free woman."

"I mean to give you away in marriage, not slavery. Now get some sleep. We leave in the morning."

Eiriksson heaved his huge frame and turned away from her. Audrey peeked under the sheepskin to fully appreciate his flexed glutes.

"I will not go with you," she said. "But keep watch for my shipwrecked kinsmen along the way. May luck be with you, so you may find them."

# CHAPTER FOUR
## Tales of Exploration

*There was much talk about Leif's Vinland journey, and his brother, Thorvald, believed that the country had not been sufficiently explored. So, Leif said to Thorvald, "If it be your will, brother, you may go to Vinland with my ship." Then Thorvald got ready for the voyage with a crew of thirty men, consulting all the time with his brother Leif. They fixed up the ship and sailed away, and nothing is reported to have happened before they got to Vinland. At Leif's camp, they laid up their ship and spent a pleasant winter, getting their food by fishing.*

*—Saga of the Greenlanders*

Peggy Volkov buzzed around her B&B home with blissful anticipation. She hummed a series of traditional tunes as she shifted from dusting to dishes to decorating. Luc was applying a topcoat of paint to the exterior window-sills. He chastised her for stepping onto her deck before its stain was completely dry.

"Luc, you don't know what it means to me to have you here. This place hasn't looked this good since I can't say when. And we're fully booked. With all yer scientist friends taking up the fancy places, I'm getting me travel trade back. One more season like this and I can finally retire!"

Luc screwed up his face trying to scratch the orange spatter off his stubble without adding more. He had never painted a house with such vivid colours before. But by Newfoundland standards, Aunt Peggy's navy and ginger exterior was tame.

Her delight was diminished by the sight of him, wearily focused on the task at hand and totally bereft of joy. He hadn't been the same since he came back bruised and bloody from St. Anthony a week ago. She recognized the signs. His heart was bruised and bloody as well.

"G'wan then, finish up and I'll make us a celebration supper. Tourist season starts with a bang for you and me this long weekend, and we may not get a chance for another." Luc began to wipe off his brushes. "Why don't you invite that friend of yours, the brunette you brought with you from Winnipeg?"

He looked up in alarm. "Audrey?"

She sniggered. "Unless you snuck in another one I don't know about."

"That's not going to work, Aunt Peggy. I beat up her boyfriend."

"From what Lenny Anderson told me, he deserved it."

Luc almost knocked the orange paint over the deck. "You talked to the Mountie? What the hell, Aunt Peggy!"

She walked as far as she dared past the patio doors. "Don't worry, luv, I've known Lenny since he was only this high," she said, leveling her hand at her hips.

"Since he was a fetus, then."

"You see, Luc? That's a Newfoundland sense of humour, right there. Now yer coming 'round."

"What about my girlfriend, Gabrielle?"

"That would be a bit like bringing her home to Mum, wouldn't it? You ready for that? I just want to make sure yer friend from Winnipeg gets a home-cooked meal in her every once in a while." Aunt Peggy could see the hopeful look in Luc's eye as he pondered the proposal. Now she could smile without guilt.

To Luc's surprise, Audrey accepted the invitation. He was also surprised at how nervous he was, waiting for her outside the Views of Vinland Hotel, as if it were a first date. He peered through the passenger window tentatively as she dashed up to the truck, half expecting her to throw something at him. Her curled hair bounced around her shoulders and perfectly framed a radiant face.

The relief was overwhelming.

Within seconds, they were chatting convivially as if the last seven days had never happened.

Once they were back at the B&B, Aunt Peggy placed a hefty Jiggs dinner before them: salt beef and pork riblets boiled with turnip, cabbage, potatoes, and carrots. It was accompanied by a savoury pease pudding created with yellow split peas and spices.

Audrey poured the wine she brought with her and offered a toast to the significant season ahead.

Then Aunt Peggy broached the subject she most wanted to discuss. "So, tell me about yer parents, Audrey. I used to watch that TV show they were on for so long. About Egypt and all those strange places. What was it called?"

Audrey almost swallowed a riblet whole. "*Ghosts of History*," she managed, before washing it down with wine. "If you saw the show, you pretty much know all about them. In fact, they'll be here on Saturday."

"Will they now? Isn't that news?" Peggy Volkov's gregarious smile covered it well, but she was incensed at people she hadn't even met yet; parents so distant that either their daughter couldn't tell them what she'd been through or, if she had, they wouldn't tear down heaven and earth to get to her sooner. "So, what's the occasion?"

"Since L'Anse aux Meadows opens to tourists at the end of the month, we've been working like crazy to clear the protective sand from the original structures. The full site will be on display for the first time in over thirty years. Mother and Dad will be hosting a live, two-hour TV presentation of the event on Victoria Day."

"Well, that'll be nice for you, luv. To have yer parents here for a time."

Audrey replied eagerly and innocently. "Yes, it will. They even booked a room in Views of Vinland so we can stay together for the whole weekend."

Aunt Peggy had to run to the kitchen with the dishes to hide her tears. *A whole weekend. What a sacrifice!* she raged inwardly.

"Pardon me, luv," she explained when she returned to the table. "But as me Russian fadder used to say, '*Wer rastet, der rostet.*' He who rests grows rusty."

Audrey was confused. She understood the phrase, but knew it to be German.

Luc refilled Audrey's wine glass and led her out to the now-dry deck overlooking a stunning view of St. Lunaire Bay.

"Wow, look at this! You painted this three-story yourself?" Audrey marvelled.

"Yep," he replied, holding his beer tight to his chest as he admired his work. "I'm handsome *and* handy." The dimple was now a deep line in his cheek.

She turned toward the sun-washed bay. "Magnus and I are finished."

Luc threw his head backward in angst and then forward in embarrassment as he turned seaward as well. "I'm so sorry, Audrey. Please forgive me."

"It wasn't you. It was me. He said I was too scary to have as a girlfriend."

"Wha-a-at?"

"Do you know what Magnus does in his spare time in Iceland? He races formula off-road dune buggies on the lava fields. Have you *seen* the online videos? And *I'm* too scary!"

Luc's eyes were pasted on Audrey for signs as to whether he should quip or commiserate. She continued.

"I *am* a scary date. I have a computer brain inside a girl's body. I know everything, and I understand little. I've been everywhere, and I don't have a home. I fear almost everything, except what I should. My parents are famous. And my best friend's a smoking hot journalist who can rip you up with his words or his fists."

Luc stopped breathing. It was the first time she had ever complimented him physically.

"And Magnus doesn't even know I talk to dead people," she added.

Luc exhaled and asked softly, "How's that going, by the way?"

"Well, Leif Eiriksson and I had a nice chat last week." Audrey grabbed the deck rail and looked panic-stricken. "Luc, will you please help me prepare for this live broadcast? I don't want to pee on my shoes in front of the whole country."

He wrapped his arm around hers like he did the night of the Scoff and Scuff and spoke in French.

"Come to my boudoir, mademoiselle, and let me show you my etchings. Or at least my recently delivered Diploma of Applied Arts in Creative Communications from Red River College. It will prove that I am fully qualified to help you be the perfect model in front of any camera. Clothing is optional."

\*\*\*

The television crew arrived at L'Anse aux Meadows with a fleet of trailers, an army of personnel, and even a small air force consisting of a helicopter and two camera-equipped drones. As usual, Luc had taken on two jobs: the first, behind the scenes as a site-savvy technical advisor to the network, and the second, on camera as a media-savvy tourist guide.

The production was on a scale that would petrify media veterans. Except Audrey's parents, that is. Lachlan and Hanna Vincent joked with archeologists and producers alike while grips set up lights around them and make-up artists dabbed their noses.

They had recommended Alexis as a youthful spokesperson for the archeological team because they knew her to be knowledgeable and fearless. When they discovered Dr. Olsen had chosen their daughter instead, they bartered Audrey's participation down to a staged swordfight with Cody Murphy, the blacksmith re-enactor and occasional swordsman from Norstead Village. Audrey was an experienced fencer, and the producers were keen to avoid an accidental decapitation during a live broadcast.

After forty-eight hours of staging, pre-recording video cutaways, and countless rehearsals, the director of production instructed the cast to take their positions. Audrey's parents stood gazing toward the sky in front of the replica longhouse. It was almost sunset. A drone flew in from the south, its camera catching the waves crashing on the shore and the cast of characters, both students and professionals, dispersed over the site. It hovered long enough for the opening title to appear on screen, then zoomed in for a close-up of the Vincents welcoming the audience to this special televised presentation.

The moment the director called for a cut to commercial, a blaze of activity broke out in the mobile control centre. Luc couldn't contain his glee; this was the epitome of his career ambitions for the past four years. Not a single classmate could claim to have been where he was now during a live national broadcast.

Despite his training, it was still difficult for him to discern what was happening in the babble of voices, the spectrum of lights on the sound and vision mixers, and the bank of monitors displaying a dizzying array of images. Luc was there to provide a split-second answer to any question the director might have about the site or its staff. This was his primary responsibility until he was scheduled to appear by the Meeting of Two Worlds sculpture for his interview about the impact of the Norse arrival on the island's Indigenous people.

Audrey was chatting with Cody Murphy in the shadows by the longhouse. Cody's obvious terror mitigated her inward nervousness. As he spun his replica Ulfberht sword in his hand and rocked from foot to foot, he spoke Newfinese at an incomprehensible speed.

Audrey checked her gear. She and Aunt Peggy had shared great fun concocting a shieldmaiden costume, composed of laced-up leather boots, black britches, a blue silk blouse, and tanned hide vest, bound by a giant leather belt. She styled her hair in a messy mass of locks and braids, and smeared a bit of kohl around her eyes.

Alexis stood near Complex D-E, her turf during the excavations. She was ridiculously overdressed in a gold voile blouse draped over a low-cut and too-tight velvet camisole. She gave no thought to the crane hovering over her, or the cameraman strapped to it, who practised how far and how fast he could zoom into and out of her cleavage.

As the production progressed, the participants began to recognize which segment was coming up next based on their many rehearsals. When the time approached for the sword fight, a production assistant, tablet under her arm, came for Audrey and Cody. She had to grab Cody and physically position him on his mark. When Audrey saw how many times Cody wiped his sweaty palms on his britches, she realized executing the choreographed swordplay was no longer possible. But improvising a television-worthy fight was.

Luc had permission to leave the mobile unit because his segment was soon after Audrey's. He had planned to stand behind her camera to give her moral support, and then sprint to the sculpture during Alexis' intervening on-camera presentation.

When the huge HMI lights fired up, turning evening into day, and the cameras were moved into position for the fight, Audrey leaned into Cody. She barked his name a couple of times before his green eyes met her now steel grey ones.

"You have only one thing to worry about for the next three minutes," she said.

"What's that?" he squeaked.

"Getting butt-kicked by a girl on national television!" Quickly glancing beyond her helmet's metal nose guard, she saw the somewhat alarmed production assistant counting down before the cameras went live. On cue, she leapt back into position and yelled, "Prepare to die, swordsman!"

Audrey began to circle Cody, who matched her moves defensively. She reached in with her sword and tapped his legs playfully, startling him with her speed and agility. Then Audrey laughed. And Cody lost it. The fight was on.

Cody clenched his sword and swung hard. Audrey countered with her shield and pushed him away. Then he surged forward with a mighty, right-handed thrust. She stepped aside and kicked his feet out from under him.

"What the fuck?" exclaimed the director of production inside the control centre, as he contacted the production assistant with Alexis to prepare her for a possible quick cutaway.

"What the fuck?" breathed Luc as he watched nearby, horrified by the improvisation.

Cody picked himself up and lunged at Audrey several times. Each time, she used her shield and pointed her sword at Cody's breast. Between parries, she caught sight of a figure standing beyond the camera. He was also in costume, arms outstretched, and hands folded over the hilt of his sword that rested on the tip of its blade in the soil before him.

Her attention was divided between an enraged Cody, a frightened production assistant, and the amused stranger. Her veins turned to ice as she heard the sound of an approaching train. *Oh no, not now!* she pleaded silently. She was distracted long enough for Cody to knock the sword out of her hand with a sideways slash that came within centimetres of her face.

In a move often seen in martial arts films, Audrey bent over backwards, the top of her helmet grazing the ground, as Cody's second swing passed over her, causing him to lose his balance. She allowed herself to roll back onto her shoulders, curled her knees to her chest and then sprung to her feet again. Before Cody could recover, Audrey caught sight of a shining sword twirling through the lights toward her. She held her breath and heightened her mental acuity, so she could time the revolutions in the air. At the perfect moment, she reached up and grabbed the incoming sword by its hilt.

"Okay, we're gonna stay on the sword fight a little longer," the director dryly communicated to Alexis' production assistant, over the exclamations of admiration in the mobile control centre. "Tell your girl to cut her presentation in half."

Audrey let Cody score a few more points before she wielded her new sword and sliced his shield in two. Both combatants halted in surprise. Hanna Vincent was speedily dispatched to conduct a post-fight interview with her daughter, who was shaking hands with Cody and bending over to remove her helmet. She straightened up, flipped her hair back, and tucked her helmet under an arm. While her astonished mother approached, Audrey stared beyond the lights at the beguiled stranger who clapped his hands at her performance before disappearing into the darkness.

"That was quite the battle!" her mother proclaimed, smiling professionally at the camera while inwardly reeling. "And now, my husband and I have the great pleasure of introducing this Viking shieldmaiden: our daughter, Audrey Vincent, a second-generation archeologist who will be working on the excavations this summer at L'Anse aux Meadows. Now, tell us, Audrey, even though shieldmaidens appear frequently in contemporary fiction and television, how authentic is this image of Norsewomen as warriors?"

Once again, Audrey decided to go off-script.

"Shieldmaidens are mentioned in several Norse sagas and poems, and there are a few historical references to Norsewomen taking part in battles during the Viking Age as well. The Danish historian Saxo Grammaticus, for example, recorded that shieldmaidens fought in the Battle of Bråvalla in 750. In 971, a Byzantine historian reported that armed women were found among the dead of the Norse Varangian guard, an elite group of mercenaries.

"A recent study of Viking graves in northern England revealed there were more women present than originally thought, including one buried with a sword and a shield. And a small silver figurine discovered in Denmark just last year depicts a pony-tailed woman, also with a sword and shield."

Hanna Vincent was flummoxed by her daughter's unrehearsed response that was contrary to the prevailing view of many Vikingologists. "But isn't it likely these references are as legendary as the Valkyries themselves, mythical women with helmets and wings who selected the bravest warriors on a battlefield and flew them off to Valhalla? And even Valkyries were depicted with spears, rarely with swords, which are associated with masculinity."

Audrey countered, "The Norse were described in reports of the day as being significantly taller than medieval Europeans, so Norsewomen would have been well-matched to their opponents in stature. I think it's quite conceivable that some learned to wield these masculine symbols of power very well and could hold their own on the battlefield."

The director cut from the mother and daughter duo to Alexis standing in the excavation of Complex D-E. A north breeze had picked up offshore, sending bits of sand and debris swirling into the air. It also whipped the collar of Alexis' blouse as she spoke, alternately revealing too much bosom or not enough face. Alexis battled through it all professionally. She even managed to compress her presentation on modern excavation techniques into a comprehensible fraction of its original length.

Meanwhile, Luc and Audrey's father waited impatiently for their cue near the Meeting of Two Worlds sculpture. They had only met a couple of times previously, and this occasion was equally as uncomfortable. Lachlan Vincent wanted to be open-minded, but could not believe such a virile young man could maintain a platonic friendship with his pretty young daughter. Yet he and his wife relied on Luc to provide support for Audrey when they could not. It was a strange and somewhat strained arrangement.

Luc was wearing the uniform of a Parks Canada guide. Acknowledging an awkwardly oblique request from Ryan Miller, he wore his long hair in braids to accentuate his Indigenous heritage. He also endured his third shave of the day right before the show to remove the constant stubble that was a legacy from his French ancestors.

Before long, their production assistant signaled a countdown. Lachlan smiled into the dead camera with relaxed professionalism. When the camera light came on and the production assistant pointed to him, he projected boldly and clearly.

"Welcome to the iconic Meeting of Two Worlds sculpture at L'Anse aux Meadows. This spectacular work of art heralds the place where Europeans and North American Indigenous peoples may have met, perhaps for the very first time, over a thousand years ago.

"With me is Luc Laliberte, a Young Canada Works student, who is a guide at the visitor centre here. So, Luc, tell us about the Indigenous population that once inhabited the northern peninsula of Newfoundland."

Luc addressed the camera with equal poise. "As a matter of fact, Dr. Vincent, evidence of five or six Indigenous groups has been found, stretching back five thousand years—particularly artifacts from people of the Dorset culture, who were here at least two hundred years before the Vikings."

Opening a box, Luc pointed out the tools and pottery shards found in the area and described their origins. "If the Norse sagas are accurate, it may have been the Beothuk who encountered the Vikings. The sagas describe attempts at trade that ended in conflict. In 2010, a team of European researchers discovered a previously unknown DNA sequence in Iceland, which they suggest might have come from a captured Beothuk woman. One theory is that the Beothuk shied away from the Europeans who arrived centuries later because of what happened to them at the hands of the Vikings—one of many factors that may have led to their extinction in the early 1800s."

Lachlan Vincent then asked, "Yet there hasn't been any evidence found of Indigenous peoples being here during the time of the Norse encampment. Isn't that correct?"

Luc replied carefully, but confidently. "Even if there wasn't an Indigenous presence here at that specific time, it would've been like building a house in someone's backyard when no one was home. Conflict would've been inevitable once the inhabitants returned."

Their production assistant counted them out of their segment, then gave word to the grips to strike the equipment. Lachlan and Luc briskly walked to the beach for the closing segment of the show. The sun had just set.

The *Snorri* cargo ship had been moved from Norstead Village to the beach behind the L'Anse aux Meadows interpretive buildings. Drs. Olsen and Miller conducted an extensive on-camera interview of Finn Murphy, the Viking shipmaster, who, to everyone's relief, was far less nervous than his twin. Then another drone was dispatched for an aerial view of campfires on the beach now populated by an eclectic mix of archeologists, Norse re-enactors, Young Canada Works students, and Parks Canada personnel. The Vincents, with Audrey between them, walked to their marks and were flanked by all the on-camera presenters. They invited viewers to L'Anse aux Meadows to experience the site in person, see the excavation in progress, and relive history. While the closing credits rolled, fireworks exploded over the ocean in celebration of Victoria Day.

When the director of production declared, "It's a wrap," a cheer surged across the beach. Participants collected around the fires and champagne toasts were made.

Audrey kept searching for the costumed figure who had watched the swordfight. Eventually, she sat on a bench to examine the sword tossed to her. To her alarm, she discovered it had a steel blade. *That's why it cut so cleanly through Cody's shield*, she mused.

Luc hurried to her side. "Holy fuck, Audrey, that swordfight looked real!"

"Cody froze solid. I had to goad him into a real fight or we would've been staring at each other for three minutes. Oh, damn!" she exclaimed. "Here comes Mother. She's angry too."

"Hell, yeah! You could've been seriously hurt!"

"Oh, she's not upset about the fight. She's incensed because I was supposed to say Viking shieldmaidens are pop culture myths. Now would be a good time for you to get me a glass of champagne."

Luc turned to see the Vincents advancing. "I think it's okay. Your Mum is smiling."

"That's not a smile. She's baring her teeth."

"Going for champagne now."

As Luc left, Lachlan Vincent approached and hugged his daughter before his wife's barrage could begin. "*Halò, mo ghràidh* (Hello, my dear)," he said in Gaelic.

"*Halò, dadaidh* (Hello, Daddy)," she replied in kind. Her mother's words were loud and clearly in English.

"*What* were you thinking?" Hanna Vincent reprimanded, her blue eyes raging while her shellacked brown coif remained resilient in the breeze. "Who do you think you are to challenge the studied opinions of experienced Vikingologists?"

"I'm a woman capable of defeating almost any man on this beach—with or without phallic weapons—because of the martial arts training *you* paid for. So, I couldn't very well stand in front of a television audience and say all Norsewomen were nalbinding hearth-keepers!"

Lachlan Vincent bit his lip and turned his eyes toward the other fireworks. It took a while before his wife could recover enough to speak. "From whom did you learn it was acceptable to speak to me like that?" she asked.

Audrey glared at the ground, jaw clenched, because she knew her mother was inferring that the bad influence in her life was Luc. Since she had to ask a favour on his behalf, she chose her next words carefully.

"From university professors who taught me to challenge conventional thinking and seek my own answers," she said.

"Ha!" Hanna Vincent snorted. "I knew letting you attend that lightweight university was a mistake."

Audrey looked up and smiled wryly. "Actually, I was talking about you and Dad."

Lachlan gave his daughter another squeeze and shifted his gaze to his stupefied wife. Before either could speak, Audrey continued. "I assure you, there's nothing 'lightweight' about the University of Winnipeg's anthropology department and its integration with one of the finest Indigenous studies programs in the country. Especially since Canadian archeology is going to be my focus. Shall I assume, then, you won't be attending my convocation ceremonies?"

"Audrey, dear, let's leave that discussion until the morning, shall we?" her father pleaded.

Audrey shook her head and stared at the sand knowingly.

In a botched attempt at being conciliatory, her mother said, "It's only an undergraduate degree, Audrey. You won't really be missing anything important."

Audrey stood up in her shieldmaiden's gear, sword in hand, and stared straight into her mother's eyes. "You're right," she said. "I won't be missing anything because I'm going."

"We changed our schedules so we could be here for this event. And we're coming back at the end of July. To make another trip, is just not—" Hanna Vincent stammered.

"But Luc will be with you, won't he?" her father interjected. "Isn't he graduating at the same time?"

"He can't afford the airfare. But there *is* something you can do for him." Audrey produced his silver flask from a pouch. "This has been in Luc's family for several generations. Would you be able to verify its authenticity and determine its worth?"

Her father picked it up at once, his thumb going over the crest just as Audrey's had done. Her mother leaned in for a good look as well.

*Artifacts, the bright shiny things of archeologists*, Audrey mused.

"That's the Bourbon coat of arms! It was probably 'liberated' from the royal family during the revolution," her mother said.

"Or Luc could be the Dauphin," defied Audrey, who didn't like the disparaging reference to Luc's surname. "Now, if you'll excuse me, I believe the next king of France has a glass of champagne waiting for me."

When Audrey arrived at the bonfire, Luc noted she was upset, as she usually was whenever her parents were around. "This should cheer you up," he said, as he held up his phone. He had navigated to her blog where he had uploaded an image of her in shieldmaiden attire. "Have a look at the visitor numbers."

Audrey was stunned. "They've quadrupled!"

"And, look at your other social media stats. A star has been born."

Audrey was also distracted. "Are the producers still around? I'd really like to find out who threw me this sword."

Luc walked Audrey to the mobile control centre and re-introduced her to the director of production who was supervising the striking of sets and equipment. "Ah, the shieldmaiden," he said. "I should scold you for not sticking to what we rehearsed."

"No need," Audrey replied. "Luc and my mother have already done that for you. But I *am* interested in finding out who threw me this sword. I wasn't expecting it, either."

"Let's pull up that video and see what we can find."

It wasn't long before video from her fight appeared on two monitors from two different camera angles. The switcher synchronized it, so he could play both angles simultaneously for review. In one, the sword seemed to appear out of nowhere, but from the second angle, the shadowy outline of a rotund man, wearing a beige jacket and white cap, could be seen throwing it. The director downloaded the segments onto a flash drive for her.

Back at the bonfires, Audrey told Dr. Olsen about the sword and video. Olsen told her to take both to Views of Vinland where they would examine everything in the morning.

Moonlight streamed into Audrey's room, polishing every surface with shades of blue, grey, and silver, except the darkest corners that remained defiantly black. She luxuriated in a long, luscious muscle stretch as she turned toward the window. She stared at the sword leaning against the wall, gleaming with power and purpose.

"It's beautiful, isn't it?" he said in Old Norse.

A shock of adrenaline mainlined through her body, driving her to sit upright and fight for air. With eyes barely connected to their sockets, she saw the costumed figure from beyond the cameras, now seated at the foot of her bed.

"You watched the swordfight," Audrey whispered, so no one could hear outside her room.

"I did," he said, as he removed his boots. "My brother was wrong about you pretending to be a shieldmaiden. You are the best I have ever seen. But he was right about your beauty."

"You're Thorvald Eiriksson," she said.

He stood up and let his cloak fall. "I am."

"Why are you here?"

He removed his linen shirt. "A Norseman's heart is always with his sword."

"This is *your* sword?"

With one pull of a drawstring, he dropped his trousers and stepped out of them.

"Yes," he smiled, as he climbed under the duvet. Audrey scrambled to the opposite edge of the bed.

He seemed surprised. "Leif said you liked to share a bed, although he was fool enough not to touch you." Then he reached for Audrey, and she felt a shard of ice stab her heart.

She awoke with a long, drawn-out gasp as if she'd been underwater and had just broken the surface. She was alone, except for the sword shining in the moonlight.

***

Three weeks after the Victoria Day long weekend, Luc and Audrey were in St. John's on their way to Winnipeg for their convocation ceremonies. Luc was still giddy about his prop plane ride from St. Anthony. The photo Audrey had taken of him posing with the stuffed polar bear in the St. Anthony airport lobby was posted to his social media accounts along with the airport's identifier code: YAY.

Now they stood at separate check-in terminals in St. John's: Audrey, with the blasé automation of a seasoned traveller, and Luc with the attention to detail of a novice. So, it was Luc who noticed the change in their status. "It says we're in first class!"

When they checked with the desk attendant, they learned they were indeed booked into first-class seating, to and from Winnipeg.

"I thought your parents were using their mileage points to send us to grad?" Luc queried.

Audrey gave him a sardonic look as she lifted her carry-on to her shoulder. "We got the guilt upgrade."

"Your parents can afford this?"

"Definitely. Consider it your grad present for babysitting me through university. Now let's get our free drinks in the lounge."

Luc's own guilt was soon assuaged as he availed himself of every perk offered to him. Audrey watched with amused affection. She was glad he was finally able to enjoy a little luxury. So, she reluctantly reached into her purse and extracted a certified cheque. "I have to ask one more time," she said. "Are you sure you want to do this?"

Luc sat on the edge of his seat. "You have the cheque already? This is amazingly awesome!"

"I take that to be a 'yes,'" she replied in defeat, as she handed it over.

He stared at it, wonderstruck. "Four years of university debt, gone!" he said, as he snapped his fingers. Then he snapped a photo of the cheque with his phone.

"Oh, you're not putting that on social media!" she scolded.

"That was my bank app. I deposited it into my account."

"Sorry. I guess I'm just disappointed that you wanted to sell that flask. It was such a precious heirloom."

"You have no idea what this means to me, Audrey. I thought that debt would be around my neck forever. Right now, for this moment in time, Luc Stanislas Laliberte is debt free!"

He leaned back in his leather lounge chair, craft beer in one hand and phone in the other to take a very proud selfie. Then he closed his eyes in peaceful contemplation.

Luc's dimple returned as he came back to life. "Moment over!" he announced, as he set down his ale glass and began to text furiously. Several messages were transmitted over the next few minutes until a brilliant ear-to-ear grin split Luc's face in two. With immense pride, he stuck his phone within an inch of Audrey's nose. "Look what I just bought!"

She stared at the image of a shiny black truck with oversized wheels and ornate rims. "That's a lot of chrome," she remarked.

"And this is what I'll be wearing to grad," he said, as he swiped to another image.

"You bought your own tuxedo?" She dropped her head to her chest.

Luc was hurt by her disapproval. "Ah, excuse me, but I desperately need a vehicle. Slobbering Cousin Joe is a car salesman now. He alerted me to a super sweet deal on that one-year-old, low-mileage, fully loaded beauty. Because I'm using cash to pay it off in full, I save even more.

"It did *not* make sense to use the flask money to pay off my student loan that has a much lower interest rate than a car loan. But I *did* put some into a savings account, equal to three months' salary at the new job I just landed at APTN."

Audrey looked up in joyful surprise.

"The news director saw my interview on the live broadcast, remembered me from my internship, and offered me a job in the newsroom. As for the tuxedo, I recently produced a video for a fashion designer in Winnipeg who launched a shop in The Exchange District. To demonstrate his skills on camera, he fitted me for a custom tux at half price. I needed a suit for a whack of weddings anyway. Now I can pay it off."

Audrey smiled. "I should've known that money wouldn't spoil you."

***

After flying most of the day and picking up Luc's tuxedo on the way, they finally arrived at Audrey's impeccably restored art deco apartment. Luc had given up his drab bachelor suite when he took the job at L'Anse aux Meadows, so it only made sense for them to stay here, within walking distance of the University of Winnipeg. Luc had to appear at the campus early in the morning to don his cap and gown and be briefed on his ceremony. Audrey's ceremony would follow in the afternoon.

Since they had sated themselves on planes and in airport lounges, there was nothing left to do but prepare for bed. Audrey showered first, then pulled out the sofa bed when it was Luc's turn.

When he returned to the living room, towel wrapped around his waist, and saw the sofa bed, he froze in disappointment.

"Something wrong?" Audrey asked. Luc stopped towel-drying his long black hair.

"I just thought—" He looked at the sofa bed and then back at her bedroom. "I hoped we'd spend the whole three days together—and the two nights."

When Luc glanced sideways into her bedroom, she was struck by how much he looked like an ancient Egyptian with his bronzed, V-shaped torso disappearing into a white towel and ebony hair falling over his shoulders.

"Friends with benefits?" she asked.

"I think we've become more than just friends, don't you?" he replied.

Audrey's eyes seem to change from violet to green. "Don't say that! Don't you *dare* say that! I have never used the term '*just* friends'. Not once! I moved halfway across the world—alone—and enrolled in university at fifteen, so I could use the last chance I'd ever have to make friends." Tears flowed as she said, "I made—" Her voice broke, and she could only mouth the word "one" as she held up a single finger in front of Luc. "I can't risk losing you. I just can't." She ducked her head and tried to slip past Luc.

Luc reached out to hug her. She threw up her arms in protest.

"As your friend, as your friend!" he assured her, until she relented.

She buried her tear-damp face into his bare chest as he kissed the top of her head.

After a time, she started to half laugh and pull back, but still couldn't bring herself to look at him. "I just realized that, had I knocked your towel off, my big speech would have been for nothing. Good night." She waved over her shoulder as she entered her bedroom and closed the door.

Luc folded his hands over his head. "Couch, it is," he said to himself.

\*\*\*

About 2:00 a.m., Luc was awakened by a loud thud in Audrey's room. He hurried to the door and called her name. When he heard another thud, he entered quickly and flicked on the light.

Audrey was face down on the floor with one of her suitcases at her feet. He sprinted to her, calling her name, but she didn't respond. He touched her hair and recoiled. She was wearing a black, tightly curled, shoulder-length wig with a gold headband and straight cut bangs. When he turned her over, he saw that her eyes, heavily outlined in dark black eyeliner, almost looked brown. Her lips were stained red.

"What the fuck!" he exclaimed. He glanced over to her dresser and saw open containers of makeup scattered among the coloured glass perfume bottles. She began to speak, but he couldn't make out the words. Her pupils were completely dilated.

"Audrey! Can you hear me? It's Luc."

He tried to get a grip on the gauzy, transparent nightgown she was wearing that revealed everything. Eventually, he managed to get her to her feet. Luc finally realized she was asleep.

Then she reacted to him, raising her hand to his face. She asked him a question in a strange language. When he didn't answer, she began to act very seductively, caressing his face and naked chest. He grabbed her hands and placed them back at her side. Then she undid the sash of her gown and opened it wide.

"Oh no! Girls back in the kimono," he said, as he tried to cover her breasts. She looked at him quizzically, took his hands and tried to lead him to bed.

Using the word for 'sweetheart' common to both the Cree and Michif languages, he said, "*Nicimos*, if I thought for a minute you'd remember any of this, I'd be in there so fast—"

He got her into bed and tucked her in. She touched his face, smiled as her eyelids closed, and said, "I love you," in English.

Luc was breathless. He decided to remove all the makeup containers and anything else that could create a hazard.

"Note to self," he mumbled. "When she and I are finally lovers, remember the Cleopatra costume."

***

In the morning, Audrey gently shook Luc to waken him. He was lethargic, but when he did open his eyes and saw her leaning over him, he half shrieked and scrambled against the back of the couch. She howled. "Well, good morning to you too. Like some coffee?"

She passed him an oversized porcelain cup. He took it cautiously, then leaned forward and looked for traces of the heavy makeup he saw the previous night. There were none. She was clear-eyed and annoyingly cheerful. He shook his head, wondering if he was the one who had been dreaming.

Once they arrived on campus, they entered the 118-year-old, castle-like, sandstone Wesley Hall. Inside, they could only share a few moments before they had to part. Luc was scheduled to sit with the arts graduates during his ceremony in the morning. After sharing tea and refreshments with him on the front lawn at noon, Audrey would join the science grads for her ceremony. They wouldn't be together again until suppertime.

"Here's a little something for you," Audrey said, handing Luc a tiny wrapped box. "I just thought of this last night, and it didn't cost me anything, so please don't feel obligated to reciprocate."

Luc took the gift, as female classmates walking by openly flirted with him and male classmates either elbowed him or patted him on the back.

"Should I open this now?" he asked. She nodded.

He did and was speechless. Inside rested solid gold cufflinks with inset bloodstones.

"They were left to me by a great-uncle. I never knew what to do with them. When we picked up your tux and you chose French cuffs for your shirt, I remembered. And bloodstone is your birthstone too, so they were meant to be yours."

Luc was embarrassed because he didn't realize French cuffs needed cufflinks, and he didn't know how to put them on. Audrey sensed this and attached them expertly. He leaned in for a kiss, then remembered the previous night's speech, so he gave her a bear hug instead.

During Luc's ceremony, Audrey found it difficult not to cry; Luc was so happy and his family so proud. She tried to take the best pictures she could with his DSLR camera.

When it was time for her ceremony, Luc joined the professional photographers on the gym floor to catch Audrey at her best. When she was called forward to receive her parchment and identified as "Manitoba Jones" as well as a Rhodes Scholar, most of the audience applauded politely. The Lalibertes cheered and cried out, "That's our girl!" Luc was extremely touched when she smiled joyfully and waved to them in the stands.

After the ceremony, when he noticed parents buying bouquets of flowers for their daughters from tables near the exit, he presented her with a dozen red roses. He said it was because they matched her shoes, but it really was because he was finished pretending.

Luc's family had reserved a room at a steakhouse for the post-grad supper. Luc and Audrey were the stars of the show and their parchments were prominently on display.

After dinner, at Luc's suggestion, Audrey spoke privately with his maternal grandfather, Gerald Ghostkeeper.

"You know my last name is the English version of the Cree name Kanachakhtwin, meaning keeper of the spirits?" he said. Audrey nodded. "And you know about vision quests?" Audrey nodded again.

"In residential school, I was told that, if I saw a spirit guide, I'd be sent to the punishment closet. But if I saw Mother Mary, I'd be sent to the Pope."

Audrey wasn't sure if she should smile or not, but Gerald Ghostkeeper did.

"I'm told you see spirits. Do you have native blood?"

"Yes. M'ikmaq and Dakota Sioux."

"Was it a Dakota man you saw at The Forks?"

"Actually, it was."

"Are you seeing spirits now?"

"Yes. Vikings."

"Do you have Viking blood?"

"Actually, yes."

"Ah well. You can't choose your family, eh?"

They both chuckled.

"But you can choose your friends," the elder Ghostkeeper added. "You and Luc have chosen well. He's a good boy. And he doesn't scare easy. He says you're smart, so try to stay out of the punishment closet."

"I'll try, but looking for spirits is what I do for a living now."

"So, you're a ghostkeeper too. What other ancestors do you have?" he asked, as they headed back to the dining room.

"German, Scottish, French and Irish."

"Good luck with that."

\*\*\*

Luc paid the cab driver for the ride from the steakhouse and raced to Audrey's door. It was open before he arrived, and she already had one lovely leg adorned with a sparkling scarlet shoe perched on the cement.

He bent over and reached inside for her hand. In doing so, he was looking down at that exquisite porcelain face and a hint of the breasts he had briefly become acquainted with the night before. He now knew what every inch of her looked like, from the firm haunches he had captured on camera that first night in St. Anthony to her well-toned stomach and delicate, denuded mons.

*Now I've done it*, he scolded himself silently. *So much for getting any sleep tonight, either.*

He watched her stride in her ruby slippers and shimmering dress to the brass-trimmed entrance to her apartment building where she used a vintage brass key to open the door. The sound of tittering giggles distracted him. He looked to a side street and saw two young women, also dressed for the night they just had on the town, leaning into each other for support as they waved and smiled coyly at him. When Audrey pivoted to witness the scene, he was adjusting a cufflink and acknowledging them at the same time with a broad, white-toothed smile.

*Damn. With those cheekbones and that smile, he could make the cover of GQ*, she mused. She watched as he turned back toward her, lowered his head sheepishly, and picked up his pace until she could feel the heat of him standing next to her. That's when she knew everything had changed.

As Luc followed Audrey up the three flights of stairs to her apartment, they both had their heads down, contemplating what they were going to do and say once inside.

"What would you like to drink?" she asked, as she placed their leather-bound parchments on the coffee table and headed for the kitchen to wrap her roses for transport.

"I think I'm done," Luc said as he sat down, loosened his bowtie, and stretched his arms along the back of the couch as if embracing his date for the evening.

"How about some Newfoundland glacier water?" she asked.

"You know, that sounds perfect."

She returned with two brandy snifters full of clear liquid and set them down on the coffee table. Then she flipped the leather covers of their parchments around and set them up as triangles facing the couch. After scrolling through the music on her phone, she selected the song, "*Time after Time*," which issued from all the speakers in her apartment. She picked up her glass in one hand and reached out for Luc with the other.

They stared at the degrees they had earned together, while holding hands and listening to Cyndi Lauper sing. Luc teared up as four years cascaded by, with no memory more precious than the first. He had ducked into what he thought was an empty classroom so he could bang his head against a desk for draining a year's worth of savings on textbooks and a curriculum he couldn't understand. Then he felt a tiny hand on his shoulder.

He looked up and there she was. Luc couldn't believe his own recollection of how young she was; that little girl with mascara drizzled on her cheeks from crying. But her violet eyes displayed nothing but concern as she looked at him and asked quietly, "What's wrong?" And when she found out, she gave him a smile that touched his heart. "No problem. I'll tutor you. I may not look like much, but I have a very big IQ."

Then there were the lessons he gave her in return. He designed fake identification for her, but also taught her how to look eighteen, act eighteen, and handle men in bars. It gave him a sad, insightful appreciation of the precarious world of young women. He certainly remembered getting schooled on the dance floor by the fifteen-year-old who had learned to samba in Rio de Janeiro.

The song's refrain repeated before it faded out. With his eyes fixed on his degree, he squeezed Audrey's hand, almost to the point of pain, his emotions were so strong. She squeezed his hand in return, acknowledging she couldn't have done it without him, either. When the final note retreated into silence, she clicked off her phone.

"About what I said last night. I want you to forget it. Forget it all," she said. "I realize now the word 'friends' doesn't begin to describe what we are. And everyone but me seems to know that. Now that I'm legal, even in Newfoundland, I think it's time we did something about it."

Luc's eyes were still watery as he leaned toward her. Audrey kept her eyes locked on his as she leaned forward as well. Then, completely overcome, Luc could do nothing more than tip his forehead against hers, while cupping her head in his hands.

*Oh no*, Audrey thought. *I overdid it with the Lauper tune.*

She really began to panic when she saw the odd look on his face, as if he were about to renege on every overture he had ever made to her. She kissed his impassive face quickly, warmly, and incessantly, as if she was trying to melt an iceberg.

Then Luc's trademark grin reappeared, made even more potent by the lovingly covetous gaze in his brown eyes, as he gathered her up in his arms. As he carried her to the bedroom, Audrey did something she had wanted to do since the first time she had seen him smile. She traced his dimple from his cheekbone to his chin, letting her finger slide gently over the stubble all the way to his Adam's apple.

\*\*\*

As the morning sun heated up behind the bedroom curtain, Luc collapsed on top of Audrey in yet another post-orgasmic heap. She softly kissed his shoulder and stroked his hair.

When he managed to open his eyelids again and focus, he looked down at her. Then he slowly rose on one arm, elevated by alarm.

"*Non, non, non! Ni Mihtatayn,*" he apologized in Michif, as he extricated himself from her.

Audrey, who was drifting off to sleep, whispered, "What is it?" When she didn't get a response, she glanced up at Luc, who was staring wide-eyed at her neck and chest. She raised her head and tucked in her chin awkwardly to see what was wrong.

"I should've shaved before we made love," he said.

He whipped the duvet back to see if she was red and raw anywhere else. "Flip over," he commanded. She grabbed the duvet and whipped it back. "I'm not an omelet!"

"Maybe it's my cologne?" he wondered. Then his eyes grew wide with worry. "You couldn't be allergic to me, could you?"

From what she could see on her breasts, Audrey was almost certain she knew what it was, but rose to go to the bathroom for a closer inspection. Luc inquisitively tiptoed after her. While she was examining the red spots in the mirror, part of his black mane and one big brown eye peeked tentatively over her shoulder. She pursed her lips.

"It's your fault, all right," she said, and then paused for effect. "It's an orgasm rash."

Luc's distress increased. "You're allergic to orgasms?"

Audrey quelled the urge to laugh. "Quite the opposite. But the rash doesn't happen all the time, so, in the future, please don't think you must… keep going until you see it. As it is, we barely have time to get to the airport."

Wisely, he stopped himself from comparing her to the high striker carnival game where the goal is to hit the pad hard enough with a mallet so the light at the top turns red.

"Enough time for a shower," he said, as he wrapped his hands around her waist and marched her toward it.

# CHAPTER FIVE
## Passage of Promise

*In the spring, Thorvald told his men to get the ship ready. He sent some of them out with the long boat and asked them to spend the summer exploring the coast to the west. They found that it was a lovely wooded country and that the woods ran almost down to the sea, with a white sandy beach. The sea was full of islands and great shallows. Nowhere did they find any vestiges of men or animals, except a wooden granary on one of the islands to the west. They found no other human product, and in the fall, they turned back to Leif's camp.*

*—Saga of the Greenlanders*

Luc and Audrey launched the return journey from their convocation with breakfast at Stella's in the Winnipeg James Armstrong Richardson International Airport. Luc ordered almost everything on the menu, while Audrey asked for two non-fat extra dry cappuccinos with a dash of cinnamon. She planned to order more on the other side of the security screening area.

He couldn't stop grinning when he looked at her, even while he ate. He stretched out his hand to peek under the scarf wrapped around the rash on her neck. She slapped it. His behaviour had the aura of conquest about it, which she found irksome.

On the way back, Luc bemoaned missing out on first-class privileges because all he wanted to do was sleep, until Audrey informed him that sleeping comfortably was the primary attraction of first-class travel. Attendants on each leg of the flight, in the lounges and in the air, smiled when they covered them with blankets because, even in their sleep, they kept reaching for one another.

On the prop plane to St. Anthony, Audrey asked about who was picking them up. When she saw Luc blush for the first time ever, she shook her head. "Not Gabrielle?"

Luc became exceedingly uncomfortable.

"Awkward," Audrey chimed.

To Luc's enormous relief, Finn Murphy showed up instead. Finn didn't explain why and no one asked. Luc was dropped off first in St. Lunaire-Griquet, then Audrey at Views of Vinland. Finn lifted her luggage from the truck, then tried to brace her for his news.

"There's something I should tell you," he began. "First, Cody wants me to thank you for not making him look like a complete tool on that television show. I thought you gave him a pretty good spanking, but he says it would've been a lot worse if you hadn't woke him up first. Second—"

As he was speaking, Audrey watched Magnus run up to Gabrielle on the lawn of the hotel and throw his arms around her. Finn followed Audrey's line of sight in time to see Magnus pinch Gabrielle's buttocks.

"Okay," Finn said, without moving his head. "Maybe that should've been first."

He looked back with trepidation for the shieldmaiden's reaction.

"That escalated quickly," Audrey said.

"I t'ink that Icelander's got a death wish, meself, poking both you and Luc in the eye like that. Either one of you can clean his clock."

Audrey smirked. "I'll let him live. And I'll break it to Luc."

"Oh, thank Christ! No b'y wants to be the one to tell a b'y that his girl's been cheating on him with another b'y."

Audrey managed to keep a straight face when she replied, "I understand."

Finn tweaked the peak of his ball cap. "Best get on the go then." He scrambled into his truck and drove off. It reminded her of Captain Brian touching his white cap before he left her and Luc at the dock in St. Anthony.

Lugging her carry-on and toting her roses, Audrey headed to her room and the prospect of a rejuvenating sauna. Dr. Olsen intercepted her and asked to meet for a drink on the deck once she was settled. Then Magnus intercepted her and asked to meet at the cove past the bush line. Then Gabrielle intercepted her and asked her to stop by her room. She scheduled the requests in order of their arrival.

"Double graduation ceremonies! I am sure it will be a day that you and Luc will always remember," Dr. Olsen said, handing Audrey a shot glass of Aquavit.

Audrey nodded and hoped it wasn't her turn to blush. "Thank you for giving me time off to attend it."

"*Skål*," Dr. Olsen said, as she tapped Audrey's glass. They both downed their Aquavit and Olsen poured her another.

"I have great news about your sword." She smiled. "It has finally been returned with its documents of authenticity and put on display at the visitor centre. A genuine Ulfberht sword from the first millennium—now the most valuable artifact ever found at L'Anse aux Meadows."

"It was thrown at my head. I don't know if that qualifies as a find."

For the first time, Audrey heard Dr. Olsen's laugh. It sounded like wind chimes.

"There were a few skeptics who thought your scene was staged. Everyone connected with the show went on record to say it was not. Your video footage seemed to verify that."

"I cut Cody's shield in half with it. If I thought for a second the sword was real—"

"No need to worry, Audrey. We believe someone who was part of the production found the sword at the site and thought it was a replica. When you lost your sword, they simply tossed you another one."

Audrey wanted to sigh in relief, but she knew that theory helped to obscure the truth. Now both the rune stick and the sword were pointing to the encampment as being the burial site.

"Were there any trace elements found on the sword?" Audrey asked.

"In fact, there were," Dr. Olsen said. "What made you ask?"

"It looked like someone tried to polish it or something."

"You have a good eye," Dr. Olsen replied, guardedly. "There were traces of some kind of cleaner."

"So, between the time the sword was found and the time it was thrown it to me, someone tried to polish it?"

Dr. Olsen became very cold and reserved. "There are enough mysteries at L'Anse aux Meadows that we do not need to open additional lines of inquiry."

An image of Corporal Anderson, sitting in the booth at the coffee shop, entered Audrey's mind. "Follow the money," he was saying. "Two million dollars is a helluva motive. Find out who benefits from that, and you just may find the person who planted that clue."

Dr. Olsen was already benefiting.

Then she heard the voice of Gerald Ghostkeeper. "Try to stay out of the punishment closet."

"*Skål*," Audrey said, as she raised her glass and downed her Aquavit. Dr. Olsen nodded without taking her eyes off Audrey's.

The next stop was Wheeler's Cove. The sun was setting. Audrey was losing patience with Magnus, but knew she needed this forensic specialist as an ally. He emerged from the bush, swatting mosquitoes, and cursing in Icelandic. She couldn't help but laugh.

"How do you Canadians stand these bloodsucking creatures? They are driving me crazy!" He swore in Icelandic and scratched ferociously. When she saw the enormous welts over his face and neck, she felt sorry for him.

"The bush at sunset in June is not the best meeting place," she giggled. "It's a good thing we had our trysts in May, before they hatched, because it seems they have a taste for your virgin Icelandic blood."

"I have news for you," he said. "They have really increased security at L.A.M. since they put your Ulfberht sword on display. Now they have infrared sensors and cameras everywhere. I would not recommend sneaking in there again, under any circumstances."

Audrey tried to look casual. "That's good to know."

"I must swear you to secrecy on the next piece of information." Magnus cursed again and slapped a mosquito that exploded on his neck. "I conducted tests on the sword before they sent it away for authentication. Someone tried to clean it with polish."

"Why are you telling me this?"

"Because something is up. Dr. Olsen told me not to tell anyone. I trust you. You are the kind of person who does the right thing even if it means getting in trouble for it. I do not want to be standing next to you when you do it anymore, but I certainly respect you for it."

Audrey smiled graciously. "Why Magnus, I do believe that's the nicest thing you've ever said to me. Did you happen to identify the polish?"

Magnus grimaced as he scratched. "I knew you would ask, and you were the only one who did. I have a printout of the chemical composition for you. I dare not look it up myself. This is as far as I go." He handed the printout to Audrey.

"Anything else?"

"Yes," he said, lowering his voice in shame. "Please tell me that you and Luc hooked up in Winnipeg, so I know he will not kill me for seeing Gabrielle."

Audrey laughed aloud. "What made you think we would?"

"Because, despite what both of you say, Luc is not your big brother, and you are not his little sister."

Audrey fumbled around in her purse and withdrew a tube of mosquito repellent. "This is the best stuff for keeping away the nippers, as Newfoundlanders call them. It has a lot of DEET in it, but that's why it works. And I'll make sure Luc stays away from you too."

"Thank you!" Magnus exclaimed, as he grabbed the tube. He looked at her regretfully. "I wish you and Luc all the best. You are a good match." And then he bolted for the Views of Vinland Hotel.

After watching the sun set over the cove, Audrey made her way to the hotel as well. She knocked on the door of the Snorri—the room Gabrielle shared with an archeologist from Memorial University in St. John's. Gabrielle invited her in. Her roommate was not there.

"How was your graduation?" Gabrielle asked in French.

"It was wonderful," Audrey responded in kind. "Two days of flying for one day of celebration, but it was worth it."

"I just broke up with Luc on the phone."

Audrey didn't respond.

"I really liked Luc, but I soon learned he was in love with you. When I found out he was staying at your place in Winnipeg, it drove me crazy. No one likes to be the second choice."

"Gabrielle, I had told you the truth about our relationship."

Gabrielle started to cry a little. "Is it still the truth?"

Audrey lowered her eyes.

"You see? I knew that would happen. Neither one of you expected to hurt me, I know, but I could see it coming. That is why Magnus and I are together now. He is the perfect summer boyfriend. In the fall, I go back to Quebec, and he goes back to Iceland. No strings."

"I am sorry, Gabrielle. Perhaps you saw it coming, but I did not."

She half laughed. "You are still very young. You are more experienced than me when it comes to archeology, but not in affairs of the heart. I cannot be around Luc for a while yet, but I would still like to be your friend."

Audrey was shocked. "I would like that very much."

Gabrielle smiled through her tears. "And maybe, if it does not bother you, you can give me some tips on how to, um, accommodate Magnus. He is the biggest man I have ever encountered."

It took Audrey a moment to catch her meaning. Then she picked up her phone, inputted several website links, and sent them to Gabrielle. It was her turn to be amazed.

"How is it you know these things and yet have so little experience?" Gabrielle asked, while scanning the sites on her phone.

"I had a few well-meaning au pairs in places in the world where such education is considered part of the lessons of life. The instruction was theoretical at the time, but has since proven valid in practical applications."

When she finally returned to her room, Audrey cleaned up and collapsed into her bed with her laptop. She checked emails and posted social media updates. Just before she closed the lid, a text popped up from Luc: *Miss u.*

She smiled in the immediacy of the message, but then worried about the long-term implications. As much as she cautioned others not to fret about the future, it was her default mindset. If he truly missed her after just a few hours, how would he react to a two-year absence while she was at Oxford? Or a lifetime of absences unless he abandoned his career to join her, or she gave up hers to join him?

*Wow, I really didn't think this through*, she mused. But, for the first time, she felt lonely in her own bed.

She responded: *Miss u too.*

***

After his three-day leave, Luc showed up early at L'Anse aux Meadows to check his time-lapse footage, afraid that Gabrielle may have let her video vigilance lapse when she decided to dump him. He was relieved to discover she had not.

Then he rushed to the visitor centre to see its star attraction: Audrey's Ulfberht sword, now properly cleaned and encased in a dazzlingly lit, security protected display. Luc was so mesmerized by it that he didn't hear a small cadre of his colleagues approach, some Young Canada Works students, others Parks Canada employees, all of them Indigenous.

"Good thing they got that sword off his white girlfriend or she might've sliced this Apple in two," Joe Snook teased. Luc stiffened when he heard the derogatory term for someone who is Indigenous in appearance, but appears to have abandoned his culture (red on the outside, white on the inside).

"Which white girlfriend was that, the French one or the Viking?" laughed Jackson Pardy.

Luc smiled wryly as he turned to face them. He knew a certain amount of teasing was common to many Indigenous communities. But this group had been cool toward him since he arrived because they believed he had taken a job that should have gone to someone from the province.

Snook, Pardy, and a female student were Mi'kmaq from Newfoundland, while the other man and woman with them were Innu from Labrador.

Joe held up his hands defensively. "Don't worry, Luc, we've come to bury the hatchet. That's an Indian term, you know."

Luc smiled. "I know."

"I hear Luc's pretty good at burying his hatchet. Or was it that his girl-friend's pretty good at handling a sword? I can't remember," Jackson sniggered.

Luc realized he better end this chatter before he had to defend either Audrey's honour or his own.

"What's the matter, my brothers and sisters? Did you miss me?" he grinned.

Joe stepped forward. "We know we've given you a hard time since you got here. But we just found out you were a last-minute replacement for a Southern Inuit guy from Labrador who broke his leg playing hockey. So, you're okay now."

The group chuckled as Joe took a box from Jackson's hands.

"Seriously, we liked the way you handled that interview on the TV show, and we're proud you got your university degree, so we got you a gradua-tion present."

Luc graciously accepted the box and opened it. His marquee grin appeared as he lifted a pair of handcrafted sealskin mitts from the tissue paper. "Thank you!" he beamed. "You have no idea how much I'll appreciate these during a Manitoba winter!"

One by one, they walked up to shake Luc's hand and then silently went back to work.

***

Canada Day, July 1, broke clear, sunny and searingly hot. The maple leaf flag hung limply at half-staff over the red-and-white bunting that festooned the visitor centre at L'Anse aux Meadows. In Newfoundland and Labrador, the first of July is also Memorial Day. It commemorates the catastrophic losses sustained by the Royal Newfoundland Regiment that was nearly wiped out on the first day of the Battle of the Somme in the First World War. Parks Canada personnel held their own memorial service on site before raising the flag and preparing for the tourist blitz to follow at noon.

Locals said the sun was "splitting the rocks." They also found the lack of wind unsettling as they bundled bits of red-and-white cake and prepped Canadiana trivia quizzes for children. Archeologists rushed to ready their excavations, securing protected areas but offering others for close-up views by the curious. There were even mini "dig pits" or sandboxes where young treasure-seekers could sift through the sand and search for plastic "artifacts."

Their preparations were quickly breached by a tidal wave of tourists who swept over the site. The queue to see the well-publicized Ulfberht sword meandered along the boardwalk to the visitor centre. Water fountains flowed constantly to fill ever-emptying bottles as parents tried to cool crying babies and quench the thirst of sweating toddlers.

Audrey soon regretted acquiescing to Ryan Miller's request for her to don her shieldmaiden costume from the Victoria Day television broadcast. She sweltered in her leather boots, wool britches, and hide vest. She even agreed to pose for photographs with tourists near the sword's display case in the air-conditioned visitor centre rather than suffer the heat outdoors. Luc kept mouthing "I'm sorry" every time he took his own images of her celebrity-style selfies with strangers who had no qualms about wrapping their arms around her or asking her to autograph articles of clothing. He had always wanted to make her a star. He was beginning to rue the success he was having.

"God save me from another sticky-fingered child!" Audrey grumbled, as she held out the seams of her stained silk blouse.

Luc caught up with her outside the women's restroom. "I can't believe you'd rather do this than handle questions on the excavation site."

Audrey shot him a remonstrative glance. "You don't remember the last time I had heatstroke at a dig?"

It wasn't the air conditioning that made Luc shiver. If he had been the only one to see her that day, clutching a vessel with artifacts and conversing with an unseen Dakota chief on the banks of the Red River, it wouldn't have been so bad. It would have been like finding her face-down in her bedroom wearing a Cleopatra costume and trying to seduce him in an ancient dialect. Surprising, but not deleterious.

Unfortunately, several archeologists also witnessed her first incident. She was very nearly dismissed from The Forks's dig and the University of Winnipeg's anthropology program because of it. A heatstroke diagnosis saved her from both personal and professional embarrassment.

"Go ahead and splash some cold water on that black stuff melting around your eyes. You're starting to look more like Alice Cooper than Aud the Deep-minded," Luc suggested, referring to the legendary woman of Norse sagas, after whom she had been named.

***

Standing in the living quarters of Complex F-G, the prime area that Audrey normally supervised, Alexis was initially happy to hold court with the visitors crowded along the roped-off edge of the excavation. She was relatively cool within its earthen walls, while the sun blazed halos around the faces of her onlookers. Until they started asking questions.

"Where was the sword found?"

"Is this where the sword would have been kept?"

"Who did the sword belong to?"

"Did you touch the sword?"

"How heavy is the sword?"

Before long, Alexis was forcing grimaces into grins at every mention of the weapon that had sliced out her heart as soon as it landed in the hands of her now openly reviled nemesis. She couldn't even enjoy this literal moment in the sun, because Audrey had already upstaged her.

When she tried to change the topic to anything else, people would drift away from the site, bored by the bareness and relative banality of it. All the while, Lonny MacLeod of the *Northern Pen* dutifully snapped publicity-style photos of her. He was desperately trying to duplicate the success Luc Laliberte had achieved in scoring with the international media as well as with Audrey.

When the midday heat had driven even the hardiest history buffs away, Alexis dropped all pretenses, including the fake grin.

"Keep smiling," Lonny urged, as he continued to shoot. Alexis reached for her water bottle, poured cold beer down her throat, and fired Lonny a glance that scorched hotter than the sun directly above him. He lowered the camera, baffled.

"Give it up, Lonny," she snarled, as she lifted her Canada branded cap to wipe her brow. She was more disgusted at his lack of success than her own. Luc had beaten him to every story in every news outlet in every medium. They both knew this should have been Lonny's big break. Instead, a come-from-away had robbed him of it just as Alexis imagined that Audrey had snatched the Ulfberht sword away from her.

In the torment of her jealously, she was convinced that Audrey's parents had merely pretended to give her a plum assignment on that fateful Victoria Day broadcast. In fact, Alexis was the author of the rumour that the sword discovery was staged.

"Are there any more tourists up there?" she called out.

Lonny looked around and shook his head. "I think they're serving cake now at the visitor centre."

Alexis waved him down to the floor of the excavation. She watched in disgust as he stumbled into it, knowing that the athletic Luc Laliberte would have made the leap gracefully.

"It's time to face facts, Lonny," Alexis said. "We've been had."

"Whaddaya mean?"

"This whole thing is a setup. Dr. Olsen faked the rune stick to get invest-ment for this dig in the first place. Then she and the Vincents conspired to get an Ulfberht sword into Audrey's hands during a television broadcast to gain international attention."

Lonny reacted in disbelief. "G'wan. That's… that's—" He hesitated to use the word crazy because he had already begun to doubt Alexis' sanity. Not that that would stop him from sleeping with her if she gave him the chance.

"Think about it!" she said, tapping her temple almost as heavily as she wanted to smack his. "Audrey arrived with her own publicist, for fuck's sake!"

Lonny stared in the direction of the visitor centre where he imagined Luc was now photographing Audrey with the Ulfberht sword, pretending to cut a giant Canada Day cake with it—just the kind of image that would make the national news. Again. He began to consider Alexis' theory, just as he shared her jealousy.

"Not much we could do about it, even if it was true, wha?" he said.

"If it were true, how big of a story would *that* be to break?" Alexis taunted.

Lonny faced the fierceness of Alexis' wolf blue eyes. His mouth went dry just thinking about it.

Luc wove his way through sunburned tourists to the prospect windows of the visitor centre where he spotted Joe Snook facing seaward. He walked up to him, but Joe never moved, never spoke. There was something about Joe's pensive scan of the horizon and the way the muscles twitched around his unblinking eyes that chilled Luc to his core. He had seen that look before on the faces of his grandfather, father, and uncles, while fishing in the middle of expansive Lake Manitoba. It always preceded an abrupt end to the trip and a hurried dash to shore. Sometimes they outran the storm clouds his elders had sensed were coming; sometimes they were bailing their boat while golf ball-sized hail battered them bloody.

"How long do we have?" Luc asked.

"An hour or two. Maybe less."

"That's not a lot of time to clear the visitors and protect the dig sites."

"If Whitey doesn't see clouds on his radar app, he's not going to believe us."

"How bad is it going to be?"

"Bad."

"High winds? Rain? Lightning? Hail?"

"Yes."

Luc gulped. He had hoped Joe would pick just one or two options out of the list. "Then I better convince Whitey."

***

Ryan Miller studied the cloudless sky and calm sea before him. Then he glanced back at the tourists, children and elderly among them, who packed the visitor centre and dotted the hectares around it.

"I mean no disrespect to the Indigenous staff, but I can't close this place down on a hunch. Not on the busiest day of the year," he said.

Luc hoped his voice sounded as fearful as he felt. "I'm told there's not enough time to close it anyway. Best we can do is make sure everyone seeks shelter, in here or in their cars. And we can tarp the dig sites. Maybe. Before it hits."

"Radar is showing a disturbance, but it's well east of here and heading away from us," Miller said, as he thumbed his phone.

"Imagine the publicity if that storm turns and hits us, if people are hurt and the site is damaged, when you were warned ahead of time and could've done something to prevent it."

Miller scowled. "Is that a threat, Luc?"

"We can tell the visitors there's a heat warning so they have to seek shelter. In the meantime, we secure the sites. If nothing happens in an hour or so, we resume normal programming."

"It will be like herding cats."

"I'll organize the cat wranglers. I'm sure your crew can batten down the hatches pretty quick."

"You're just a student, Luc. I'd have to put staff in charge."

"I can outrun Snook and Pardy, plus I know all the YCW interpreters and most of the archeologists. I can get to the right people faster."

Miller stared at Luc's anxious face while tapping his foot a couple of times. Then he nodded. Luc dashed out of the nearest door.

***

Audrey raced to Complex F-G, waving at Gabrielle and Magnus to join her along the way. Her pace quickened as the temperature dropped.

"An hour is not enough time to secure these sites properly. We have artifacts on display. They should be packed up first," she called out to Luc, who ran beside her.

"The locals swear there isn't time. Just stick a lid on everything and head for shelter as soon as you can." Luc reached out to encircle her waist. He stopped briefly to kiss her. "You're already a heroine, so don't stay out here any longer than you have to."

Audrey responded. "That goes for you too."

"Don't worry, I've no intention of being a heroine." Luc grinned before turning and racing down the boardwalk to the southern edge of the site.

Audrey ordered Alexis out of Complex F-G and instructed her to secure her own area, Complex D-E, nearby. As the assembled archeological crews began pulling out tarps and collecting stakes, the Canadian flags and bunting around them started to flap in a robust breeze from the east.

Before long, the sky had darkened and icy raindrops were stinging their faces. As they worked, the clouds boiled blacker, and the crews had to shout instructions to each other over rumbling thunder. The rain fell harder and faster, turning the bog beneath them into a slippery quagmire. Day soon turned into night, with lightning bolts providing the only light by which they could see. Gales now threatened to rip the wet tarps from the workers' hands.

Just after her team finished and rushed to the interpretive buildings, Audrey noticed a corner of a tarp tear away from its stake. She grabbed more stakes to secure it, but could barely catch hold of the bouncing tarp against the force of the wind. Twigs and unsecured objects had become airborne missiles.

Alexis saw her opportunity and took it. She picked up a two-by-four, hit Audrey across the back of her skull, and pushed her into the pit. Then she poured the rest of her beer over her, secured the tarp over her motionless body, and ran for the visitor centre.

***

Audrey awoke on sheets of rough linen with a soft sheepskin hide draped over her. She couldn't focus her eyes. Her head throbbed. She reached up to touch it and felt a strip of cloth instead. The oddness of it made her fight to clear her mind as her fingers walked along the cloth to the back of her skull, where the pain was at its worst. It felt damp. She immediately brought her hand to her face and saw blood.

The man lying next to her reached out to encircle her waist. He stopped briefly to kiss her. "How do you feel?" he asked. "You were wounded, shield-maiden, trying to be a *hetja*."

Audrey jolted into lucidness upon hearing the Icelandic word for hero. She saw a tanned man with long hair leaning over her as he softly stroked her face. His muscular V-shaped torso disappeared under the sheepskin that covered them both. She recognized him as Thorvald Eiriksson.

"So now I have landed in your bed instead of you crawling into mine," she whispered huskily. Thorvald saw the blood on her hands.

"You need a new bandage. And some ale."

He peeled back the sheepskin hide and rose in the darkness. He poured ale from a flask into a hollowed-out horn and handed it to her. Then he lit a whale oil lamp and walked to a cavity in the wall. He withdrew strips of clean linen, a small wooden container of ointment, and some moss. He fashioned a poultice and returned to the bed.

Alarmed in her reverie, Audrey searched the eyes of this spectre to ascertain his intentions. She saw no malice, only warmth.

"Drink the ale, shieldmaiden," Thorvald instructed. "This may sting a little."

He unwound the linen strip that circled her forehead and the back of her skull until he reached the last layer that bound an old poultice to the wound that had started to clot. With a quick tug, he pulled it from her hair and flesh.

Audrey winced and drank the ale. Thorvald examined the gash.

"Good, it is healing," he reassured her. He began to apply the new poultice. Audrey raised her hand to stop him.

"Pour some ale over the wound first," she said.

Thorvald laughed. "You think your wound needs a drink, too?"

Audrey smiled. "Yes. I do."

When Thorvald grinned, Audrey thought she saw a trace of a dimple in his left cheek. He tipped some ale over the wound, applied the fresh poultice, and deftly rewrapped the linen.

"I understand. The ale masks the smell of the ointment," he said, as he picked up a lock of her hair and held it to his nose. "It is not as pleasant as your scent, however. I have sampled many goods from many parts of the world, and never have I smelled a perfume as intoxicating as yours."

"Perhaps it is just your intoxication." Audrey nodded to the ale by his bedside. He laughed and poured some for himself. Then they began to chat.

They discussed his reasons for visiting this place—Vinland, as his brother Leif had named it. The goal was to establish a lumber camp here, since the Norse had nearly stripped Iceland and Greenland of their forests. As Vikings continued to expand their territories, the demand for more longships and longhouses made harvesting lumber a lucrative enterprise.

"But the men my brother assigned to me are not interested in commerce," Thorvald said. "They are only interested in conquest. They cannot wait to encounter the Skraeling so they can do battle with them." He swirled the ale in his hollowed-out horn pensively.

"It would be wiser to trade with these people instead of fight with them," Audrey said. "There are far more of them than there are of you."

"You know this to be certain?" Thorvald queried. "We have not seen a one, although we know they must be here. Every time we leave this camp and return, our utensils and equipment go missing."

"So, you have things they want, and they have things you want. Is that not a good basis for trade?"

Thorvald searched Audrey's blue eyes. "You would make an ideal wife for a man of commerce, shieldmaiden. And I don't even know your name."

"I am Aud—Hannasdottir," Audrey replied, quickly making up a matronymic surname by attaching the word for daughter to her mother's first name.

"I have heard the stories of Aud the Deep-minded. You are well-named." Thorvald leaned in for a kiss and Audrey allowed it, aroused by the contrast of rough skin and a gentle touch. "Last summer, I sent the men to explore the west side of this land. They said it was beautiful, like Norway, with its wooded cliffs and fjords. I want to take you there, away from the men in the camp who are jealous of me, and the women who are jealous of you," he said, as he nodded toward her bandages.

"I thought it was an accident…" Audrey instinctively reached for the back of her head. She remembered the storm, the pelting hail and rain, the flying debris, and then the pain. Now she recalled a blurry face at the corner of the roof before it was sealed over her.

"You were hit while trying to protect this dwelling in a storm. The edge of your wound is too sharp and straight to have been made by a branch or debris. You were hit with a weapon. A man would have dragged you off to his bed, so it was definitely a woman who hit you and left you for dead."

Audrey struggled to recall the face.

"Come with me, Aud," Thorvald urged, as he kissed her hand. "My men told me there was a granary on one of the islands, but they did not encounter Skraeling. If we do, perhaps you could interpret for me."

The tender but persistent urging to follow his wishes was reassuringly familiar. She kissed his shoulder and stroked his hair. "If you ever engage Skraeling in battle, it will not go well for you, Thorvald. Promise me you will try to control your men so that does not happen."

Then Audrey gave up trying to return to another life and gave in to her desire to make love to him.

***

Audrey scanned the exquisite vista before her, its steep, tuckamore-covered terrain plummeting into slivers of indigo sea that sliced some of the cliffs into beach-encircled islands. She began to distinguish the Rock Ptarmigans as the birds scurried among the stones that camouflaged them. The ceaseless screeching of Great Black-backed Gulls called her back to the present.

Then a well-tanned, bearded face popped into view. It looked at her inquisitively, a white-toothed grin masking the misgivings that surged behind it.

*Skraeling*, Audrey mused. The figure offered her a glass of red wine. *Maybe that's why Leif called this place Vinland*, she chuckled inwardly.

"Now that you're no longer taking your meds, you can enjoy a drink. *Santé!*" he said.

"*Skål*," Audrey replied, as she accepted the glass.

Luc watched her drink and wondered if she was slipping back into Icelandic again. Audrey focused on the Ptarmigans.

"What are you thinking?" he asked gently.

"I'm thinking you were right about this place. Gros Morne is indeed beautiful. And the landscape is different from anything I've ever seen in Canada. No wonder it's another UNESCO World Heritage Site."

Luc exhaled in relief when she responded in English, until she added, "How did I get here?"

"Who am I, Audrey?" Luc asked, swallowing the tears he wanted to shed.

She managed a faint smile. "You are Setka. You are Mato. You are Thorvald. You are Luc."

"Bingo!" Luc responded in jest. At least, he hoped he had sounded jovial, when he really wanted to cry out in despair.

Her smile was pensive, knowing that he failed to understand. She lifted her nose to the crisp, salt air and inhaled the present.

"What do you remember last?" he queried, even though he was warned by the doctors in St. Anthony not to force her to recall anything before she was ready.

"I remember the storm. I remember running to the dig site with you beside me. I remember your kiss."

A tear welled in his eye.

"I remember you telling me not to be a *hetja*."

The tear fell.

"I mean a heroine," Audrey corrected. "We tarped the site and ran for cover. But a corner of the tarp ripped loose. I ran back to fix it. Then I felt a sharp pain at the back of my head and I tumbled into the pit."

Luc saw Audrey close her aqua eyes to replay the scene in detail. He despised the journalist within him who forced him to ask, "Anything else?"

"When I looked up, before I passed out, I saw a face."

"Whose face?"

"A cold face. A woman's face. She poured something on me and replaced the roof. I mean the tarp."

"She poured something on you?" The revelation disturbed him. "Then what?"

Audrey tried to sort what might have been remnants of reality from her reveries of the past. "When I came to, I realized the back of my head was bleeding. But I kept slipping in and out of consciousness. I'm not sure what was real and what was imagined."

She dropped her head in embarrassment.

Luc grasped her hand and squeezed it. "You've suffered a concussion. That's normal," he said.

"Could you please just tell me what really happened?" she begged.

Luc hesitated as he considered how much he should recount. "I was stuck with a group of obnoxious tourists on the lee side of a knoll, the only protection around. It was the longest afternoon of my life. They wanted to run across the open bog to their cars in the middle of a Nor'easter. For some strange reason, I didn't let them."

At least Audrey giggled. He continued. "When the storm let up, I set the tourists free and headed for the visitor centre. When you weren't there, I checked the interpretive buildings. Gabrielle and Magnus were inside, but you weren't. Magnus, the bastard, didn't bother to make sure you were safe."

"It wasn't Magnus's fault. It was a woman who hit me."

"Who *hit* you?" Luc repeated in alarm.

Audrey's eidetic memory was fractured, reduced to bits of images and sounds. Running footsteps. A flash of lightning. The edge of a blond piece of lumber. The sight of red canvas sneakers as she fell. The blurry face. A red maple leaf.

"We searched everywhere for you, at least everywhere above ground. I was frantic. Dr. Miller didn't want to remove the tarps protecting the sites, but I forced him to. And there you were, lying on the floor of the leader's room in Building F. You were out cold, with old bandages wrapped around your head. *Really* old bandages." Luc searched her face warily for a response. Audrey seemed distraught.

"It looked like part of a wall had given way in the rain, uncovering some linen cloths and ointments. You had wrapped the stuff around your head. It was another find, Audrey. A primitive medicine chest or something. Because the stuff was organic, your high-tech ground-penetrating radar didn't pick it up."

"I wrapped artifacts on my head?" Audrey repeated. She preferred her dream-like memory of the events.

Luc paused before revealing more. "A few of the archeologists wanted your head—pardon the pun—for doing that, Alexis leading the pack. She even suggested you were drunk when you fell into the pit because you smelled of beer when we found you. She added that you drank a flask of rum every night when you two shared a room."

Audrey eyes and mouth widened.

"But the doctors said you didn't have any alcohol in your system. They speculated that you found some old Viking booze and knew enough to pour it on your head to kill the germs before wrapping those mouldy bandages around it. They said if you hadn't, you would have lost a lot of blood before we found you."

"Did they say what hit me?"

"No, but Magnus examined you."

Audrey's eyes grew even wider.

"Just your head! Just your head! After all, he is a forensic scientist," Luc exclaimed, and then they both laughed. "He says the wound was too sharp and straight to have been made by a branch or debris."

The words were identical to Thorvald's. Now Audrey was beginning to wonder exactly when she was unconscious and where she was having her visions—in the pit or in the hospital.

Audrey finished her wine and asked for a refill. Luc allowed her several more sips before he added, "There's more. The sword's gone missing."

She dropped her wine glass. Luc's lightning reflexes snatched it out of the air before it hit the rocks.

"How?" she stammered.

"The storm knocked the power out. The lights were out in the visitor centre and the alarms were off around the display case. Even the security cameras were out for ten to fifteen minutes until the backup generator kicked in."

"Who—"

"No idea."

"Where—"

"It hasn't shown up anywhere. The Mounties are combing the island. Everyone who signed the guest book has been interviewed. Border officials have been placed on alert. Hell, Dr. Olsen even has Interpol on it!"

Audrey threw her head back, but the sudden motion made her dizzy. Luc quickly slipped his arm around her.

"I'm an asshole, Audrey. Sorry. I shouldn't have said anything."

Audrey rubbed her throbbing temples. "Why are we here? Why aren't *you* at work, at least?"

"Dr. Olsen knew you'd try to come back to work as soon as your feet hit the hospital floor. She also knows I'm the only one who could keep you away from the site. You need a vacation." Luc's voice trembled slightly. "And I need to know you're okay."

Audrey laid her aching head on his chest. Luc resisted the urge to squeeze her as hard as he wanted and kissed her hand instead. After a moment, he said, "I remember that Mato dude was the Dakota chief from The Forks dig in Winnipeg. But who the hell is Setka?"

As usual, Luc made her laugh through her tears. Audrey touched the cartouche around her neck. "That's another vision for another time. Let's just concentrate on this mystery, shall we?"

***

Luc and Audrey spent a week camping in Gros Morne National Park in a two-person tent on loan from the Murphy brothers. They hiked trails at a leisurely pace to restore Audrey's balance gradually. They walked white sand beaches where they built fires and marvelled at the spectacular night sky. In one secluded cove, they swam nude and experimented with making love in the water. Audrey was impressed with Luc's stamina given the still-chilly temperatures of the fjords.

Her fragmented memory, as well as her scalp, healed with each passing day. At her frenetic urging, the doctors did not shave a large patch in her chestnut tresses before stitching her wound. Instead, they cleared a small area in the immediate vicinity, allowing the hair above to flow seamlessly over it. Luc dutifully checked it each night and brushed her hair carefully so she wouldn't disturb the stitches.

"The hole in your head is healing nicely," he proclaimed on their last day. "And the stitches are dissolving."

Audrey's eyes were closed and she almost purred, like a cat getting her fur brushed. "I could handle having you groom me like this every night."

Luc was struck with a deep longing to make their togetherness permanent. Audrey spun around in his arms until they were almost nose to nose.

"Have you ever conducted a thorough search of me?" she asked.

"Just when I thought your memory had returned!" he laughed. "Well, there was the night after convocation, a couple of rendezvous on Wheeler's

Cove, about a dozen visits in Views of Vinland, and don't tell me you've already forgotten our underwater adventure. That was my best performance to date."

Audrey deadpanned her response to his mockery. "Online. I meant an online search."

"I have a few apps monitoring online mentions. Why?"

"Have you ever researched anything about my childhood? My travels with Mother and Dad?"

"Strangely enough, no," he said, cocking his head slightly at the revelation.

Audrey straightened up. "Then I should 'get out in front of this', as you put it. And explain the story you may find when you do."

"Okay," Luc replied apprehensively. As she spoke, his eyebrows arched incrementally higher.

"When I was four, I wandered away from my parents at a dig near the Giza plateau. Egyptian authorities launched a nationwide search, but they didn't find me. For three months. Then a tourist spotted me sitting in the doorway of the Sphinx temple. Doctors examined me and said I was fine—well hydrated and well nourished. No sign of foul play.

"I was wearing the clothes I disappeared in, except for this cartouche of my name on this gold chain. News stories of the time said I had no memory of where I'd been or what had happened."

Luc could only manage a meagre, "Whoa," in response.

"That wasn't quite true. I remembered walking away from Dad. Mother is still blaming him for that, by the way. I followed a falcon I thought was calling me from the sky. It flew to the Great Pyramid, where a man in a white turban and lavender *galabia* beckoned to me. I followed him into a very dark, dank passageway. I lost him and spent a long time stumbling around, terrified. Eventually, I found some *Shabti* dolls. They're little figurines of servants that were often buried with pharaohs in their tombs. Egyptians of the day believed these dolls would transform into humans to serve their pharaohs in the afterlife. Some Egyptologists believe *Shabti* dolls replaced a more ancient practice of burying real servants alive with their dead pharaohs."

Luc winced.

"What my four-year-old self remembers is that those *Shabti* dolls did come to life. They led me through the passageways, out of the Great Pyramid, and into the Egypt of about 2500 BCE."

As Audrey took a long sip from her rune-marked water bottle, she kept her eyes focused on Luc. "In the three months I was missing, I have memories of living an entire lifetime in ancient Egypt. From a four-year-old girl, to a grown woman with children, to a dying grandmother. Then the *Shabti* led me back into the pyramid and back to this time.

"When I told my parents what I thought had happened, Dad cried. He believed I was so traumatized by being alone in the dark for so long, that I fashioned an alternate reality out of the stories he told me of ancient Egypt. Mother developed her own alternate reality. She believed this babbling child who appeared out of nowhere was switched for her real daughter, despite DNA proof of my identity."

Audrey hung her head, still feeling guilty for fracturing her family. "Police believed someone found me and considered holding me for ransom, until they learned how high profile the case was. Then they changed their minds and returned me to Giza. Interpol thought the cartouche was a clever way of identifying me without leaving any physical evidence on a note or anything that could be traced."

For the first time, Luc scrutinized her cartouche. It looked very old. "What do you think happened?" he asked.

Audrey smiled oddly, then chimed, "There was a young lady named Bright, whose speed was far faster than light. She started one day, in a relative way, and returned on the previous night."

Now both of Luc's eyebrows were at his hairline.

Audrey laughed. "It's a limerick that one of the very first professors at the University of Manitoba—Reginald Buller—wrote about Einstein's Theory of Relativity. Stephen Hawking even paraphrased it in a lecture on space and time warps. Did you know that matter slows down time, and that the heavier the object, the more it drags on time?"

"I'm an arts grad, Audrey. I only know about Stephen Hawking because of The Big Bang Theory—the television show, not the actual theory."

"It's been proven that time moves more slowly when you stand next to the Great Pyramid, the heaviest object on Earth." She narrowed her eyes when she looked into his. "Imagine what it must be like to stand at the very centre of it."

Luc struggled to comprehend the concept.

She added, "My eidetic memory stretches back to the cradle, but that three-month period is definitely an anomaly. Egyptian doctors did tell Dad it might've been possible for me to live inside the pyramid that long on the four-thousand-year-old beer and honey I found in clay pots. So, you see, I have a history of finding what I need to survive when trapped in archeological sites."

Luc scrutinized Audrey's pupils to discern any sign of dilation or loss of focus. There was none. "Why are you telling me this, Audrey?"

"I'm answering the question you asked a week ago."

Luc was at a loss.

"You asked, 'Who the hell is Setka', remember? Well, Setka was a scribe who served the Pharaoh Khufu in the period of the Old Kingdom. Most archeologists believe that it's Khufu who is buried at the Great Pyramid." Audrey looked at Luc lovingly and added, "During my life in ancient Egypt, Setka was my husband."

"Okay…" Luc responded tentatively. "Maybe that explains the Cleopatra costume I found you wearing the first night at your apartment, *before* convocation."

"What Cleopatra costume?"

"I heard a loud noise in your bedroom. When I checked, I found you on the floor, wearing a curly black wig, a see-through housecoat, and black makeup around your eyes. You were speaking a language I couldn't understand."

Emotionless, Audrey responded, "I don't own a costume, Luc. Or a see-through housecoat."

They eyed each other suspiciously.

"I'm thinking now's probably a good time to call it a night," Luc said. Audrey nodded and curled up in his arms.

"By the way," Luc added. "What does four-thousand-year-old beer taste like?"

\*\*\*

In the morning, the pair packed up and trekked to Rocky Harbour, where Luc had parked the rental car Dr. Olsen had provided for their getaway. Neither Luc nor Audrey wanted to extend the conversation of the previous night, so they buried themselves in the present.

They savoured baked beans and bologna for breakfast at a popular restaurant that also had a gift shop. As Newfoundlanders would describe it, Luc and Audrey had great fun "twacking," or casually browsing through the souvenirs.

"What the hell is this? It looks like a voodoo doll!" Luc exclaimed, as he picked up a handmade doll crafted of brightly-coloured felt and cotton, with what appeared to be a kerchief tied over its head.

"That's a mummer doll." Audrey laughed. "Newfoundlanders dressed like this travel from house to house around Christmas time. There's even a Mummers Festival in St. John's. Didn't you do your cultural research?"

"I confess I missed this. Do mummers show up at kitchen parties? Aunt Peggy is having one in a couple of weeks, and we're invited."

"They've started to show up at kitchen parties in the summer to entertain tourists. People play whatever instruments they have, sing whatever they know, and dance any which way they want. Tell me you brought your fiddle!"

"I don't leave home without it," he jested, overjoyed to find Audrey in high spirits again. He picked up a couple of mummer dolls as souvenirs—or cultural references, should Canada Revenue Agency question his tax claims.

Audrey arrived at the till with two small boxes and six bottles of golden wine.

"Look at this wine! A national and international award winner, made from the local fruit Aunt Peggy calls bakeapple and Scandinavians call cloudberries," she announced to Luc. "For decades, people believed Vikings must have landed in the States first because they described finding grapes that made excellent wine. I believe cloudberries were the Norse version of grapes, and this fruit wine is why they called this place Vinland."

She became immobilized at the sight of maple leaf-shaped sugar candies on the counter.

"The woman who hit me was wearing red sneakers and a ball cap with a maple leaf on it," Audrey recounted without expression, closing her eyes to recall the image again. She opened them as she announced, "It was Alexis."

Luc searched her face to ascertain her state of mind. "Even if I can verify what Alexis was wearing from photos of the day, we still can't prove anything," he replied.

"I know. And Mother thinks *I'm* unstable. Her pet student is bat-crap crazy."

Before Luc closed the car trunk on their purchases, he presented Audrey with a mummer doll. "I have gifts for us too," she said, as she opened her little boxes. She slipped a silver chain with a strange-looking symbol around her neck. Then she placed another one just like it on Luc.

"What's this?" Luc asked, as he examined the pendant. "It looks like an arrow with the feathers broken off the right side."

"The Icelandic rune for romance," she answered as she stood on her tiptoes to kiss him.

# CHAPTER SIX
## Theatres of Conflict

*In the second summer, Thorvald sailed his vessel along the coast to the east, into some nearby fjord mouths, and headed for a jutting cape that rose high out of the sea and was all covered with woods. There they anchored the ship in a cove and laid down a gangplank to the shore. Thorvald went ashore with all his company. Then he said, "This is beautiful, and here I should like to build a home." After a time, they went back to the ship. Then they caught sight of three little mounds on the sand farther in on the cape. When they got closer to them, they saw three skin-covered boats, with three men under each. They split up their force and seized all the men but one, who escaped in his boat. They killed all eight of them, and then returned to the cape. Here they saw a number of mounds in the fjord and guessed that these must be human dwelling places.*

—Saga of the Greenlanders

By mid-July, Parks Canada personnel and archeological teams had repaired the minor damage inflicted by the Canada Day storm on the L'Anse aux Meadows buildings and excavations. Drs. Anna Olsen and Ryan Miller presented the Indigenous staff, including Luc Laliberte, with special awards for using their knowledge to predict the storm and protect the site and its visitors.

Even though he was one of the award recipients, Luc still managed to sell the story to several news sources. His personal blog and online interview by APTN went viral, although that had more to do with his looks than his content. Lonny MacLeod was assigned the personally and professionally excruciating task of interviewing Luc for the *Northern Pen*.

The wall niche Audrey had discovered in Building F had been meticulously excavated and its remaining contents exhumed. Three similar niches, also used for storing personal grooming aids and medical supplies, were discovered in other complexes. As well, doctors declared that Audrey's health had been restored, and she could return to work.

The only thing that hadn't been restored was the Ulfberht sword. A multi-force investigation by the Royal Newfoundland Constabulary, Royal Canadian Mounted Police, Canadian Coast Guard, and Interpol was ongoing.

"It's exquisite," Audrey said, as she examined the framed Mi'kmaq artwork that Olsen and Miller had presented to Luc. "So much for my telling you not to be a hero."

"I sure as hell wasn't!" Luc exclaimed. "My *Nicimos* gets whacked on the back of the head and I'm half a mile away, babysitting strangers. I should've stayed with you."

Audrey's grey eyes narrowed. "Then we both might've wound up in the pit, and those tourists would've been fried by lightning."

"I would've taken that bitch," Luc snarled, referring to Alexis.

"I have four black belts. What makes you think you would've fared better than I? And please don't use the B word, Luc. It's too easy to throw around. You don't know how many times it's been hurled at me."

"Who would call *you* a bitch?" Luc asked in surprise. "You're the sweetest, most well-mannered—"

"—wimpiest nerd you've ever met?"

"I wouldn't say that. Especially now I know you have four black belts. Really? *Four?*"

"Khmer Kung Fu, Silat, Brazilian Jiu-Jitsu, and Krav Maga."

Luc whistled. "Those are the deadliest martial arts on the planet! Damn bae, forget this archeology shit. I'll give up journalism to be your manager in the UFC!"

Audrey smiled shyly until Luc added, "You really *are* Lara Croft!"

Her grey eyes darkened to a tourmaline green. "Don't. Ever. Call me. That!" she hissed through clenched teeth.

Luc exaggerated his fear only slightly as he backed into the edge of his dresser. He stayed there, pinned, until her anger abated.

When it did, Audrey apologized. "I'm sorry, Luc. It's just that I've been dismissed by being called Lara Croft as often as I've been denigrated by being called a bitch. If a woman is deemed too good at something for her own good, she's labelled as either eccentric or evil. Or both."

Luc brought his hand to his heart. "You have to admit, *Nicimos*, you know a lot of cool shit most people don't."

Audrey rolled her eyes. "Because I've lived a life most people wouldn't want. I went missing for three months when I was just four years old. Not scary enough for my parents to change professions, but it made them pay for martial arts lessons to 'protect me'. While they excavated in the Middle East, I learned Krav Maga. While they studied the Gunung Padang pyramid in Indonesia, I learned Silat. While they explored Angkor Wat, I learned Khmer Kung Fu. And while they looked for the Lost City of Z in the Brazilian Amazon, I learned Jiu-Jitsu, as well as how to samba. What a minute…"

Luc waited.

"The night before convocation, when you said I was wearing a see-through housecoat and a Cleopatra wig. Could that've been a see-through body leotard with strategically placed sequins and a feather headdress? I was in the Rio Carnival parade."

"Can you air express them here for verification?"

Luc was saved by a knock on his bedroom door.

"Audrey, luv," said the voice on the other side. "If yer finished looking at Luc's etchings, I'd like a word in the kitchen before all hell breaks loose."

***

Peggy Volkov sat at the head of her aluminum-rimmed Arborite kitchen table with the contents of a sizeable mahogany tea caddy spread over it. The caddy, with its key lock, had been converted into a storage chest for important papers. The black-and-white pictures and ribbon-bound documents it contained still smelled of Darjeeling.

"As much as I hates to trouble you, luv, I've had this mystery on me hands since me fadder died. Now I finally knows someone who can help me solve it," she began. "I t'ink I told you me fadder, Kiril Volkov, was Russian. He was a submarine hunter in the Red Navy. He married me mudder right after the Second World War."

Audrey scanned the documents before her. "Some of that, yes, you did," she answered, silently noting all the documents were in German.

"Fadder always told me and Luc's grandmudder that he came here after torpedoing a U-boat somewhere in the channel north of L'Anse aux Meadows. He captured the U-boat captain and took his papers off him before turning him over to his comrades. But then he decided he didn't want to return to the Soviet Union, as it was known back then, so he jumped ship and swam to shore."

Luc was taken aback. "Great-grandpa Volkov was illegal?"

Aunt Peggy cautioned, "You must remember, we were all so isolated back in those days, we never knew who 'longed to where. In 1949, when Newfoundland joined Canada, fadder just became a Canadian along with everybody else."

The bracelet on Aunt Peggy's right hand caught Audrey's eye. She had difficulty concentrating on the story as Luc's great-aunt continued.

"Me fadder always said he wished he could return the papers to the U-boat captain's family in Germany so they'd know what happened to the poor bugger. But he never did. And I have no idea as to how to go about it. So, I was hoping you'd know, luv. Do you t'ink you can help?"

Audrey assembled a few photos of the U-boat commander from among the yellowed, curled up documents. In two of them, he was identified as Kapitan Zur See Karl Gustav Wettin of Dresden. Luc also sorted through the papers with interest.

"Would you happen to have any documents or photos of your father, as well?" Audrey asked. "It might help me repatriate these papers if I can verify the identity of the man who gained possession of them."

"I don't have much, luv, not even wedding photos of me mudder and fadder. He was some camera shy and understandably so. Would you like me to look for them now?"

"*Wer rastet, der rostet,*" Audrey said, with a smile.

Aunt Peggy beamed. "Fadder's favourite saying! Luc's right, you're not too mossy. I'll be right back!" She trundled off to her bedroom.

Audrey shot Luc a quizzical glance.

"I think that means you're intelligent," he said. And then he added, "What's up? I know that look, Aud."

Audrey dropped her voice to a whisper. "All of this is odd. There's far more documentation here than you'd expect a U-boat Kapitan to carry at sea. And why would your great-grandfather protect the papers of an enemy when he jumped ship, but not his own?"

Luc spun the papers around to take a closer look. "Is that why you're asking for pictures of him?"

"Yes. And the fact that *wer rastet, der rostet* is German, not Russian."

Luc gave Audrey a playful yet meaningful glance while raising one finger at a time as he recounted, "English, French, Icelandic, Gaelic, German…"

Aunt Peggy returned with her father's Canadian citizenship papers, driver's licence, Canada Pension details, and his death certificate. There was but one blurry black-and-white photograph that was taken in the sixties. "That's all I have, I'm afraid," she said.

"Then that's what I shall work with," Audrey replied cheerfully. "I'll get Luc to duplicate these documents so you won't lose the originals. Now, would you mind terribly if I had a really close look at your beautiful bracelet?"

"Not at all, luv," Aunt Peggy answered, as she slipped it off. To her surprise, Audrey pulled a jeweller's magnifying glass from her purse, placed it expertly in her eye socket, and scrutinized the bracelet from a few millimetres away. Its elaborately twisted strands of silver ended in wolf heads that faced each other.

"May I ask where you found such a gorgeous piece?" she queried, without looking up.

Aunt Peggy was flustered. "It was a gift from the fella that brought you here, Brian Rickman."

The magnifying glass fell from Audrey's eye. Once again, the image of bulky Captain Brian touching his white cap before he left her and Luc at the dock in St. Anthony sprang to mind. Then she recalled the pixelated video image of a rotund man wearing a white cap who threw her the Ulfberht sword during the Victoria Day broadcast. Now she imagined him slipping a silver Viking arm ring on Aunt Peggy. Her eidetic memory often put the pieces of a puzzle together for her.

"That's quite the gift," Audrey replied, hoping she didn't sound judgmental.

Aunt Peggy blushed. "I thought so too, when first he gave it to me, but he swears it was just a trinket he picked up at a flea market in St. John's."

Then Audrey had to make the most difficult decision of her life. She glanced first at Aunt Peggy, the lively lady who had treated her more like a daughter than her mother ever did, who helped her craft her shieldmaiden's costume, and spent a memorable day with her at the local fish market. Then she looked at Luc, leaning casually and confidently on the table, an alluring bicep extended and his big brown cow eyes peering out from under long lashes and wickedly thick black brows, one cocked inquisitively at her hesitation.

Audrey thought hard and swallowed harder before she spoke. "I suspect this bracelet is very valuable. It's expertly crafted in pure silver. I could have it appraised at our lab for you, if you like."

It pained her to see the jubilant smile break across the face of the hard-working woman who owned few luxuries. "Oh my! Valuable, you say? Certainly, luv. Go right ahead!"

And it broke her heart to see the loving half-grin from Luc who thought she was bestowing a favour upon his aunt.

Just then the B&B guests noisily returned from their bus tour to L'Anse aux Meadows. Aunt Peggy jumped up to greet them.

"Luc, be a dear and pack those papers in the caddy and return it to me bedroom, would you? Those are me guests, so me musicians and mummers won't be far behind."

While both were out of the kitchen, Audrey forced herself across the worn tiled floor and opened the cupboard door under the sink. With trembling hands, she extracted a dinted can of silver polish and noted it was over a decade old. She snapped an image of its label with her phone, and replaced the can.

*** 

Aunt Peggy's B&B guests were seated in chairs around the perimeter of the dining room, now cleared of tables to make room for dancing. Propped against the walls between the chairs were strange devices called ugly sticks. Brooms, mops, and toilet plungers were festooned with bells or wooden noise-makers, topped off with coffee-can faces or mummer doll heads, and glued into boots or cast-off shoes. Empty beer bottles, rinsed-out plastic buckets that once held salt beef, and metal spoons stood at the ready.

While the come-from-aways took photos of these homemade instruments, Audrey asked permission to play the upright piano in the corner. Aunt Peggy looked at it fondly. "Me fadder's pride and joy," she said, as she nodded her agreement. Audrey sat down and noted that it was a high-quality Bechstein.

She played the scales as Luc began to tune his fiddle. Without missing a note, he leaned over and teased, "So how many instruments do you play?" When Audrey fired him an angry scowl, his signature dimple appeared. He mouthed, "Bitch!" then immediately launched into the Red River Jig.

Audrey dropped her head and snickered as she accompanied him masterfully. As aggravating as he could be at times, she had to admit that Luc Laliberte was the perfect man to keep her balanced.

At that point, the local musicians arrived. They respectfully stood against a wall and listened to Luc and Audrey play. When the duo finished and everyone applauded, the leader of the group announced, "Well these two really know what they're doing, so we must be at the wrong place." All the local musicians turned at once and pretended to leave. The ensuing laughter masked Luc's statement to the leader. "Play whatever you like. We'll just tag along."

And that's what happened. Over the next half hour, the music improved rapidly in quality and tempo. That was the cue to break things off and encourage the guests to use the homemade instruments around them. The musicians transformed into veteran comedians who soon had everyone roaring. Luc put down his fiddle and picked up his DSLR, shooting stills and video, especially of Audrey playing the piano. Then he put down his camera and surprised everyone by picking up the spoons.

A spontaneous spoon-playing contest erupted. Luc won it handily and the locals were duly impressed. Then the front door opened and someone bellowed, "Any mummers 'lowed in?" On cue, the musicians launched into *The Mummers Song* as seven extraordinarily attired visitors entered the room.

The guests couldn't contain themselves at the sight of them. They jumped up with their phones and tablets, shooting nonstop. Three of the mummers had their faces obscured by pillowcases with holes cut out for their eyes and mouths. One had a crocheted doily suspended from a top hat. Another wore an old-fashioned, on-the-face goalie mask and a St. John's IceCaps toque, while two sported Halloween masks under elaborate lampshades. One of the pillowcase mummers wore an overstuffed housedress with an enormous pink bra on the outside. The goalie mummer wore a baby blue housecoat, oven mitts, and goulashes. Some layered jackets, skirts, and jeans, while one fellow wore long underwear under a tutu.

Once the song ended, they engaged in practiced banter, all the while obscuring their voices and exaggerating their actions. Some of the men pretended to be women, while the three women among them lowered their voices and mimicked male behaviour. Audrey recognized the goalie mummer as Captain Brian.

Aunt Peggy questioned them as to who they were and all denied their true identities. Captain Brian announced in a high-pitched voice, "We're just here to perform a traditional set dance from Harbour Deep called *Running the Goat*." The seven mummers paired up as couples on the floor, leaving Top Hat without a partner. He reached out for Audrey as the musicians began to play a very lively tune of the same name.

It was fast-paced and furious; part square dance, part step dance, and part Schottische. Audrey did remarkably well since she was at least familiar with Scottish country dancing and jigging. Top Hat, whose doily did not disguise his ginger Murphy hair and freckles, expertly guided her through the spins and turns. Occasionally, she strayed off course or turned the wrong way, but Cody quickly retrieved her before any collisions occurred.

Of course, Luc captured the entire dance on camera—all seventeen minutes of it. At the end, the dancers collapsed into the nearest available chairs while the come-from-aways rose to give them a standing ovation. Drinks were dispensed at once.

When all were refreshed, the mummers announced their departures. Before he left, Cody Murphy reached out for Audrey once more and whispered in her ear, "You taught me a lesson in sword play; I taught you one on the dance floor. Now we're even."

The musicians soon followed. When Aunt Peggy reminded her guests that breakfast would be served at the usual time, they left for their rooms. Luc and Audrey helped restore the dining room to its original state.

"Thank you truly, you've been right dolls, you have," she gushed. "Now aren't you just the best fiddler ever picked up a bow, Luc! And oh, me gawd, Audrey, you could dance on a plate! You did me proud, the two of you. Now head off to bed. Just mind I'm on the other side of the wall, and I've got toutons to cook in six hours' time."

She left the couple staring at each other since Luc had planned to drive Audrey back to Views of Vinland. He merely cocked his head and raised his arms questioningly to determine what she wanted to do. Recognizing that Luc was tired and had consumed a few drinks, Audrey smiled demurely and nodded.

So, she was quite surprised at his surge of energy and desire as soon as she slipped off her dress and slid under his sheets. His hands and lips immediately went for her most sensitive and responsive spots, having quickly learned what moves and touches aroused her most effectively. She struggled against him as he tried to wriggle off her underwear.

Pointing to the wall behind the headboard, she barely breathed, "Your aunt's right there!"

"I know," he moaned, too loud for her liking. "And it's making me even hornier."

Audrey soon realized her struggles were having the same effect. As her body began to writhe and Luc's lips were starting to slide south, she silently mouthed, "Stop!"

"What's the matter?" Luc teased, in a whisper she thought sounded like thunder. "Are you afraid you'll wake the guests?"

She reached down quickly and grabbed his testicles to get his attention. She raised an eyebrow as she admonished, "I'm not the noisy one!" She soon realized submitting was her only option without getting into a debate that would awaken Aunt Peggy anyway. So, she turned the tables and used the techniques Luc reacted to the most, hoping to get him off as quickly and quietly as possible.

She grabbed the hair at the back of his head with one hand, kissed him ferociously, and then unclasped her bra with the other. She lowered her bra strap and panties, then quickly switched hands and completely disrobed, never letting her lips leave his.

Just as musicians and dancers alike had shown off their skills all evening, this was one last challenge. Each tried to bring the other to a climax first. When it seemed as if Luc was winning and he was riding Audrey's undulating abdomen and mons like she was a mechanical bull, she collapsed and wrapped her legs around his waist. This sent him far deeper, far faster than he anticipated.

It was his turn to arc backwards, eyes closed and mouth opened wide. He was silent at first, but Audrey knew this wouldn't last. She desperately looked around for something and spotted the mummer doll he had purchased in Rocky Harbour. Reaching out to the nightstand, she grabbed the doll and stuffed it into Luc's mouth. He bit down hard.

His cry was duly muffled, but at a high cost. When he unclenched his teeth, the cloth-covered head rolled off the doll and under the bed. For a moment, Audrey and Luc stared at each other. Then they quickly piled all their pillows, blankets, and the handmade quilt over their heads to insulate their laughter as best they could.

***

The mobile lab at L'Anse aux Meadows was filled with boxes of potential artifacts and soil samples to be tested. Magnus gave them an anxious glance and then Audrey a frustrated one. He didn't feel beholden to her anymore, but he still couldn't resist her requests. Everything she brought him was a far greater mystery than the odd bead and broken nail uncovered by the other archeologists.

"What does a German U-boat commander have to do with Vikings?" he mumbled as he saved the black-and-white images she had emailed him onto his hard drive.

"They share common ancestors, the same linguistic origins, and have a thing for conquest in boats," she replied nonchalantly, while keeping watch by a window.

"This a good way to start more rumours about the two of us. I do not need Luc on my face again."

Audrey turned her head toward Magnus and bit her lip. "I think the preposition you want to use in that sentence is '*in*'. You don't need Luc *in* your face again."

Magnus looked up at her, perplexed. Poking his finger into his face, he asked, "How could Luc be *in* my face?"

"Just trust me on this one," she replied as she turned back to the window. "And don't worry. If my suspicions are correct, he'll be in *my* face."

Magnus lined up an image of Kapitan Karl Wettin beside the digitized photograph of Kiril Volkov that Luc had enhanced as much as he could. Then he ran his facial verification software. Within seconds, the software pinged, signaling it had completed its task. Audrey dashed to the screen.

"We have a match," Magnus observed.

"Now try the image on the driver's licence against the other two photos of Wettin," Audrey ordered. Magnus did, and the software matched them as well.

Audrey sighed. "Thanks, Magnus. Just send me the report and then delete the images and history."

"Way ahead on you."

Audrey decided to let that linguistic lapse slide. "Now I have a tougher request."

Magnus looked up and cowed at the sight of the arm ring. "Please tell me that is a replica."

"No, *you* please tell me it's a replica."

"Where did you find it?"

"You don't want to know."

"You are right. I do not."

"Can you date this on your spectrometer?"

"Like the sword, I can only determine its age in rough parameters. And like the sword, we would have to send it away for neutron activation to obtain more accurate results."

"Understood."

"This has been cleaned, likely with some kind of polish, just like the sword," Magnus, said, as he studied it under a microscope.

"Could you please run the same chemical analysis of the residue so I can compare the results to the printout you gave me?"

"Damn it, Audrey! Why are you doing this? Why are you risking your career?"

Audrey was astounded by his passion. She didn't think he still cared. "Despite what everyone thinks, I didn't become an archeologist to be famous. I did it to uncover the truth. And so far, the most valuable finds at this site are turning out to be ones we didn't uncover. Which means someone else is digging them up."

"A local has found a horde?"

"With a man's arm ring, his sword, and a grave marker that reads, 'Below this stick rests the body of Thorvald Eiriksson.'"

"Son of a bitch!" Magnus exclaimed.

"No, son of Eirik the Red."

***

Luc waited anxiously at what had become his and Audrey's favourite table overlooking the wharf at The Cod and Claw in St. Lunaire-Griquet. Each time he saw the laminated menus and the lobster crates at the edge of the bay, he couldn't help but recall the first intimate dinner he and Audrey enjoyed together. It seemed so long ago when it had only been three months, but a lifetime had elapsed in between.

"Hello, Luc," a sugary voice said. He turned to greet it with a smile, but the smile soon became a sneer.

"Alexis. What are you doing here?"

Both Luc and Audrey had been openly hostile to Alexis since Canada Day. She deduced they suspected it was she who had knocked Audrey into the excavation pit. And she also determined that Audrey's allegations must be too weak to take to the authorities or they would have done so by now. So, she believed she still held the upper hand.

"I'm going on the same whale-watching excursion as you are, evidently. May I join you?"

Luc cocked an eyebrow. "No, you certainly may not!"

Alexis struck a coquettish pose, pursed her red-stained lips, and batted her lacquered eyelashes. "I don't know what you've been told about me, but I've done nothing to earn such hostility. I admire your loyalty to your friend, but you must know she's not quite well."

Luc stared down the wolf blue eyes. "She's perfectly well. As brilliant and talented as ever, thanks."

"Hmmm," Alexis purred. "The Professors Vincent confided in me, you know. They were *so* worried about her coming to this dig. It must be hard to follow in the footsteps of famous parents. Especially when a traumatic incident happens when you're very young. Archeology is a difficult profession. It can be tough to leave the past in the past," she said. Then she walked off to join the other archeologists and students at the bar.

He couldn't stop his eyes from following her, or his mind from wondering how much she really knew about Audrey—and how much she might be right. He was still staring at Alexis when Audrey rushed in and breathlessly sat down across from him. She followed his line of sight.

"Damn! She's not coming too, is she?" Audrey asked. "Talk about having to watch your back."

Luc turned to Audrey. He was already concerned because of her inordinate interest in the origins of Aunt Peggy's father and the silver bracelet. She seemed to be finding a mystery in everything. Too many mysteries. Too many anomalies. As a journalist, he was trained to be suspicious of this. He manufactured a smile. "Any results for Aunt Peggy?"

Then he recognized the look on her face. "What's up?"

"I sent you a link to a CBC radio documentary about U-boats in Canada during the Second World War. They were all along the coasts of Newfoundland and Labrador. A few even made it up the St. Lawrence Seaway," Audrey began. "There were reports that some surfaced near Newfoundland and their officers came ashore for reconnaissance or simply to have a pint at a nearby pub."

Luc frowned in disbelief.

"Apparently, they passed themselves off as Russians. As Aunt Peggy said, most Newfoundlanders were very isolated back then, without much knowledge or news of the world, so they believed them. There were rumours that some Germans even returned a few times and had relationships with the local girls—"

Luc could see where Audrey was headed. "No!" he countered in disbelief.

"I used the latest facial verification software on all the photographs. It's different than facial recognition. It's designed specifically to determine if various images are of the same person, even if they're taken decades apart or they appear in different media. It's helpful in archeology when you want to match a skull to a grave mask or an image of a young man to that of an old man, for example."

Luc held his breath.

"There's a 97.2 per cent chance that the images of Karl Wettin *and* the two images of your great-grandfather taken years later are of the same person."

Luc stared in wide-eyed disbelief. Audrey continued.

"I checked the records of the German navy. A Kapitan Karl Gustav Wettin was identified as lost at sea. I'll likely never get a response from what is left of Soviet naval records, so I believe the best way to proceed is to contact Kapitan Wettin's family in Dresden, send them copies of the documentation, and ask for a DNA sample. Then test Aunt Peggy and your grandmother against it. I have the Wettins' current address."

Luc was thunderstruck. "Are you saying I'm part Nazi?"

Audrey was diplomatic in her usual, informative way. "Nazism was a doctrine, not a race, and not everyone serving in the German armed forces believed in that doctrine. Your great-grandfather may very well have jumped ship because he didn't."

She took a sip of water before proceeding. "Think about it. The first names 'Kiril' and 'Karl' are very similar. And 'Volkov' is derived from the Russian word 'volk' or wolf. Groups of U-boats sent to attack Allied convoys were known as wolf packs."

Luc clapped his hands on either side of his head and leaned forward on the table to ponder everything he had heard. "At the very least, I didn't need to go through life with the middle name Stanislas," he finally managed.

Audrey winced. "I have another theory about that. The full name of Louis XVIII, the last king of France, was Louis Stanislas Xavier Bourbon. Of the same royal family that owned the silver flask you had. I think you were named after him, not a phantom Russian submarine hunter."

Luc leaned back in his chair again. It all seemed logical, but fantastical at the same time.

"What about the bracelet?" he asked.

To her credit, Audrey kept her eyes locked on Luc's while she explained. "I had a spectrometer analysis conducted on it. The arm ring is made of nearly pure silver, as I suspected. And it appears to be about a thousand years old, as I also suspected. The design is definitely Norse. To be certain, we'll have to send it away for further tests. But it appears to be a historical artifact, not a replica."

"You turned it in?" Luc asked with alarm.

"No, not yet. I also compared the chemical analysis on the polish Aunt Peggy used on the arm ring to what was used on the Ulfberht sword. Both were a match to the old silver polish I found at her place. There's nothing like it on the market anymore."

"*What?*" Luc shouted, as he pounded the table with his fist. Everyone in the restaurant and adjacent bar stopped talking and turned their way. Audrey had never seen Luc so angry. His gentle cow eyes turned black and hard, glowering at her under fiercely knitted brows. His brilliant white smile became a threatening snarl. He terrified her.

Alexis couldn't help but smirk as she sipped on the straw in her mojito.

In the excruciating silence that followed, people slowly returned to their conversations. Audrey couldn't move, nor could she stop the tears from spilling down her cheeks. She never imagined her best friend and now lover could ever be this hostile toward her.

"You investigated a member of *my* family to this extent without consulting with *me* first?" Luc ground out through clenched teeth. "How *dare* you!"

He leaned forward so that Audrey could feel the force of his anger, even though he had to lower his voice. She leaned as far away from him as her chair would allow.

Audrey couldn't face Luc anymore. Not able to turn toward her colleagues inside the restaurant, she turned toward the bay, where the same idyllic scene she had witnessed three months earlier appeared before her. Only now, the view was bereft of all its beauty. She pressed a knuckle into her upper lip to silence her sobs, and shut her eyelids tightly so that all her tears would drain at once.

Frustrated, Luc threw himself back against his chair and automatically looked away from her. When his eyes focused again, they were on Alexis, perched on her bar stool and casting a distinct "I told you so" look his way.

He glanced back at Audrey, who turned to face him. Instead of seeing a passionate and mature lover, he saw the distressed and sobbing fifteen-year-old he met at university four years ago and the disoriented and incoherent eighteen-year-old he found on the banks of the Red River. It hit him hard that maybe Audrey was not the wise and capable woman he thought she was, but rather a damaged little girl who never really made her way out of the utter darkness she found herself in so many years ago.

Nevertheless, it broke his heart to see the mascara drizzled on her cheeks from crying. "Listen, Aud, I'm sorry I blew up like that." Luc reached out for her. She threw up her hands, just as she did at her apartment the night before convocation—the night she said she didn't want to be his lover because she couldn't bear to lose him as a friend.

Audrey summoned all the inner strength she had acquired from her martial arts training. She managed to calm her voice, but still couldn't bring herself to look at Luc directly. "If one of my colleagues had spotted that arm ring on Aunt Peggy before I did, the issue would've been out of both of our hands. It's against the law in Newfoundland to acquire historical artifacts by any means. The penalty is up to $50,000, a year in jail, or both.

"So, I gathered all the data that could potentially be used against her. Now you have a chance to clear her before it even gets reported. Ask her if she ever cleaned up an old sword for Captain Brian. If so, then this is all on him. If she denies it, then either Captain Brian stole her silver polish or she's covering for him. Either way, let me know by tomorrow evening. I'll have to make a full report to Dr. Olsen."

Then Audrey hastily gathered up her purse and rose to leave the restaurant. Luc was so anxious to catch her eye as he stood up, he didn't see her leave a gift box on the table. He tried to stop her before she left, but she dashed out before he could. He dug a twenty-dollar bill out of his jeans to cover his drink tab, while looking at the door and wondering if he should chase after her. When he started out, he heard the waiter from their first evening at The Cod and Claw call after him.

"Thanks, buddy, but you forgot something."

When Luc looked back, the waiter was waving the gift box in the air.

"That's not mine," Luc replied.

"Then it belongs to yer lady friend, the ball crusher."

Luc collected it, thanked the waiter, and then exited the restaurant. He bumped into Gabrielle and Magnus on their way in.

"Aren't you coming on this whale-watching trip?" Gabrielle queried.

"Another time," Luc replied tersely.

"When will there ever be another time to go whale watching in a Viking ship?" Gabrielle laughed, while Magnus anxiously tugged on her arm. He suspected he knew the reason for Audrey's, and now Luc's, hurried departures. Gabrielle caught on to Magnus's signal and followed him inside.

Luc opened the gift box outside the restaurant. In its satin lining rested a sterling silver replica of the wolf head bracelet. The card inside, addressed to Aunt Peggy read, "Not as authentic as the original, but I hope it will be a suitable replacement. Love, Audrey."

Luc threw his head back in exasperation. His heart wanted to pursue Audrey, but Alexis had successfully sowed a seed of doubt in his mind regarding both her stability and her sanity. When he weighed a rare opportunity to go whale watching in the *Snorri* against a desire to console her, he reluctantly returned to the restaurant.

***

The next day, Audrey almost tiptoed into the nearly empty visitor centre at L'Anse aux Meadows after closing time. She was afraid to disturb Luc, seated at a couch near a window, since he was evidently immersed in Ingeborg Marshall's book, *A History and Ethnography of the Beothuk*. She was fearful because of the news she was bringing, as well as of the history he was reading. But Luc sensed she was there and looked up, his eyes watery with sorrow.

She was contrite. "I'm sorry, Luc. I really am. But I have to act on the bracelet now or be judged as part of a cover-up."

Luc was also contrite. He was sorry for having yelled at her so publicly in the restaurant. He was sorry for having enjoyed the whale-watching excursion without her—and with Alexis. And he was sorry for the clash of cultures that had resulted in the extinction of a race of people.

He had to clear his husky voice before speaking. "I talked to Aunt Peggy. She understands and wants to thank you for the substitute bracelet." Then his voice turned cold. "I, on the other hand, cannot."

The words cut like an Ulfberht sword, but Audrey remained stoic.

Luc continued. "Aunt Peggy says Captain Brian did give her a sword to polish when he gave her the bracelet over a year ago. He said the sword was for a mummer's costume. She assumed both came from the same flea market in St. John's, but he didn't provide a name or location. On the night of the kitchen party, she asked him why he didn't have the sword. He told her he lost it."

When Audrey turned away and rolled her eyes, Luc's anger was inflamed again. "It's more plausible than my great-aunt's boyfriend being a Viking grave robber! And if he was, why the hell would he throw the sword to you during a television broadcast?"

Audrey forced herself to scan his dark, desolate eyes. "You and I have the same job, Luc. We both seek the truth. It's just that our timeframes are a little different."

"The present means a hell of a lot more than the past, Audrey!" Luc snapped.

Audrey nodded toward his book. "Does it?"

Luc threw the tome down on a table and rubbed his face. "So, you've read this? It's horrific! The last Beothuk woman, Shanawdithit, said white settlers routinely attacked her people. She was shot when she was just a child. Her aunt was abducted. Between the hatred and the disease inflicted on them, all the Beothuk of Newfoundland were completely wiped out."

He glanced up at Audrey, realizing the import of what she had been saying. "I guess it does matter that people know what happened to the Beothuk."

"Yes, it does."

"And whether someone's father was an Allied submarine hunter or an enemy U-boat commander. When Aunt Peggy found out, she said her sheltered childhood suddenly made sense."

Audrey dropped her head in case a steady gaze was misinterpreted as an "I told you so."

"But whether Thorvald Eiriksson was buried at L'Anse aux Meadows or somewhere else—?"

"I didn't know Captain Brian was Aunt Peggy's boyfriend."

"Since they were teenagers, she said. But her U-boat commander father didn't approve. Called him a *schlingel* or something like that. Aunt Peggy just thought he was too Russian to say scalliwag."

"Schlingel *is* German for scalliwag. Earlier this summer, didn't your aunt tell you her B&B was finally booked up because all the scientists were taking up the 'fancy places'? That one more season like this meant she could finally retire? And Captain Brian repositioned his tour boat up here instead of competing for tourists like he normally does in St. John's. That wouldn't have happened if that rune stick hadn't shown up at L.A.M."

Luc straightened up and became a journalist again. "Motive?"

She nodded, then echoed the words of Corporal Anderson. "Follow the money."

"Do you think any of this could hurt Aunt Peggy?" Luc asked.

"Not unless Captain Brian was *schlingel* enough to steal the sword back and your aunt is in on it. Do you know if she told him we were asking about the bracelet and the sword?"

"I asked and she said, 'Why? What's he done this time?' I said we were just trying to track down the origins of both items; that it was best not to say anything until we knew more."

Audrey pointed to the chair across from him and asked if she could sit down. Luc nodded reluctantly, resigning himself to a conversation he'd rather not have given his current mood.

"It seems Aunt Peggy is taking all of this better than you are," Audrey began. "She'd rather know who her father really was. She'd rather have a sterling silver replica than a banged-up artifact. And she's even accepted that her long-time *schlingel* boyfriend may have done something wrong—again."

Luc crossed his arms defiantly, incensed at being chastised.

Audrey tried to broach the subject of their own relationship without becoming emotional. Her voice broke anyway.

"What I don't understand, Luc, is why you're ignoring a story you should be investigating. Why you can publicly chastise me, your friend for the past four years and now your lover, to protect a woman you didn't even recognize three months ago. And why you can't forgive me for doing my job, even though you've pushed me as hard as you dare to be a success at your own."

Luc stared out of a window at the horizon while he tried to gather his thoughts.

"You don't know what it's like, Audrey," he began. "Growing up poor in a community where you're not expected to amount to much." He turned to face her. "My parents were upset when I told them I wanted to go to university. Not because they expected me to do badly, but because they expected me to do *well*. They were afraid I'd be gutted when I found out that hard work and good marks wouldn't be enough. They were afraid that, when I moved to the big city, I'd be treated like someone who didn't belong there, in his own homeland."

Audrey was chastened by Luc's despondency. He was normally so upbeat, so hopeful. This side of him seemed foreign and foreboding.

Luc pointed to his skin. "When I'm wearing my winter white, I'm a funny French-Canadian that guys like and girls flirt with. But when I lose the beard and get my tan on, security guards follow me around shopping malls and women cross the street rather than walk by me.

"I've learned that I can never count on what other people think of me. I can never count on getting the recognition I earn or the respect I deserve. The only thing I can count on is my family. That's why my instinct is to protect them."

Tears fell unchecked from Audrey's violet eyes. "Now I understand why you've always accepted me without prejudice, despite all my issues. But I guess I was wrong to assume that acceptance was unconditional." She paused before adding, "Ironically, the only family that ever treated me like family was yours. And the only person in your family who can't accept me as family is you."

She stood up to leave. "Your Aunt Peggy may get a call to make a police report about how she came by the bracelet. All she needs to do is tell the truth and everything should be fine. I just have to explain why I waited a few days to report it."

It was Luc's turn to hang his head. He tried to break the long silence that followed with an attempt at contrition. "I'm sorry you missed the ride in the *Snorri*. And seeing the whales. It was incredible."

Audrey managed an equally feeble smile. "There'll be another chance, I'm sure."

***

Later that night, unable to sleep, Audrey threw on a jacket and left her room—The Thorvald—in the Views of Vinland Hotel. She stopped first at the dining room for a cup of coffee before heading out to Wheeler's Cove. Annie Coulson, who had popped by to prepare the kitchen for the next day's breakfast, was unplugging the coffeemaker and planning to dump the last carafe of the day.

"This stuff will peel the enamel off yer teeth, me darling. You don't want this," she warned as Audrey held out her mug. "I'll make you another."

"No need. The stronger, the better," Audrey urged. "I need to take a walk, clear my head. Strong coffee will help."

Annie looked at her strangely as she poured. "Mind the fairies, then. There's a full moon tonight, and they be full of the devil."

Audrey managed a quizzical smile.

"You knows about Vikings and sagas and whatnot, but you don't know about Newfoundland fairies?"

Audrey shook her head, intrigued. She did know about Scandinavian elves and trolls, and Icelandic *Huldufolk.* She wondered if there was a connection.

"Newfoundland fairies are no sweethearts, to be sure. The little fellas be about two-foot high, and they like to get people into trouble. If they hits you, you gets a fairy blast and all kinds of strange stuff oozes out of the wound. To stops them from putting a charm on you, keep some silver coins in yer pocket."

Audrey laughed and said she didn't have any coins.

Annie slipped her hands into the pockets of her apron and handed over a few. "Here, take these Euros. They be no use to me as a tip; no time for the bank."

"Ah, they're not Euros, they are Scandinavian. You don't happen to recall who gave them to you, do you?" Audrey replied, as blasé as possible, as she looked at the Norse silver. She pulled a twenty dollar bill out her pocket in exchange.

"Thank you, me darling, I appreciate this. It be a local fellow, Brian Rickman."

Audrey nodded at Annie, lifted her coffee cup, took a sip, and then expressed her thanks. She suddenly had a clear head.

Down at the edge of the cove, Audrey pulled the Norse coins out of her pocket with a tissue to examine them in the moonlight. *Damn fool!* she thought. *Now you've gone too far. I have to track you down.*

She thought she heard some laughter in the bush. She glanced up and spotted the pair of well-lit, two-and-a-half-story houses on the north side of the cove. They too were full of students and archeologists working at L'Anse aux Meadows. She smiled and assumed a young couple was using the bush for a private rendezvous.

Then laughter issued from the south side. She whipped her head around, a sudden move she hadn't made since her concussion nearly a month ago. She became extremely dizzy and nauseous. She dropped to her knees, and she dropped the coins.

As she groped in the grass for the silver, she struggled to see clearly. Her ears were ringing, first with a high-pitched whine and then with a rhythmic sound, like that of an approaching train. She forced her eyes to focus.

Standing before her was a chubby toddler with tousled blond curls, cherubic cheeks, and a mischievous smile on his face. A dark blue peaked cap with a nautical slant was perched on his head, while his belly protruded under a red-and-white striped t-shirt and over a pair of khaki pants. He flipped the Norse coins in his hands with the dexterity of an adult, all the while keeping his green eyes on Audrey.

"Are you supposed to be out here this late?" Audrey asked, looking around for any sign of adult supervision.

The child remained silent and kept flipping the coins.

"Now give those back. They don't belong to you," Audrey reprimanded, as she extended her hand for the silver.

The toddler kept grinning and flipping the coins, as if challenging her to take them. Exasperated, Audrey lunged forward. To her great surprise, she missed both the coins and the child. She heard the laughter again, this time behind her, so she spun around. She wasn't sure if there were two children now, or whether she was experiencing double vision. They appeared to be wearing similar clothes, almost a type of uniform. The first child resumed his coin flipping, while the second produced a gnarled piece of wood. With a nod and a wink to each other, the child with the coins ran for the bush while the one with the wood ran for Audrey.

She leapt over the wood-wielding cherub, but her take-off foot slipped on the dew-damp grass so she didn't achieve the height she wanted. The child managed to strike her left shin with his club. The pain was excruciating. She stumbled upon landing, but summoned all her strength when she saw the first child nearing the bush line. She dashed toward him and tackled him by his foot. He let out a high-pitched wail, but she wouldn't let go. Then he tossed the coins away and she scrambled after them.

After Audrey gathered up the silver, she turned to face the children, but all she saw was moonlight turning the sea to silver as well. Wincing in pain, she scooped up her coffee mug and hobbled up the hill to the hotel.

*It's bad enough that I bump into ghosts of the past, but now I'm starting to see little people*, she thought. *If I encounter aliens, it'll finally be time to see a shrink.*

Once inside Views of Vinland, she spotted Dr. Olsen in the dining room reviewing some papers while enjoying a freshly brewed coffee. Audrey went to her room and retrieved the wolf head bracelet. Returning to the dining room, she placed the artifact on Olsen's table.

"Is that what I think it is?" Dr. Olsen asked, in a manner that could only be described as refined horror.

"I'm not sure." Audrey only half lied, knowing that further tests would be required to confirm its authenticity. She explained how she obtained it, avoiding the exact date, and hoping Aunt Peggy would do the same. Then she told Dr. Olsen that Peggy Volkov received this present, along with an old sword to clean, over a year ago in May.

"That's when the rune stick was discovered," Dr. Olsen said, slumping over her papers, and cupping her head in her hands. It was the first time that Audrey had seen Olsen's long hair loose and spilling over her shoulders. Her informal attitude and appearance made the senior archeologist seem so much younger, more of a colleague than a boss. "An arm ring, a sword, and a rune stick that says, 'Below this stick rests the body of Thorvald Eiriksson.' A local has found the gravesite."

Amazed that her mentor expressed the same conclusion she and Magnus had come to—in almost the same words—Audrey was emboldened to offer, "I think it's time to look for Crossness."

Dr. Olsen slid her hands over her face, which muffled her response. "We cannot. All the funding and approvals cover the current search parameters only. We are not authorized to look anywhere else." Then she slumped back against the booth in which she was sitting and stared straight at Audrey. "It's depressing to think that one of the most significant archeological discoveries on this continent has already been desecrated. And God only knows what else is missing."

Audrey felt for the Norse coins in her pocket, retrieved them with her tissue, and slowly poured them on the table.

# CHAPTER SEVEN
## Quest of Fortune

*A host of boats was then heading toward them from the inner end of the fjord. Thorvald then said, "We shall set up our breast-works on both sides of the ship and defend ourselves as best we can, but do as little killing as possible." So they did, and after the Skraeling had shot at them for a while, they hurried away as fast as they could. Thorvald asked if any of his men were wounded. They said they were not. "I have gotten a wound under my arm," he said. "An arrow flew between the gunwale and my shield and struck me under the arm, and here is the arrow. This will be the last of me. Now I advise you to make ready for your return as quickly as possible. But me you shall take back to that cape which I found so inviting. It looks as if I spoke the truth without knowing it when I said that I might live there some day! Bury me there with a cross at my head and another at my feet, and ever after you shall call it Crossness."*

—*Saga of the Greenlanders*

It was Aunt Peggy who broke the silence as Luc drove her truck along the road that snaked to the St. Anthony RCMP detachment. He was taciturn and preoccupied, while she watched the colourful bog, now bright with flowers and berries, glide past her window.

"The bakeapples be just about ready," she said with a smile. "Audrey wants to spend a day with me, picking and putting down jam."

Luc cleared his throat. "I don't think we'll be seeing Audrey again." He kept his eyes on the road as Aunt Peggy rocketed hers toward him.

"Ah, whaddaya done this time, you damn fool? It's not her fault we're heading to the cop shop. It's that arsehole Brian Rickman's. And it's not the first snarl for me, neither."

Luc looked back, astonished.

"Yeah, that's right. He's put me in the middle of it more than once. Can't keep his mitts off the booze, other people's stuff, or other men's women. And it's usually me that's left on the hook."

Luc's eyebrows shot to his hairline.

"So why do I still have anything to do with him?" Aunt Peggy turned back toward the bog and the sea. "Despite it all, he ain't such a bad fella. He's never really hurt no one, except himself. Broke a few hearts, including mine, but no bones or heads. Just has the willpower of a two-year-old and the brains of a goat."

She reconsidered her statement. "Well, maybe he did get into a scrap or two over the years, but no real damage was done. To the bones, that is, not the hearts. Those don't really mend." She turned back to Luc. "Which is why you best patch things up with Audrey soon as you sees her. Apologize quick as you can and be done with it."

"Why are you assuming it's me who's in the wrong?"

"Because yer a man!" Aunt Peggy retorted. "The spat's always over yer purse, yer pride, or yer power. Or all three. This can't be about yer purse since Audrey was born to money. That leaves the other two. Let me guess. She turned in the bracelet without checking with you first."

"As a matter of fact, she waited to make sure you weren't involved first. So, it would be better if you can't quite remember when you gave it to her. A 'day or so ago' should be fine." He groaned in exasperation. "Okay, I *was* angry that she didn't check with me before she had it tested. After all, you're family."

Luc lowered his head as Aunt Peggy shook hers. "Pride *and* power. That's gonna take wine *and* roses and plenty of both. Just remember, lad, women aren't the property of the men in their lives, or their beds. We're not answerable to any of you, just ourselves. Am I clear?"

"Crystal," he responded.

As he parked the truck in front of the RCMP detachment, Luc chewed the inside of his cheek. He recalled the fight on the lawn with Magnus and the fear had he felt about Audrey's safety. Regardless of how this investigation turned out, he realized he had to make amends.

Once inside, Aunt Peggy was ushered into the room where Audrey had made her statement to Corporal Anderson about Professor Osborne. This time, a new corporal, recently assigned to the detachment, would conduct the interview. Luc made a pretense of bringing his great-aunt a glass of water before the proceedings began. Just as Audrey had suggested, he finally recognized he should be investigating this story instead of ignoring it. When no one was looking, he slipped his phone, with the audio recording app turned on, into Aunt Peggy's gaping purse.

Before Luc could leave, a big voice boomed from the entrance to the detachment. "Lawd thundering, is that Peggy Volkov's truck in the front street again? What's that nephew of hers done this time?"

The new corporal glanced up at the reception window just as an outsized head poked itself into view. The other RCMP members in the room broke into jubilant grins.

"May I help you, sir?" the corporal asked of the casually dressed stranger who dared to interrupt the proceedings. The other members jumped up and hurried out of the office doorway to greet the intruder. The overly friendly giant was chastened when he saw the interview in progress.

"Pardon me all to hell, Corporal. Sergeant Lenny Anderson here. Just came with a few boxes to gather some of the gear I left behind. Carry on. I'll keep me mouth zipped and be out of yer hair in no time."

With the awkward stiffness of age, Aunt Peggy turned toward the voice and smiled. "It's me that's in trouble, this time, Lenny. Thanks to Brian Rickman, of course."

Anderson rounded the wall from the reception window and entered the door quickly. He nodded in deference to the corporal. Despite the corporal's scowl and his hands waving at her to stop, Aunt Peggy proceeded to tell the newly promoted sergeant everything that had happened. Luc remained at her side. The members who followed Anderson back into the room scrambled to sit down and type notes.

Anderson feigned disinterest. "Just tell the corporal anything he needs to know. I'm only here to pick up me kit."

Distracted, the corporal resumed the interview, forgetting that Luc was still present. Anderson packed his boxes as slowly as possible.

Dr. Olsen had passed along most of the questions. They centred on Captain Brian's whereabouts over the past year and any interest he might have shown in specific areas of the eastern coastline. When a printed copy of her statement was presented to Aunt Peggy to read and sign, Anderson arose slowly and silently.

He was standing behind the RCMP members, but in front of Luc and Aunt Peggy. He waved at Luc to get his attention. When Luc looked up, he saw Anderson raise a finger to his lips and then point at his crotch. Then he pretended to be holding his own member and urinating against a wall. Luc's left eyebrow arched quizzically. Then, Anderson pointed down the hallway, excused himself, and covertly waved at Luc to follow.

When Luc finally figured out the charade, he once again slipped his hand unnoticed into Aunt Peggy's purse, retrieved his phone, and then meekly asked if he could use the restroom. The corporal nodded and pointed in the direction that Anderson had taken. As Luc turned down the hallway that led to the men's room, he physically bumped into Anderson, who used the opportunity to give him a quick pat down.

"Is that a phone in yer pocket or are you just happy to see me?" Anderson growled. He stuck out his hand for it. Reluctantly, Luc lifted his phone out of his jeans and passed it to Anderson, who made sure the microphone was off.

"Seems to me that Audrey Vincent is key to all this," Anderson said, as quietly as he could manage. "Has she given a statement yet?"

"Dr. Olsen called to say Audrey fell last night and cut her leg. She's at the hospital now getting it looked at," Luc replied.

Anderson eyeballed Luc with the knife-like gaze of a veteran interrogator. "How come Audrey didn't tell you that herself? I thought she dumped that white-haired wuss for you."

Luc threw his hands up in exasperation, wondering if there was anyone in Newfoundland who didn't know about his love life.

"Jaysus, b'y," Anderson muttered in disappointment. "That didn't last a jig time!" Then he resumed his serious attitude, "Listen, I can't get involved in this because it's not me shop anymore, but Audrey told me she never did believe that Viking of hers was buried at L.A.M. This other stuff's that's popped up, courtesy of Rickman, seems to be proving her point."

Luc looked at Anderson warily, not knowing which side he was on.

"That girl went after a serial rapist, collected evidence against him, and snuck into L.A.M. that very night to test the drinks he spiked despite me warnings to stay out of it. Then, cool as a cuke, she walks up to the bastard lying on a stretcher and tells him to go straight to Hades."

Luc remembered the errant image of a rain slicker that looked remarkably like Aunt Peggy's, that had appeared and then disappeared on his time lapse video of the dig site that evening. Repeating Audrey's words without thinking, he responded, "Hades was the Greek concept of hell. Ragnarok was the Norse apocalypse—endless winter."

Anderson quickly deduced that Luc still had feelings for her. "I don't think a scrape on the leg would've stopped that girl from making a statement, do you?" he asked.

Luc looked up uneasily as he recalled having to take her to Gros Morne to keep her from L.A.M. after she was knocked unconscious on Canada Day.

"Does that sleeveen Rickman know he's suspected of stealing artifacts?" Anderson queried.

"I don't think so. I told Aunt Peggy not to say anything."

"Then me guess is Audrey's trying to trick him into showing her where he found them. And I bet that Norwegian ice queen gave her time off to do it. The new b'y here will get the coast guard to track down Rickman's boat, but you check Audrey's usual haunts in case I'm wrong. Are you with me, lad?"

Luc nodded strongly in agreement as Anderson returned his phone. It was his chance to redeem himself.

***

Audrey tried not to limp as she crossed the parking lot to the St. Anthony pier where Captain Brian moored his boat. "Just what I need. More stitches," she grumbled. This was turning out to be a physically, as well as an emotionally, demanding adventure. She was even beginning to think she was getting that ulcer the rune teller had warned her about.

After her discussions with Dr. Olsen the previous evening had stretched into the early morning hours, Audrey had fallen exhausted into her bed without washing up. When she awoke sometime later and examined her shin, she was astonished to find pus already issuing from it. Olsen's subsequent suggestion of a medical appointment enabled her to delay her police statement and follow up her early suspicions about the location of Crossness.

"Gawd, this wound is fousty!" The nurse practitioner had scrunched up her face from the smell as she peeled off Audrey's makeshift bandage. Her disdain grew as she debrided the cut. "You got half the shoreline in here, you daft thing. Why the hell did you not clean it before you went to bed?"

Audrey winced as the nurse used tweezers to extricate first a splinter and then an ivory-coloured shard.

"This is a fishbone! And what in the name of old lawd jaysus is this?"

The tweezers dove into the wound again and came out with a coloured shred of yarn. The nurse looked at Audrey, aghast. "I think this is from a fairy blast, I do. I've been told about this me whole life, but I've not seen one before. You've not been taunting the little fellas, have you?"

Audrey could barely fake a smile before the application of antiseptic turned it into a genuine scowl. But the six stitches that followed did not stop her from tying back her hair and pulling on her hiking boots. She silently wished she had Luc with her as backup, but bleakly accepted that she may never have his support again.

She approached Captain Brian's boat with caution, glancing around for any sign of him. Seeing none, she began to inch up the plank that led to the deck, painfully aware of the tautness of the stitches in her skin.

"Stay where yer at till I comes where yer to!" Captain Brian's shout startled her.

He quickly crossed the prow to the plank and offered an arm to steady her. "Yer limping, me dear. What ails ya?" His chivalry made her second-guess her suspicions of him.

"Just bumped my shin a little," Audrey replied. "Nothing serious, but enough to get the day off and a chance to explore a bit." Now she worried that she was over-sharing.

"So yer alone, then?" he asked, and her nervousness returned.

"For now, yes, but Luc will be picking me up," she lied, as she forced a smile. "Do you recall me asking you what speeds you were travelling between different points along the coast when you first brought Luc and me here?"

Captain Brian's face was blank. "Nary a bit, no."

Audrey produced the paper on which he had written the speeds in knots. His face was still blank. She continued. "Anyway, I noted how long we took to get from one place to another. So, if you follow these speeds in reverse, we should get to the area I'm interested in."

"And what exactly caught yer fancy, then?"

She was unsure if he was curious or suspicious.

"I spotted a good place for hiking."

Now he was suspicious. "You bangs up yer leg, so you thinks it's a good time for a hike?"

She sheepishly delivered the excuse she had practiced. "I can't crawl around in a pit, but I don't want lay around and stiffen up either, so I thought a walk in the woods might keep me in shape."

Captain Brian shook his head as he escorted her to the cabin and started up his craft. "You Flatlanders must be tougher than you look."

As the tiny tour boat skirted the eastern shoreline, he kept trying to start a conversation with Audrey, who was immersed in her notes and pertinent passages from the Greenland saga. She also checked her watch frequently and the view from a still oily window, directly across from the one she initially peered through when she and Luc first came to Newfoundland. Once again, she was searching for that "jutting cape that rose high out of the sea and was all covered with woods."

"So, you going to the Westward Viking Festival in L.A.M. this week? Should be a good party, all in," Captain Brian remarked.

Audrey replied without looking up from her papers. "It certainly should be. My parents will be here too. They're anxious to meet Benedicte Ingstad, the daughter of the couple who discovered L'Anse aux Meadows. On Saturday, she's launching a book she wrote from her mother's notes on the original dig."

"You don't say," he replied. "And they're putting up that bloody big statue of Leif the Lucky on the harbour on Sunday. Ten foot tall he be, and covered in bronze." Then he muttered angrily, "It's a shame that damned sword went missing!"

Audrey glanced up and saw that his expression of disgust was genuine. *So, he may have moved the sword from the burial site, but not from L'Anse aux Meadows,* she mused. *Perfect. There are two thieves involved, not just one.*

After a time, he cut back the engines and Audrey looked up in surprise. She scanned the shoreline and saw only wooded knolls.

"Why are we slowing down here?" she asked.

"Time's up for this last leg at the speed you asked for," he answered. "This should be yer hiking spot."

She searched his face for any sign of deception. Either the speeds he gave her three months ago were wrong, or he deliberately failed to follow them. There was no "jutting cape" in sight.

"I must have made a mistake in my calculations," she offered. "We're not there yet. Do you mind just cruising until I see the area I'm looking for?"

Captain Brian seemed somewhat exasperated, but complied. When Audrey did spot the cape coming into view, she imagined he sped up to pass by quickly.

"This is the spot!" she exclaimed. "Could you please pull into this cove?"

Again, he appeared exasperated. But, again, he complied. "Listen, me dear, this seems daft to me. You don't know where yer going and yer phone's as useless as one side of a pair of scissors out here."

"I've travelled all over the world, Captain Brian." Audrey grinned. "I've trekked across jungles and deserts and savannas, sometimes alone. All I need is a compass, a watch, and the sun. I'll be back in a couple of hours."

"A couple of hours!" he exclaimed. "What am I to do till then?"

She tried to sound nonchalant without being flippant. "I've paid for the afternoon, so feel free to fish or do whatever you like as long you pick me up at three. Is that amenable to you?"

He acquiesced reluctantly. "All right then. But sees yer back here by three on the dot. I plans to get me beer on tonight." He anchored the boat near a rocky outcropping and helped her cross a gangplank to the shore. "Remember me beer, me dear!" he warned, as she hobbled along the beach.

Audrey searched for a natural entry point into the bush. She discovered a moose path and followed it. She knew animals always took the easiest route to any destination and imagined a group of Vikings carrying a body up an embankment would do the same.

Her progress was slower than she would have liked because of the pain. She stopped to check her phone. Captain Brian was right. There was no cellular reception. She looked at her watch, her compass, and the position of the sun before carrying on.

Near midday, she stopped again, shed a layer of clothing, and drank some water. Then she heard a twig snap behind her. She realized Captain Brian and her demons were not her only potential enemies. Newfoundland was also home to bears and coyotes. She didn't know which predators were more dangerous.

Eventually, the path widened into a clearing at the top of the jutting cape. It had a slightly artificial look to it; too wide to have occurred naturally, too overgrown to be have been kept by humans. Large animals had been bedding down here, flattening the grass into huge swirls and ensuring the trees did not regain all their original territory.

Audrey strolled to the front of the clearing and looked seaward. Peering over the rocky precipice, she admired the breathtaking outlook on the placid bay below and the ocean beyond. She lifted her phone from her pocket and backed up to take a wide-angle shot. Suddenly, she was flat on her back. When she raised her head slightly to see what she had tripped over, her feet perfectly framed a small wooden cross.

Audrey spun onto her stomach so fast, her ponytail circled her head. From ground level, she could see the clearing featured a mound in the middle, surrounded by large stones hidden in the grass. As she slowly rose to her feet, she realized the stones were forming the shape of a ship's keel. Before she reached her full height, she spied a larger wooden cross in the bush on the far side of the mound. Her heart nearly ripped through her chest.

Like dreamers in a nightmare who can't run toward the object of their desires or away from the source of their fears, Audrey had to force one foot in front of the other. She stayed well outside of the stones as she approached the larger cross. Then she issued a series of gasps in quick succession and almost cried aloud. The sod had been peeled off the back of the mound, revealing a pit of peaty soil and the mummified head and chest of a man with blond hair.

For what seemed like a thousand years, she remained transfixed, unable to move or breathe. She had known there was a chance he might be somewhat preserved had they found him in the bog at L'Anse aux Meadows, but she wasn't expecting that here. Tears fell unabated when saw the definition of his face, especially his cheekbones.

Air returned to her lungs in a rush, triggering anguished sobs. She tried walking to the head of the grave, but her legs soon failed, and she collapsed on her knees at the side of Thorvald Eiriksson.

"Why do you care so much, shieldmaiden?" Thorvald's spirit asked, as he crouched before her, tenderly raising her chin with his hand.

Audrey glanced up and searched his features. Magnus couldn't have reconstructed his face more accurately with all his tools and software. Especially those cheekbones.

"We have been lovers," she answered in Old Icelandic. And then, without knowing why, she added, "For a very long time."

As she stared into the spectre's eyes, his countenance seemed to shift in flashes, as if scores of faces were being superimposed on his in quick succession. An ancient Norse myth about true lovers living many lifetimes together came to mind as she thought she saw Luc's face among them.

Confused, she cast her eyes downward to this reality and began to examine Thorvald's body like the scientist she was. Her reverie was broken by the sight of an incision under his left arm. Automatically, she reached for the latex gloves, trowel, and brushes in her backpack. She delicately brushed the dirt off the mummified skin around the rib cage that appeared to have been sliced cleanly just under the armpit near the shoulder blade. She glanced back at his spirit, confused. "The sagas say that Skraeling killed you with an arrow that landed under your arm during an attack. But this incision was made by something as sharp and wide as an Ulfberht blade."

"Is that the story my crew told Leif?" Thorvald's spirit asked. He shook his head. "What excuse did they give for not bringing my body home?"

"They said you wanted to be buried here."

Thorvald laughed. Whisky Jacks screeched and fluttered to the sky. "And my brother believed their story?"

"He was angry with them and sent them back for you, but your men soon returned, claiming they could not find your grave again. Your brother, Thorstein, came for you too, but his crew never even found Vinland."

He was wistful. "I had very good brothers. Leif was a wise leader. Not like me. He knew not to trust his men completely. I am sure he wanted to examine my body himself, to verify what they told him was true."

Audrey had to ask. "Who killed you? And why?"

"I tried to take your advice, shieldmaiden. I tried to trade with the Skraeling, not fight them. I knew Leif, as a Christian, would want that too. But my crew believed that Leif would battle the Skraeling for this land if he thought they had killed me. I do not know which one did the deed. He stabbed me from behind."

She remembered the rune stick. "Someone in your crew was loyal to you and created a grave marker. Who among them knew *jötunvillur*?"

He smiled. "That would have been Helge Thorbrandsson. He was a friend of my father, Eirik the Red, and once a member of the Varangian guard, where such covert skills were required."

"Were you even planning to live here some day?" she asked. "It *is* a beautiful place."

"It is, but I would have preferred more company." He laughed. "The only visitors I have had in a thousand years are some strange-looking elk, you, and the man who robbed my grave."

Audrey scrutinized the area all around Thorvald's body. She began to examine a rotting sack that looked like it had been cut open. "What all did the grave robber take?"

"My sword, which was buried in stones nearby so it would not rust, my arm ring, and about a dozen pieces of silver. That is all I had of value."

"Could you describe the man who did this?" she asked through clenched teeth.

"I could, but you are about to meet him yourself," Thorvald said, as he nodded toward the path. "Take care, Aud Hannasdottir. I enjoyed sharing a bed with you, but I do not want you to share my grave."

Audrey heard another twig snap and wheeled around, still in a crouch. She felt a stitch break, but it didn't stop her from reaching into her backpack and activating a GPS distress beacon. Then she grabbed a hoe with a retractable handle, extended it, and stood up—hoe in one hand, trowel in the other. *I really hope I didn't bring gardening tools to a gunfight*, she mused.

Footsteps became clearly audible just before Captain Brian emerged from the bush. He had coiled rope slung across his torso, but no weapons that she could see.

"Quite the sight, isn't he?" he said nonchalantly. "I'd have thought he'd be nuttin' but bones or dust by now."

Audrey was worried about his intentions, but felt compelled to explain the phenomenon. "A boggy peat tends to preserve bodies. Tollund Man from Denmark, for example, was originally thought to be a recent murder victim until they discovered his body was two thousand years old"

"You don't say."

She instantly regretted using the term "recent murder victim." She quickly added, "You didn't leave him exposed like this all winter, did you?"

"Na, I tucked him in nice with a tarp and dirt when I was away. Didn't want the animals getting at him. And I didn't want anyone to get hurt. I did this," he said, nodding toward the grave, "to bump up the tourist trade and make things better for everyone."

"How did you find the grave?" she asked, stalling for time. "You don't strike me as the hiking type."

He was too distressed to laugh. "Aye, but I'm a moose hunter. Tracked them up here from the creek that flows into the cove. I've seen Viking writing before, at Norstead. When I found that stick, I knew I was on to something. I thought if I left it at L'Anse aux Meadows, someone would find it and tell the newspaper what it means. When I read it was sitting on a grave, I thought I'd be digging up one of those hordes with all the gold in it."

She turned away in disgust.

He took offense. "It wasn't for me! It was for Peggy, more than anyone. That woman's put up with me all these years, and she's got nuttin' to show for it. She was losing business at her B&B just when she needed to sell the place and retire." He sheepishly looked at the ground and kicked a stone. "Turned out the poor bugger in there didn't have nuttin' with him but a sword, and I threw that to you. Nice catch, by the way."

"Thank you," Audrey responded dryly. "So, you desecrated a grave for Aunt Peggy."

Captain Brian mocked her. "The fella's been dead for a thousand years! It's not like he's got family that gives a crap!"

Silently, she answered, *That's where you're wrong*. Aloud, she said, "Well, right now Aunt Peggy is sitting in the RCMP detachment explaining why she was wearing a thousand-year-old Viking arm ring."

He staggered back a step.

Audrey continued. "And, since her silver polish was used to clean the ring *and* the sword, she's under suspicion of stealing both."

"Did she tell them about me?"

Outraged by his selfishness, Audrey had no qualms about lying. "No. Everyone knows she's protecting you, but unless she admits it, she'll be charged. She's facing jail time *and* losing her home for good."

"Ah na. Ah na. I've done it to her again, haven't I?" Captain Brian started banging his fists against his head. "What to do! What to do!"

"How about owning up to your mistakes and apologizing to the woman who's supported you all these years?"

Audrey watched him pace up and down the clearing as he swore, kicked stones, and continued to bang his head. She wasn't expecting him to pull a large filleting knife out of his pocket.

"It seems you've left me no choice, me dear. Good thing you brought a hoe. Saves *me* from digging up the rest of him." He waved the knife at the grave. "Now get to it, wha?"

"I don't understand. Why dig up the whole grave?" What Audrey really didn't understand was why she was so calm. Evidently, dead souls scared her more than live maniacs.

Captain Brian sprayed saliva around the clearing as he raged. "Because that fucking horde has to be in there somewhere! It *has* to be! Because it's about fucking time I caught a break!"

She started digging. *I was planning to do this anyway*, she thought. *Better I excavate it carefully than a madman hack away in a frenzy.*

After half an hour of Captain Brian brandishing his knife and bellowing at Audrey to dig faster, the sound of a low flying helicopter distracted them both. She reacted first, leaping at him and wielding her hoe as if it were a sword, knocking the knife from his hand and his head to the ground.

As he lay on the grass moaning, she grabbed the rope he had dumped at the side of the grave—the rope that was meant for her—and relished tying him up with it. When the coast guard helicopter lowered a rescue basket, the paramedic that came with it looked askance at Captain Brian. He was lying on his back, hands and feet straight up in the air and bound together.

Audrey shrugged. "I've never tied up a human before," she shouted over the roar of the rotor. "Just roped calves at a rodeo!"

***

Luc parked Aunt Peggy's truck and strode over to the excavations at L'Anse aux Meadow as fast as he could without breaking into a run. He intended to consult every Parks Canada employee, archeologist, and student he encountered about Audrey's whereabouts, as awkward as that might be. Alexis intercepted him first.

She approached Luc with the intimate demeanour of a romantic partner, a position she believed she now held after their shared whale-watching experience and after his breakup with Audrey. He never confirmed that status, but didn't preclude it either.

"Well, aren't you on a mission!" Alexis cooed, as she strolled up to him and laid her arm on his shoulder. "This is an unexpected pleasure."

Luc stared at her flawless features and wondered why they seemed so unappealing. He realized it was impossible to discern her true feelings, while Audrey was incapable of hiding hers. Even when she acted a little crazy, he could always see Audrey's beautiful soul. He wasn't sure Alexis had one. "I *am* on a mission." His voice held no warmth. "Do you know where Audrey is?"

Alexis stepped back, half laughing, thinking he must be joking. "Why? Has she wandered off again?" When she saw by Luc's expression she was right, she added, "What a burden her parents have placed on you! Isn't it about time they found another keeper?"

He removed her arm from his shoulder. "I assume that means you haven't."

When he marched off toward Complex F-G, Alexis ran after him. "I'm sorry, Luc. What's wrong? Maybe I can help."

Luc stopped suddenly to put an equally abrupt end to her delusions. "You're incapable of helping anyone, Alexis, except yourself. I'm not interested in you, so just leave me the fuck alone!"

Alexis was devastated. She retreated to the tent near Complex D-E to recover. Lonny Anderson was there, reading news stories on his laptop while waiting for her.

"Hi, babe. Up for a late lunch?" He grinned.

She whirled to face him. He was a reminder that she was, once again, relegated to second best. She approached him slowly, in a surging rage, and was about to sweep his laptop off the table when his screensaver popped up. Her pupils remained fixed at their widest dilation.

Lonny turned around to see what she was staring at. Then he leapt toward his keyboard to knock the image off the screen. Alexis caught his hand in mid-air, leaving them both to stare at a full-screen image of Audrey. She was crawling on all fours, bare buttocks uppermost, wearing nothing but a suit jacket, possibly a thong, and perhaps a low-cut top, but the darkness in which the scene was shot obscured them.

"Lonny, you animal! When did you take that picture?" Alexis asked, trancelike.

"I didn't take it! I didn't take it! It was on Luc's camera."

Her eyes narrowed. "How did you get a hold of Luc's camera?"

Lonny hunted for words even faster, afraid of being accused of theft as well as cyberstalking. "He gave it to me for an image download when me camera buggered up," Lonny explained. "It was during the Scoff and Scuff, the first night all you come-from-aways were in town."

Alexis' wolf eyes lit up with pleasure. "So, he gave you permission to download this?"

Lonny was evasive. "He gave me permission to download images of the evening's events. I'm guessing he had already forgotten about this particular event."

Alexis hunkered down over the laptop and expanded the image. "Oh, this is perfect. Absolutely perfect!"

***

After checking with all his own and almost all of Audrey's colleagues at L.A.M., Luc steeled himself before entering the onsite lab. As he opened the door, Magnus did a triple take.

"Hello, Magnus. Have you seen Audrey?" Luc asked, with as much humility as he could summon.

Magnus straightened up from his microscope with some alarm. "Why do you ask? What is wrong?"

Luc didn't expect his voice to falter when he replied, "I know you've tested all kinds of stuff for Audrey. Drinks she thought were spiked. A Viking bracelet. Silver polish. Even pictures of my great-grandfather. I don't care about that. Or that you were a crap boyfriend. What I do care about is Audrey. And she's missing."

What colour Magnus did have in his face faded completely. "Oh, fuck!"

Luc tried to mask his fear with humour. "It seems your English is improving. Do you have any idea where she could be? Even if it's something she shouldn't be doing. Even if it's connected to something *you* shouldn't have done. Just tell me. I'll cover for you."

The former combatants eyeballed each other until somehow, they reached an unspoken truce.

"Believe me, Luc, I kept telling Audrey to stop investigating things no one wanted investigated. That were outside her search parameters. But she would not stop. She said the truth was more important than her career."

"She told me the same thing."

"She believes a local resident has found Thorvald Eiriksson's grave and is removing artifacts like the sword and bringing them here. Audrey believes in the accuracy of the *Icelandic Sagas*. They say the grave is at Crossness, a place on a cape along the east coast somewhere."

Just then, Gabrielle burst into the lab, obviously laden with news, but she hesitated when she saw Luc. For several awkward moments, her eyes darted back and forth between Luc and Magnus. Finally, she decided to proceed with her proclamation.

"Dr. Olsen just told me the coast guard found Audrey, and Audrey found Thorvald Eiriksson!"

\*\*\*

After his hands powerfully forced every ounce of fluid from it, he plunged the sponge back into the warm, soapy water lightly scented by tea tree oil and lavender. Then, kneeling at her feet, he delicately stroked her shin while cupping her calf muscle with his other hand. Water from the sponge drizzled down her naked leg and dripped back into the basin. He repeated the motion, again and again, occasionally stopping to massage her thighs or kiss her toes.

Light from over a dozen candles gilded her pale skin. She leaned forward, damp hair falling over her white terry robe that barely shrouded her shoulders and breasts. When her mauve eyes met his brown ones, she breathed, "This is the sexiest wound cleansing I have ever received."

Luc leaned forward and let his lips brush the new stitch on Audrey's leg. Then, peering upwards lustily, he grinned. "I certainly hope so."

Audrey fell back into the easy chair with a giggle, tilting her head as she looked down at him dutifully returning to his task. "You've been on your knees all afternoon, *mon chéri*, literally and figuratively. You don't have to beg my forgiveness."

With head still bowed, Luc glanced up with the eyes of a disobedient cocker spaniel. "According to Aunt Peggy, I do." He proceeded to mock her accent—and her indignation—flawlessly. "That's gonna take wine *and* roses and plenty of both!"

Audrey laughed uproariously before she clamped her hands over her mouth and stared at the wall opposite. When her fit subsided, she poured herself a glass of champagne from the bucket to her left and asked, "Why are you at your most romantic when there are relatives next door?" This time, she was referring to her parents who, unfortunately, had booked themselves into an adjacent room in the Views of Vinland Hotel.

Luc pushed up her robe and began sponge-bathing her thighs. "Oh, there's probably a psychiatrist somewhere with an answer to that!" He smirked.

She passed him her champagne and he finished it.

"Thanks to you, I'm acquiring a taste for this stuff," he said, as he passed the glass back and resumed his supplications. "And thanks to Dr. Olsen and UNESCO, I didn't have to pay for it!"

Audrey sighed as she sniffed a rose from the bouquet on her right. "I just wish my parents hadn't swooped in for the Westward Viking Festival. They'll try to make it all about them—and me."

"And thanks to your parents, I didn't have to pay for the roses either." He smirked again.

"I feel so guilty about upstaging the festival when so many people worked so hard on it for the benefit of the community. Even Dr. Olsen wants me to hijack Benedicte Ingstad's book launch, which is something, considering they're related."

"Audrey, I took PR as well as journalism. The grave find won't upstage the festival; it will give it worldwide coverage. You found Crossness because you studied the sagas, the same way the Ingstads found L'Anse aux Meadows. Attendance at the festival will be higher, book sales will be greater, and people will make more money because you followed your convictions."

He plopped the sponge back in the basin and scooped Audrey up in his arms. "Besides, it's a bit self-centred to think this will be all about you, isn't it?"

To prove his point, he planned to ignore her admonitions to be quiet as he plopped her on the bed.

***

The second annual Westward Viking Festival had been underway for a week. Bog berry and jam-making tours, whale watching and iceberg excursions, Norse saga and music recitals, Viking-themed art and craft shows were staged across the northern peninsula. Restaurants featured Viking burgers, tapas, and martinis. Interpreters at Norstead and L'Anse aux Meadows, who were already entertaining a peak number of guests, braced for impact once the discovery of Thorvald Eiriksson's body was announced.

Luc barely had to stoke the media fires; the news spread exponentially through local sources. Dr. Miller and Parks Canada quickly alerted national media while Dr. Olsen and UNESCO proudly announced their success internationally. Since he had become the dig's go-to resource for many of these news outlets anyway, Luc was able to steer the stories away from Aunt Peggy and directly to Audrey. He wrote copy for Audrey to post on her social media accounts and website. He just left the permissions open so she could easily add images of her triumphant weekend.

His personal pampering of Audrey took place after a news conference hastily arranged by Else Pederson. He was already deeply repentant when he heard Audrey had been swept up by paramedics and transported to the hospital in St. Anthony. As soon as her broken stitch was replaced, she was interviewed extensively by the joint task force of Royal Newfoundland Constabulary, Royal Canadian Mounted Police, and Interpol. Then, before she could clean the dirt from her face or comb her bedraggled hair, she was assaulted by a phalanx of microphones and flashing cameras. All parties avoided naming Captain Brian as the grave robber. That revelation would come after he was formally charged.

Luc was determined to whisk Audrey away from his inquiring media colleagues and her irritating parents to enjoy an evening of escape for what the locals called a beach boil-up. He sent texts to a group of their friends, asking them to shelter her from questions about the discovery or anything connected to the dig.

He was surprised at how much Audrey clung to him as they left Views of Vinland, walking close to his side or slightly behind his shoulder. As much as he wanted to protect her when they first came to Newfoundland, he had spent the summer learning how much this shieldmaiden could stand on her own.

"I'm just tired from fighting madmen, filing police reports, and fending off media," she explained. "This is one time I'm quite happy for you to hold both the sword and the shield."

"I'm sorry, Audrey, but I have to ask. Did your Viking stay buried?'

"No, but wait till you see him," she answered. "Even you'll think he could sit up at any moment and talk."

It turned out to be a glorious night. The sun stayed up almost as long as the beachgoers. The breeze was fair and fresh. Residents of the northern peninsula walked to the water's edge and began pulling up seaweed and over-turning rocks. They instructed the come-from-aways on where and how to look for their dinner.

Before long, they were boiling pots of seawater full of mussels and kettles of fresh water for tea. A few fires were built beneath cleaned and polished rocks that became makeshift grills for scallops and butter. A medley of vegetables, homemade bread, and berry-based desserts accompanied the seafood. And, of course, plenty of beer.

Once sated, the locals brought out their musical instruments—guitars, harmonicas, accordions, Jew's harps, spoons, and fiddles. Just as he had cuddled Audrey in one arm when he came to this event, Luc had cradled his precious fiddle with its moose-horn bridges in the other.

It was surprising how quickly the diverse group of musicians came together on every tune. *These people sure know how to jam*, Luc thought. It was not surprising how quickly the party-goers leapt to their feet to dance.

In a province composed of small, widely dispersed communities, homemade music had been the only source of entertainment for many decades. It had spawned its own genre of folk tunes, with regional variations depending on the ethnic origins of the inhabitants. It wasn't until the advent of television in the mid-twentieth century, not long after this unique island became part of Canada, that the music of Newfoundland was brought to the world.

Some of the young men forgot about the day's events and asked Audrey to dance. She shyly declined, simply saying she was tired so they wouldn't feel embarrassed about asking. One fellow urged her to her feet anyway, before Luc could put down his fiddle and stop him. Audrey politely shuffled from one foot to another, careful not to stress the stitches in her leg again. She soon started to feel light-headed and heard the blood pounding in her ears.

As her dancing partner spun her around, she caught sight of two chubby toddlers, possibly twins, standing by some adults near one of the bonfires. They had tousled blond curls, cherubic cheeks, and bellies that protruded over their pants. As Audrey stared at them in wonder, they smiled back mischievously. Her wound ached.

Luc came to her rescue just as the tune ended. "I claim her for the next one," he said to her partner, who left with a nod. "What were you thinking?" Luc scolded Audrey, as he led her back to their lawn chairs. "Do you want to pop another stitch?" Audrey tried to find the children in the crowd again, but didn't see them anywhere.

As the pair sat down, Magnus and Gabrielle arrived.

"*Allô*, Audrey, *ça va?*" Gabrielle called out. "I hope you are recovering well from your amazing adventure today."

Audrey greeted Gabrielle equally as warmly, even though Luc shot her a worried glance. "I am, thanks. This is certainly taking my mind off things."

"Just before we came here, we got word about changes at the site," Gabrielle began, before Magnus reminded her that she shouldn't "talk store, as you Canadians say." She apologized to Audrey profusely.

"It's fine, Gabrielle. I don't mind talking shop with you two. What are the changes?"

Too embarrassed to say anything further, Gabrielle just shook her head. Magnus continued her news. "UNESCO and Parks Canada have agreed to prepare the L'Anse aux Meadows site for backfilling as soon as possible. A specialized group has already been sent to secure the gravesite until authorities allow us to exhume the body."

"That makes sense," Audrey replied. "We were only here to look for Thorvald. Hopefully, they won't leave him on that cape much longer."

Luc dropped his head and diverted his eyes.

"What's up?" Audrey asked.

Although he tried to be evasive, Audrey did know him well. "It's not confirmed—there are only rumours at this point—but Thorvald may not be going anywhere soon," Luc said.

"Wha-a-at?" all three archeologists chimed in unison.

Forced to continue, he explained. "First of all, local Indigenous groups want to examine the site to ensure the body is not one of their kinsmen."

All three slumped back in their lawn chairs.

Luc continued. "And if the body *is* confirmed to be Thorvald Eiriksson, there may be jurisdictional disputes over it."

They gasped again and leaned forward.

"Of course, Canada is likely to lay claim to him because he's been here for a thousand years. But other countries may claim him as a citizen—Iceland, which was a colony of Norway at the time, or Greenland, which now belongs to Denmark."

All three slumped back in their chairs again.

"I think it's a good time to get another beer. Anyone want anything?" Luc asked. Audrey and Gabrielle waved him off, but Magnus raised a finger to order one. Luc didn't get far before a two-and-a-half-foot-tall, 150-pound animal with long black fur came bounding out of the darkness straight at him. He shrieked and held out his hands as the beast leapt at him and knocked him to the sand.

Still shrieking, Luc rolled around on the sand trying to grab hold of the creature and save himself. The animal was joined by its mate. The two slobbering beasts proceeded to paw at Luc's clothes and lick his exposed skin.

Magnus jumped up, grabbed a log, and advanced on the pair.

Gabrielle screamed for help, while Audrey laughed uproariously and struggled to get her phone out of her purse. When she finally did, she started recording video.

"Jumping jaysus, don't kill me dogs!" a man pleaded as he raced toward Magnus. Luc was still shrieking, pinned to the sand by his attackers. One animal had an arm in its mouth, the other had a pant leg. "Get off the lad, Brawler! Molly, come here, girl. Come here!"

The two dogs left Luc alone and jumped on their owner instead.

Luc checked his arms and legs to ensure he had two of both. Magnus stood over him with the log, confused.

Audrey doubled over in laughter. "Now I have a stitch in my side as well as six in my leg!" she guffawed, as she went to Luc's aid. "Those are Newfoundland dogs, you guys, not bears. You can stop shrieking, Luc. You're safe!"

"I'm so sorry, b'y! There's just too many people here, and me dogs are too wound up. Are you okay, b'y?" the dog owner asked Luc, who picked himself off the beach and began to dust himself off.

The dogs ran up to Luc again, who stumbled backwards. "I've seen smaller cars!" he cried.

"It's all right, *mon chéri*, I will protect you!" Audrey mocked, as she approached the dogs, petted them, and made them sit still.

Luc was tremendously embarrassed but accepted the humiliation was well worth the chance to see Audrey laugh again. Not long afterward, he suggested they leave the boil-up and retire early. He knew she needed to rest for the weekend ahead.

Once back at the Views of Vinland Hotel, the couple walked as softly as they could past the Vincents' room, The Thorfinn, but the door opened anyway. Hanna Vincent appeared and smiled pleasantly at first, but her lips froze in place when she realized Luc was returning for the night as well.

"There you are, Audrey. I'm surprised you've been away so long, given everything that's happened. You didn't get any sleep at all this afternoon," she added, staring meaningfully at Luc.

Audrey chuckled. "I'm fine, Mother. We're turning in now."

It was a milestone moment: a child telling her mother she was about to go to bed with the man beside her. They stared at each other to ensure that each knew the significance of it.

"Excuse us, Luc," Hanna Vincent said, breaking a short silence. "I need to speak with my daughter."

Audrey gave Luc an apologetic glance as she allowed her mother to lead her into the empty dining room.

"This weekend may be the most important in your entire career," her mother lectured. "Fifteen years from now, when you're showing pictures of it to your husband and children, do you want to be explaining who that strange man is beside you?"

Audrey half smiled, amused. "I thought the past was your forte, Mother, not the future. What makes you so sure Luc won't be my husband?"

"What I *am* sure of is that those pictures will last forever. Are you really certain this summer romance will?"

Audrey gave Luc a long pensive look as he stood in the shadows of the hallway. She really wasn't sure their romance would last longer than the summer, but there were a couple of things she did know.

"People are more important than pictures," she said. "Memories are more valuable than mementos. I'm not going to give up either for perfectly staged photo ops."

# CHAPTER EIGHT
## Journey of Triumph

*Freydis got into the bed with cold feet, and thereby woke (her husband) Thorvard, and he asked why she was so cold and wet. She answered, with much vehemence, "I was gone to the brothers (Helgi and Finnbogi) to make a bargain with them for their ship, for I wished to buy the large ship; but they took it so ill that they beat me and used me shamefully. But you, miserable man, will surely neither avenge my disgrace nor your own, and it is easy to see that I am no longer in Greenland. I will separate from you, if you do not avenge this!" When he could no longer withstand her reproaches, Thorvard bade his men to get up and take their arms, and they went straightway to the brothers' house. All the men there were killed, and only women remained, but them no one would kill. Then said Freydis, "Give me an axe!"*

*—Saga of the Greenlanders*

Luc awoke feeling the weight of Audrey's body on his and the velvet touch of her lips on his face. Her lavender eyes twinkled when he opened his, but she kept kissing him until she was sure she had fully awakened every part of his body.

"What would you like as an eye-opener?" she asked. "Sex, sauna, or a swim in the sea?"

He arched his broad back and lifted his muscled arms in a sumptuous stretch. "How about all three?"

She sat up, straddling him, and let her dark hair fall in tantalizing curls around her breasts, nipples already alert. Her gold cartouche and silver romance rune glinted in the morning light. "Then we better get busy," she smiled. "I received an email from Dr. Olsen this morning calling for a breakfast briefing at eight, even though it's Saturday."

She rhythmically rocked her hips over his as she slowly lowered herself over him. "You'll have to coax Annie Coulson into heating up your toutons to go," she purred.

He thrust his chin skyward as a wave of pleasure washed over him. "You've done a pretty good job of that already," he groaned.

***

Luc took a deep drink of cold water from his metal bottle and slumped his long damp locks along the cedar-lined wall of the sauna. He marvelled at Audrey's energy as she bubbled brightly in conversation with Gabrielle and several other of her colleagues he could barely remember. He watched Magnus nonchalantly dip the copper ladle into the wooden bucket and pour water on the heated rocks, spewing clouds of steam into the air. He envied how casual they all were with this luxury. The Views of Vinland sauna was the only one he had ever experienced.

There had been a couple of tense moments earlier. The first occurred when Alexis exited her room, The Freydis, just as he and Audrey were walking by, hand in hand, wearing their terry robes and slippers. Also dressed in a robe and slippers, she greeted them gregariously and joined them in the sauna, sitting next to Luc. The second came when the door to the sauna opened and, through the wafting vapour, everyone recognized Audrey's parents. They were hesitant, seeing the number of people inside, but everyone squeezed together to accommodate them. Thankfully, Alexis' attention was diverted to them. Luc only wished he could divert his attention away from the sensation of her bare leg rubbing against his.

Over the summer, Audrey had inspired many of the inn's sauna-goers to enjoy a bracing dip in Wheeler's Cove afterward. As Luc lifted each knee high and dashed into the sea, he looked forward to letting this lovely lady lead him to all the delights that life had to offer.

A brief time later, he touched his foil-wrapped toutons and bacon to his brow and waved good-bye to her while she sat with the other archeologists in the dining room. She smiled and waved back, hoping the weekend ahead wouldn't prove too much for them both.

Dr. Olsen began the briefing. "I am very pleased to welcome back Drs. Lachlan and Hanna Vincent, who hosted the national television broadcast at L'Anse aux Meadows on the May long weekend," she said. The gathering murmured with surprise. "Yes, I know," Olsen laughed. "It does seem like a very long time ago."

As the Vincents joined Olsen, Else Pedersen, Dr. Miller, Alexis, Magnus, and Audrey at their table, they were applauded by a youthful, devoted following who considered them rock stars in their field. Their fans received celebrity-style smiles and waves in return. For the first time, it didn't bother Audrey. She finally felt she had come into her own and out from under their shadows.

Dr. Olsen continued. "I know all of you have questions for the other Vincent present, but I will try to answer most of them so that she can at least finish her breakfast." Audrey managed a tight-lipped but thankful smile since she had just bitten into a molasses bun.

Else Pedersen distributed photographs of the grave taken by the archeological team dispatched to the site shortly after Audrey reported the find. The photographs were met by gasps and excited discussions that had to be silenced before Dr. Olsen could continue. Even the elder Vincents were shocked. Lachlan Vincent looked at his little girl, wondering how she climbed such a steep cape, fought off a grave robber, and handled the unearthing of such a startlingly well-preserved body. He suddenly wished she had pursued a career in music instead.

Olsen went on to explain why the body was mummified and how its blond hair, the keel-shaped stone outline of its grave, and the wooden crosses strongly indicated that it was Thorvald Eiriksson. She said preliminary DNA testing would have to be confirmed before the body could be moved to the lab at L'Anse aux Meadows.

She detailed the incidents and evidence that led to the discovery of the Crossness site, and then she cautioned everyone that a criminal investigation was underway in conjunction with the find since someone had obviously disturbed the grave, removed contents, and redistributed them to L'Anse aux Meadows. She told them Audrey could not answer any questions that might relate to that investigation. In fact, Olsen had covered the details so well that, when she finally opened the floor to questions, a long silence ensued. It was broken by Hanna Vincent.

"Dr. Olsen, it's my understanding the Ulfberht sword that was thrown to my daughter during the television broadcast, the one that was subsequently stolen from the L'Anse aux Meadows visitors centre, has yet to be recovered. Is that correct?"

Dr. Olsen hesitated. She realized she had forgotten to inform the Vincents of the rumour that had circulated all summer, that a conspiracy existed between her and the Vincents to produce a rune stick and an Ulfberht sword to attract public funds for the dig and international attention for Audrey. This question was not helping to quash that theory.

Alexis sat at what had become the head table for this meeting and stared straight ahead, face immobile, knowing that many in the room would be looking at her as the source of these rumours.

"That is correct," Dr. Olsen answered cautiously.

"Is there a chance of recovering that sword now?"

"We cannot answer that question because it is part of an ongoing police investigation."

Audrey noticed the intense, brooding look on Alexis' face and wondered why she seemed oblivious to the question. The vision of another angry woman with an intense, brooding glare appeared before her eyes. That woman was also fair-haired and blue-eyed, but without makeup or jewellery. Axe in hand, Freydis entered the ancient dwellings at Complex D-E and began to attack the unarmed women inside. In horror, Audrey watched the bloodbath unfold before her, until an unnatural and uncomfortable silence jolted her back to the present.

Everyone in the dining room of the Views of Vinland Hotel was staring at her, including Alexis with her icy wolf eyes. Audrey ascertained she must have been asked a question and people were waiting for an answer. Suddenly, she became aware of the unchewed bits of molasses bun in her mouth. She gestured apologetically, pointing to her lips, and grabbed her coffee. After she had washed the bits down, she recovered with a half laugh. "Lassy bun stuck to my teeth. Sorry about that!" Almost everyone laughed with her, except her parents and Alexis. After another mouthful of coffee, she asked, "Could you please repeat the question?"

A young archeology student called out from the back of the room. "Did it scare you when you found the body?"

Audrey smiled compassionately in recognition of the student's fears. "Yes, it certainly did," she answered. "First of all, I tripped over the grave by accident, over a small cross that led me to believe I might be at Crossness. Secondly, I didn't expect to meet Thorvald Eiriksson face to face. It was quite a shock.

"Most of us don't enter archeology expecting to be medical examiners, but occasionally, that's what we become. We expect to examine the remnants of a civilization, but it only stands to reason we may also encounter remnants of the people who created it. You just have to deal with your fears and let your training take over."

Dr. Olsen interjected at this point, even though several other hands shot into the air. "I am sorry there isn't more time for questions. The other item on the agenda is the change in schedules and assignments this find has created. Please consult the information that was sent to you this morning. The discovery of Thorvald Eiriksson during the Westward Viking Festival is both fortuitous and inconvenient. We will be encountering above-normal crowds right when we need to switch gears dramatically. Remember, if members of the media or the general public approach you with questions, direct them to me, Dr. Miller, or Else Pedersen. Do not attempt to answer any questions yourself, even if you think you know the answers. Have a great day, everyone."

After three months of briefings, the crew had learned to disperse quickly, although several people hung back this day hoping to speak with either Audrey or her parents. They were disappointed because, for the first time, Audrey was proudly and warmly embraced by both of her parents in recognition of her achievement. There was also a tacit acknowledgment of Audrey's maturity as a young woman and as an archeologist.

Alexis trembled at the sight of her mentors hugging their daughter and praising her. She finally realized that, no matter how much she tried to impress them, she would never replace Audrey in their affections. The fate of the weekend, and of Audrey's future, turned on what happened next.

Alexis was the only one from the table to be excluded from a van ride to the L.A.M. visitor centre offices for a private meeting on the Thorvald Eiriksson recovery operation. Furthermore, she endured the humiliation of being stopped from entering the van by Else Pedersen in front of all the other archeologists boarding buses or bikes in the parking lot.

She didn't show up for her shift at L'Anse aux Meadows that day. Instead, she locked herself in The Freydis and plotted the next stages of her revenge.

\*\*\*

At the meeting, Audrey discussed her discovery of Crossness and Thorvald Eiriksson in unfiltered detail while the photographs supplied were scrutinized by everyone, especially Magnus. Following the meeting, he would prepare to receive the body for examination. He pointed out that, given its mummification, specialized equipment would be required to inspect the body without destroying it. Discussions ensued about the legal, moral, political, educational, and historical implications of what they were doing. It was an exceptional learning experience for Audrey to be included in these deliberations with such veteran professionals.

It was a little disconcerting, however, when her parents interrogated her as dispassionately as they might a stranger in similar circumstances. But she appreciated their level of professionalism in being able to do so. It was not only their questions, but the way in which they asked them, that gave her insights into extracting information from someone who has made a similar discovery, whether he or she be a lay person or not.

The meeting ended just before 11:00 a.m., when it was announced the group would take a brief break before being transported to Thor's Place for lunch. When most people arose to use the restrooms, Dr. Olsen approached Audrey.

"UNESCO has received a special request for an exclusive interview with you. It's for a feature article and a short video for *National Geographic*. Would that be agreeable to you?" she asked, with an odd smile.

Audrey wondered at the smile, but agreed. The room was cleared and Audrey was given time to freshen up. As she returned to her seat and waited for the interviewer, her nervousness began to build. She closed her eyes to recall the lessons Luc had given her before the Victoria Day broadcast. They returned in a rush when the interviewer entered the room.

Without introducing himself, he sat up a tripod for his DSLR camera, all the while shooting her prurient looks from under thick, dark lashes. He looked presentable enough. His blue-black hair was captured in a man bun at the back of his head and he was wearing a crisp white shirt over fashionable jeans. But he was sporting a half day's growth of beard, like someone who had forgotten to pack a razor for an overnight liaison.

Audrey leaned back in her chair and folded her arms across her chest as she haughtily sized up the reporter. "An exclusive interview for *National Geographic*, eh? It seems you've hit the big time."

"That's correct," the reporter replied, with a grin that etched a dimple deep into his left cheek. "Print, television, and online."

Then he strolled over to her side of the table and presumptuously attached a wireless microphone to her blouse without asking for permission, allowing his fingers to slowly brush her breasts as he did so. With his nose just centimetres from hers, Luc echoed a promise he had made three months earlier: "I scored a national journalism award by breaking the story on your last discovery. I plan to nail an international award with this one."

***

Audrey had hoped Benedicte Ingstad would join their group for lunch at Thor's Place. She had already read everything she could find on Ingstad's parents, Helge and Anne Stine Ingstad. Disappointed when she didn't, Audrey was still delighted when Dr. Olsen presented her with a personalized, autographed copy of Ingstad's book, *The New Land with the Green Meadows*, which contained selected entries from Anne Stine's diaries. This English translation of the book originally published in Norwegian in 1976 would be launched at L'Anse aux Meadows later in the day.

Despite repeated pleas from Dr. Olsen for her to attend the book launch, Audrey had politely refused. She knew the media would be more interested in yesterday's discovery of Crossness than in the original unearthing of L'Anse aux Meadows in the 1960s. Olsen laughed when she eventually gave up trying to change Audrey's mind. "Wait until you meet my relative. You will soon learn you cannot upstage her."

Audrey imagined she had much in common with the Norwegian medical anthropologist, especially when she learned that Ingstad's father had once transported her from Newfoundland to Norway via the Himalayas at Christmas.

"Benedicte and her parents would be pleased with your belief in the veracity of the sagas. It is that belief that led them to L'Anse aux Meadows," Dr. Olsen said. "They would be very proud of your discovery as well."

Audrey answered warily. "I believe there's truth as well as embellishment in all stories. I just think it could be detrimental to ignore any claim when there's no evidence to disprove it either."

Olsen laughed. "You are learning to be a diplomat as well as a scientist. That skill should serve you well, but I believe it was Helge's boldness, as well as Anne Stine's knowledge, that led to their combined success. Diplomacy will only get you so far. Sometimes you need to be daring."

Audrey glanced at her parents, her slightly lowered eyelids only partially shielding an "I told you so" look. Her father met her eyes directly, in agreement. Her mother, however, turned her head away from them both.

When Luc attended the book launch that afternoon, he was fascinated by Benedicte Ingstad's accounts of the discovery of L'Anse aux Meadows. He began to understand Audrey's conviction, even her stubbornness, in pursuing her beliefs when no one else shared them. That's why he didn't understand why she wasn't there.

Audrey called Luc after the launch. "I'm in meetings all afternoon. I probably won't get a chance to see you until the Taste of Vinland Gala tonight."

"What time should I pick you up?" he asked.

Audrey hesitated before responding. "Check the outer flap of your laptop bag. You'll see two tickets to the gala. I think you should take Aunt Peggy. It might be her last chance to be 'out and about' before Captain Brian is outed as a grave robber."

Luc also hesitated. "Couldn't the three of us go together?"

Audrey sighed. "I'm afraid my life is not going to be my own for a while. My parents always demand pieces of me whenever they show up. Now UNESCO and Parks Canada have claimed the leftovers."

"I don't mind tagging along."

"It's Aunt Peggy who needs someone to stand by her right now. And I don't like the idea of you standing in front of the cameras with me, instead of behind them where you belong. I couldn't bear it if my success compromised your journalistic integrity." Audrey realized she was telling Luc to stay out of her publicity shots, exactly what her mother asked her to do. She really hoped she was acting out of concern for Aunt Peggy and Luc, and not because her mother had successfully manipulated her.

Luc agreed with her on both points. "I'm sorry I squandered so much of the time we could've spent together. I wish there was a way I could make it up to you."

"Enough already, *mon chéri*. You're forgiven." Then a smile crept into her voice. "As long as you make me look good in those *Nat Geo* interviews."

"You'll look like the star that you are," he replied. "Someone must have trained you well. Which reminds me: I'll send you more shots to post online. Don't forget to blog about the day's events, even if you can't mention anything about the find. Your numbers are blowing up!"

***

For the first time since she was ten years old, and only in the interest of a possible mother-daughter reconciliation, Audrey let her mother do her hair for the Taste of Vinland Gala. She regretted it at once and sprinted to Gabrielle's room for a quick coiffure resuscitation. Gabrielle couldn't stop laughing at the teased and shellacked monstrosity as she brushed it out and braided Audrey's mane instead. As she did so, she noticed Audrey looking down at the black tights she was forced to wear to under her dress to hide the stitches on her leg.

"Those tights blend seamlessly with your black and chrome shoes. They look very stylish," Gabrielle remarked. When she saw that Audrey was unconvinced, she went to her closet and retrieved a long black scarf. Wrapping it loosely around Audrey's neck she declared, "There! Now you are balanced from your head to your feet. Just don't let your mother near your hair again!"

Aside from the scarf and the tights, Audrey was wearing the same ensemble she wore on the night the ale protection rune saved her from being drugged by Professor Osborne. She wondered if she should paint it on her nails again.

Believing that curse was behind her, and knowing her mother would recognize the rune, she decided against it.

She had to acknowledge that the rune teller had been exceptionally accurate in prophesizing the drugged drink, the journey where she would find love, all the heavy thinking and near ulcer, and most importantly, the discovery of Thorvald Eiriksson. There were only two prophecies that had yet to be fulfilled: an unplanned dunk in the sea and problems with a moose. Since she didn't consider Osborne's moose encounter to be a problem for her, she thought that hazard might still lie ahead. She cautioned her father to be extra careful when driving his rental vehicle around the northern peninsula.

***

The Tastes of Vinland Gala was held at the visitor centre at L'Anse aux Meadows. Billed as an evening of culinary collaboration and cultural celebrations, it featured local and Scandinavian musicians, a variety of products and services from regional businesses, and delectable samples of Newfoundland, Icelandic, Norwegian, and Viking fare. Audrey and her mother were thrilled to see Manitoba's Icelandic community well represented by a talented folk singer and an equally skilled chef who specialized in creating multi-layered vinarterta cakes.

Viking re-enactors, both locals and Young Canada Works students, mingled with the guests and spun their yarns to great effect. These guests included representatives from Parks Canada, UNESCO, the Royal Norwegian Embassy, and the Historic Sites Association of Newfoundland and Labrador. Since the Leif Erikson International Foundation of Seattle had donated the replica of August Werner's ten-foot-tall Leif Eiriksson statue to be erected on the harbour the next day, their representatives attended as well.

The event was designed to be a meet-and-greet affair, and most attendees wanted to meet and greet Audrey. Her parents masterfully guided her through the glad-handing. At one point, Audrey and her mother excused themselves and visited the restroom together. As they were primping in front of the mirror, Hanna Vincent noticed the new silver chain around Audrey's neck that disappeared under her scarf. Before Audrey could stop her, she had pulled it out.

"What is this?" she asked in Icelandic. "The rune for *ást*? Really, Audrey. Do you think you are in love now?"

Audrey touched the silver pendant she had purchased in Rocky Harbour and adjusted it below her cartouche. "Don't worry, Mother. I'm not giving up my scholarship to Oxford and Luc has just been hired by APTN in Winnipeg. We won't be getting married anytime soon."

The elder Vincent's jaw dropped. Audrey laughed and lifted it up again with her finger.

"I should hope not!" was all her mother could manage before she hurried back to her husband's side.

Once in the main room again, Audrey searched for Luc and Aunt Peggy. She brightened at the sight of them and began winding her way through the crowd.

"Aren't you just a princess in that dress, luv! A glittering star, indeed!" Aunt Peggy cooed as Audrey arrived.

Audrey took Aunt Peggy's hands in hers. "How are you holding up?"

"Oh, don't you worry about me, luv. I'm just so sorry I put you through the mill." Aunt Peggy's eyes teared up in shame for bringing Brian Rickman into Audrey's life.

"You've given me nothing but joy since I arrived," Audrey said, as she kissed Aunt Peggy's cheek. "If anyone dare think ill of you, just let me know. I'll go after them in full shieldmaiden battle mode!"

Aunt Peggy cackled loudly. "I heard you trussed up Rickman like a Christmas turkey!" she whispered in Audrey's ear. "What I wouldn't have given to see that. You didn't happen to take a picture, wha?"

Audrey shook her head. "But just keep that image in your mind if anyone gives you grief about him."

"I will, luv. I will."

Luc then took Audrey aside. "A friend of Aunt Peggy's will be taking her home tonight. Can you get away soon? I've arranged to make amends for a prior transgression. Please allow me the opportunity to repent."

Audrey looked at him in exasperation. When Luc appeared to be sinking to his knees to beg, she reacted quickly. "Get up! Get up! My mother's already freaked about our romance runes. If she sees you on your knees, she'll think you're proposing."

Thankful for the idea, he dropped a knee to the floor. People around them were beginning to stare.

"Okay, okay, okay!" she cried. "Just tell me where and when."

"On the beach, beyond the interpretative buildings, in half an hour." Luc stayed on the floor.

"I'll be there! I'll be there!" Audrey tried to pull him up with both hands. When Luc finally arose, gala guests in the immediate vicinity clapped, thinking she had agreed to a marriage proposal. Audrey left flustered and Luc left laughing. He raised his phone, sent a text that read, "*It's on,*" and headed for the door.

***

After apologizing to her parents, Dr. Olsen, and Dr. Miller for leaving the gala early, Audrey slipped on her trench coat and headed for the rocky beach. Thankful for her sturdy, if elevated, chrome-toed booties, she proceeded to the area beyond the interpretative buildings. She could see Luc standing there, staring out to sea.

The sun was just at the point of turning pink, painting the cirrus clouds in front of it with streaks of gold, rose, and lavender. The sky behind was deepening into a dark mauve, like her eyes. The sea below was beginning to swell in an ever-stiffening breeze. Its blue waves were on the verge of turning a steely grey.

Audrey was beginning to think she could predict this maritime weather. Usually, the sea grew calmer as night approached, but if it didn't, a storm often followed. Although the air was mid-summer warm, she turned up the collar of her coat. When she reached Luc's side, she was anxious.

"I prefer my mysteries at least a hundred years old," she said.

Luc smiled silently and peered seaward again.

"If you don't tell me what's going on, I'm leaving," she warned.

Luc pointed out to sea with his nose. Audrey followed his gaze and saw the dot of a ship on the horizon. Before long, she could also see a sail.

"Is that the *Snorri*?" she asked.

Luc nodded. "It's scheduled for the beach bonfire and fireworks in a couple of hours' time, but I convinced Finn and Cody to bring it here early so I could give you that whale-watching ride you missed."

Audrey thought of her mother as her jaw dropped. "How many people are needed to row it?"

"As a matter of fact, the oars are only used if there's no wind. And Vikings used the smallest crew possible so they could transport more cargo. With a good wind like tonight, Finn and Cody said they'd only need an extra hand or two. They might pick up a few more from the gala for the return trip."

At the point where Luc and Audrey could see three heads in the ship, they also started to hear screaming. The head in the middle had long blond hair, the ones on each side were red. As the breeze brought them closer, they could see the blond was waving something and could hear that she was screaming for help. It was Alexis. Finn and Cody were staying well away from her, holding out their hands in supplication. Alexis' shirt was ripped open.

Luc raced to a floating dock where he knew a motorboat was moored in case the *Snorri* should need a tow back out to sea. He leapt in and fired it up. Audrey jumped in after him. It took some time to reach the ship because Finn and Cody had decided to steer it away from shore and the visitor centre. Luc and Audrey continued in pursuit. They were farther out to sea than Luc would have liked by the time they drew near to the *Snorri*. Alexis recognized Luc and screamed for him to help her.

"I can't hold them off any longer!" she bellowed, as she waved what appeared to be a sword at Finn and Cody.

"She's crazy!" Finn yelled. "We haven't touched her!"

"Tell her to jump!" Audrey shouted to Luc, who glanced back as if she too had gone mad. "Tell her to drop the sword and jump," Audrey repeated. "You'll save her!"

"Are you *kidding* me?" Luc answered, as he brought the motorboat alongside the *Snorri*. "I can't swim!"

"*What?*" Audrey exclaimed. "You spent your life on Lake Manitoba!"

"In boats and Bombardiers! Fishers try to stay out of the water," Luc retorted.

"You seriously can't swim? You were in Wheeler's Cove this morning."

"Only up to my neck! Is this really the time for a debate, Audrey?"

"Fine. Tell her to drop the sword and jump. That *you'll* save her. Then she'll do it and *I'll* save her. I'm a distance swimmer, remember?"

Luc looked at Audrey sceptically until Finn yelled. Luc looked back in time to see Alexis smack a bare breast with the sword and then swing it at Cody. He ducked and she embedded the weapon in the gunwale.

"Jump, Alexis! I'll save you!" Luc called out, now afraid that she might seriously injure one of the Murphy brothers.

Alexis tugged at the sword a couple of times, then abandoned it and jumped into the ocean. Audrey, who had already ripped off her coat, booties, and Gabrielle's scarf, dove in after her.

The water was bitingly cold, but Audrey was too pumped full of adrenaline to feel it. She knew her biggest problem would be trying to see Alexis in the darkness of the deep. She stayed under water for several minutes but saw nothing. She came up for air. By this time, Finn had focused a spotlight on the area. Audrey repeated the process three more times until she saw Alexis' ripped blouse floating on the surface. She swam up to it, filled her lungs, and executed a vertical dive at the site.

Once at the greatest depth she dared to reach, she circled around 360 degrees. She discerned a large, dark shape looming near a rock. It startled her, causing her to lose some precious air from her lungs. However, curiosity overcame her, and she swam toward it. She could see it was stationary and made of metal. Swimming a bit closer, she noticed a jagged hole in its side. As she headed for the surface and the air she was beginning to need, she glimpsed a white cross with what appeared to be the outline of a Viking longship on it.

With the longest, most powerful strokes and kicks she could muster, she headed for the light above. Audrey broke the surface and gasped loudly for air. Luc was frantically searching the waves for her. When he saw her, he pointed to Alexis floating face down nearby.

Audrey swam to her briskly and flipped her over. She came up behind her, hooked her arms under Alexis' armpits, and braced her head in her hands. Then she swam on her back using powerful whip kicks with Alexis lying on top of her.

Luc cut the engine, reached into the water, and hauled out both women. He fired up the engine again and headed for the dock, with the *Snorri* following silently behind him.

\*\*\*

A month passed. Luc and Audrey were sitting on the rocky edge of an island in St. Lunaire Bay, leaning back on their elbows and staring across the sea to Norway.

"I really fucked things up, didn't I?" Luc said.

Audrey took a contemplative sip from her cobalt bottle of iceberg lager. "You tried hard to, but you've pretty much mended everything since."

"I thought you were here to cheer me up."

"Most of it wasn't your fault. We encountered quite a few people who were—what's that saying in Newfinese?"

"Snapped right off?"

"That's it. Snapped right off." She adjusted her elbows to avoid the sharp pebbles. "Most people would call me 'snapped right off' if they knew I talked to ghosts, but at least I treat both the living and the dead with respect. As opposed to Captain Brian."

"He was my fault."

Audrey turned her head and admonished him with sea blue eyes. "Now, there you go again. Taking the blame when the blame isn't yours. As your Grandfather Ghostkeeper told me, you can't choose your family, and you can't choose the people your family chooses to pick you up." She thought she saw a trace of the dimple in his left cheek.

She continued. "Then there's Alexis McQueen."

Luc threw his head back in disgust until his unbound, blue-black hair touched the rocks. "And to think I went whale watching with her."

"You went whale watching with over a dozen people. One of them happened to be Alexis."

Luc looked wistfully at Audrey. "And one of them wasn't you."

Audrey stared at the sea. "But you tried to make up for that."

"By almost getting you drowned!"

"Hey, it's the thought that counts." She gave him a sideways glance and grinned.

Luc was forced to grin back. "I did get you into the *Snorri*, eventually."

Audrey laughed aloud, sending the Black-legged Kittiwakes scurrying. "Yeah, when the Murphy brothers needed help to row it back to Norstead!"

Luc glanced down at the pebbled beach so he wouldn't laugh too. "We gave you some time to recover."

"And you picked a day with no wind so we couldn't use the sail at all!"

Both stared at the pebbles, smiling at the memory, if not at each other.

"That Ulfberht sword caused a lot of grief," Audrey recalled. "Captain Brian nearly dissected me before a live TV audience, and either Alexis or I could've killed Cody with it. I think we used it more than Thorvald Eiriksson did."

It was Luc's turn to take a swig of lager. "After everything you guys did with that sword, I couldn't believe how long it took your colleagues to remove it from the *Snorri*. You'd think it was Excalibur."

Audrey tilted her head, pondering the analogy. "But now the Ulfberht sword is back in its stone, or at least its glass case, at L'Anse aux Meadows. Something else that's been restored," she said with meaning, while staring straight at Luc. "And Alexis is back under psychiatric supervision."

"Alexis is my fault. I should've shut her down right at the beginning, but I didn't." Luc picked up a stone and hurled it into the sea. "Because she pumped my tires."

"Interesting euphemism." Audrey pretended to scrutinize Luc questioningly, who returned a look of horror. She sniggered. "My parents were the ones who recommended Alexis, so she's my fault."

"You can't choose your family, remember? Or their pet students."

"Right."

"Which reminds me, Aunt Peggy heard from her newfound cousins in Dresden, the Wettin family. They're coming for a visit next spring when the navy tries to raise Great-grandpa's submarine you found. Weird that it has the image of a longship on it, eh?" Luc said.

"Not so weird, actually," Audrey replied. "A whole flotilla of U-boats stationed in Norway used that emblem. With the theme '1200 years of Viking history'. Norse culture was part of Nazi mysticism."

"More examples of snapped right off," Luc continued, by rote. "Like Professor Osborne. That pervert should never have been invited here. Your Dr. Olsen should've checked him out better."

Audrey flicked some sand off her wetsuit. "I have a feeling she knew about his sexual proclivities. He may have even accosted her when she was in university. But there wouldn't have been anything she could've done about it, then or now. Professors still pursue students and barter marks for sex. If any of the women complain, especially in the sciences, the male governance can always find a reason to get rid of them. My mother warned me about that."

Luc stared at Audrey, knowing that he had abetted the same sexual harassment of her. "Lonny MacLeod was definitely my fault," he managed weakly.

"How so?"

"I should've supervised what he was downloading when I gave him my camera at the Scoff and Scuff."

"That was my fault, remember?" Audrey said. "I came over to whine about sharing a room with Alexis."

"I swear I totally forgot about that shot of you in the truck. It's bad enough Lonny used it as a screensaver, but to give it to Alexis, who was able to post it on all your sites because *I* left the permissions open? I got your scholarship revoked." Luc downed his beer and was about to hurl the bottle into the ocean as well until Audrey stopped him.

"My scholarship has been reinstated," she reminded him. "You can't blame yourself for something that didn't happen."

"Only because you replaced that shot with one of you in the see-through bodysuit from the Rio Carnival parade." He paused and then glanced at her warily. "Which is not the Cleopatra outfit you were wearing the night before convocation, by the way. That's still a mystery."

Audrey merely shrugged.

"The blog you wrote for it rocked, though!" he smirked. "Challenging the scholarship committee who said bare butts and cleavage contravened their moral character criteria. Calling them out for calling themselves anthropologists. It was reaction to that post—and Dr. Olsen's petitions—that made them change their minds. I was no help at all."

"*Au contraire, mon chéri.* A wise PR advisor once told me to get out in front of any story that goes sideways. Go big or go home." Audrey stared at Luc to emphasize her point. "I just took your advice. The president of the Oxford Student Union said I should be welcomed as 'a student superhero who put a predatory professor, some stuffed suits, and a missing Viking in their proper places.' I'll have a little higher profile than I would've liked, but I'm back in."

Luc stood up. He was bare-legged and bare-chested, exposing bronzed skin burnished by a summer's worth of sun. "I should never have taken that shot."

"That's the one thing you've said so far that I agree with. Why did you?"

He looked at Audrey with longing as he paraphrased his photography instructors. "I've been trained to capture any image that's engaging, exquisite, or extraordinary. You're definitely all three."

Audrey stood up beside him. "I've read reports about Indigenous peoples in various parts of the world who believe that cameras steal souls. When I thought of how many people downloaded that image for their own lascivious purposes, I felt they had captured part of me."

Luc stared upward in torment. Audrey picked up his hands. "But you've spent the past month expunging every copy of it you could find from every corner of the Internet when it wasn't even you who put it out there. I forgive you, and no harm came of it."

"Why did this amazing summer have to end so badly?" Luc lamented.

Audrey brushed a strand of his long hair from his face. "It *was* an amazing summer, but it did *not* end badly. I found the Viking I was looking for, plus a U-boat I wasn't, and you scored international bylines on both stories. You landed your dream job at APTN, and I kept my Rhodes Scholarship." She glanced back out to sea and thought of Bjarni Herjolfsson. "Maybe we need to be blown off course every once in a while. It can open up a whole new world."

Luc gently guided Audrey's chin back toward him. "What about us?"

She smiled. "You've got a career to start and I've got an education to finish. How about we reset as friends and see what next summer brings?"

With a hand still in his, she began to lead him around to the other side of the island. Luc followed without thinking about their present situation, only the immediate past and future.

"What about Christmas? Can't we get together then?"

Audrey sighed. "Unfortunately, my parents have already claimed that. They want to spend a 'Dickens of a Christmas' in England with me and then Hogmanay—the Scottish new year—in the Highlands."

"What about spring break?"

"Haven't planned that far ahead. And neither have you, from what I understand." Audrey studied Luc's face, after finally broaching the reason she was on the island with him.

He stopped walking. Tears congealed on his thick, dark lashes. "Didn't think there was a reason to," he whispered, his voice nearly breaking.

Audrey instinctively threw her arms around him and encircled his sun-warmed body. He made no effort to move his arms in return.

"Normally, this would arouse me," he said. "But it feels like being hugged by an eel."

Audrey looked down at her wetsuit and released him. Then she asked, "Do you know how old I'll be when I get my master's from Oxford?"

Luc shook his head.

"Barely legal in the United States, don't you know," Audrey said, mimicking the barmaid from their memorable double date at The Bait and Catch.

"Really?"

She nodded. "So I don't think I'm ready for marriage."

He was jolted out of his dejection. "Who said anything about marriage?"

"Now I've got your attention!" she laughed. "But isn't that what you thought you'd lost? The chance to be with me permanently?" She could see Luc was confused now, which meant he was no longer certain of his intentions. She pounced on the opportunity, picked up his hand again, and resumed their walk.

"Maybe Vikings were wise to not believe in a future, just the past and the present," she noted. "As I said on the first day we arrived, 'we shouldn't spoil the present by worrying about something that might not even happen in the future.'"

Luc walked like an automaton, devoid of emotion. "You're right. I didn't plan ahead. I don't even have a place to stay in Winnipeg anymore."

Audrey lifted his hand, kissed it, reached into a pocket of her wetsuit with her left hand, and pulled out a ring with vintage brass keys. "I vouched for you to sublet my apartment. It's right across from the mall with a heated, indoor parking space for that beautiful, chrome-covered truck of yours. It's the same place APTN parks their vehicles because the station is just on the other side. You're also within walking distance of the arena for your beloved Winnipeg Jets." She pressed the keys into his hand.

Luc perked up at the mention of his truck. With everything that had happened in the past thirty days, he had forgotten all about it. Then he felt guilty for being "such a guy", getting excited at the prospect of seeing his truck and the Winnipeg Jets again when he was losing the chance to see Audrey. And he remembered convocation.

"Your apartment is so cool, and I appreciate the offer, but I couldn't," he replied. "There's just too much in there that would trigger too many memories."

"Not anymore, there isn't," Audrey said. "I had a service pack up my stuff and put it in storage. Then the landlord painted the walls, refinished the floors, even replaced the kitchen cabinets. You won't recognize a thing."

Luc was taken aback.

"I did leave a few dishes. I thought you might need those."

"Did you happen to leave your sound system?"

"Don't push it."

For the first time in weeks, Luc's dimple reappeared. "This calls for a celebration!" He grabbed their two empties and sprinted around a granite outcropping that obscured the view of the bay behind it. As he returned with two fresh bottles of lager, he rocked backwards on his heels, threw his head back, and roared, "*Whoa!*" His eyes were saucers.

Audrey worried that he had become manic, swinging from desolation to exhilaration.

He raced up to her, shoved a bottle into her hands, and spun her around in time to see a breached fifty-foot humpback crash into the sea. Then another whale breached, and another, and another. About a dozen enormous creatures frolicked in the pod.

Luc and Audrey sprinted to the northernmost point of the beach to watch the spectacle. It was like standing at the edge of an IMAX stage. The cetaceans put on quite a show while the couple stood hip to hip, one arm around the other's waist and the other free to clink their blue bottles at every breach.

When the last spray from a blowhole faded in the distance, Luc and Audrey wordlessly strolled back to the outcropping. They were content now that they had experienced the best the northern peninsula had to offer, and that they did it together. Luc spoke first.

"So, what's up next, Manitoba Jones?"

Audrey whirled around, incensed, but Luc roared so heartily she could not bear to chastise him. It was such a relief to hear him laugh.

"I hear Parks Canada is mounting an archeological mission next summer to find the wrecks of the *HMS Erubus* and *Terror*," she announced. "Those ships comprised the famous Franklin Expedition that disappeared in 1848 while searching for the Northwest Passage. I'm going to do what I can to get on board."

"Not sure how I could crash that party," Luc replied.

"There *is* an angle that APTN might be interested in. Polar explorers have been looking for those ships for over 160 years, when the British admiralty first posted a reward for their discovery. But up until now, searchers ignored the stories of local Indigenous groups who claimed to have knowledge about where they sank. This will be one of the first expeditions to take those stories seriously, much the same way Anne Stine Ingstad took the Greenland sagas seriously and found L'Anse aux Meadows."

"Keep me updated. I may very well join you there." Luc grinned.

When they reached the beer box on the beach directly across the bay from Aunt Peggy's B&B, they placed their empty bottles inside with the other four. Audrey looked eastward, saw her tracks in the sand, and realized she had circumnavigated the island.

With compassion and love, she gazed at Luc and gently noted, "It seems you owe Aunt Peggy a rowboat." Luc's face flashed crimson, ashamed at having set the boat adrift and at what he had contemplated in coming here.

Thankful that he was now embarrassed and over the brink of despair, Audrey cupped her hands on both sides of his face and kissed him deeply. Then she calmly announced, "Well, Mr. Lake Manitoba. Here's where you learn how to swim."

\*\*\*

Audrey Vincent was the last guest to leave the Views of Vinland Hotel. The first semester at the University of Oxford didn't begin until October, so she helped to wrap up the excavations at Crossness and L'Anse aux Meadows before the latter was closed for the season.

It also gave her a chance to say her good-byes. Since he did manage to splash and thrash his way back to his great-aunt's B&B, and because his job in the APTN news room started the day after Labour Day, Luc Laliberte was one of the first to leave. He and Audrey tried and failed to make it a tearless departure at the St. Anthony airport. Neither one of them could utter the airport's identifier code—YAY—with any enthusiasm.

"If that grand-nephew of mine doesn't put a ring on yer finger by the time you graduate, I'll be some vexed! You keep me posted, wha?" Peggy Wettin Volkov pretended to be angry at Luc to hide her own emotions when she clasped Audrey's hands for the last time. Captain Brian Rickman had pleaded guilty to all charges, so he received a five-year prison sentence plus a $50,000 fine for acquiring historical artifacts. "I plans to sell me place and puts me feet up in Florida long before that wharf rat sees the light of day," Aunt Peggy promised.

Audrey bade Gabrielle Bédard adieu with tears, and a new black pashmina scarf. "You are my first and only girlfriend," she confided in French. "I do hope we can stay in touch."

Gabrielle was overcome. "But of course, my dear friend. Please tell me everything about Oxford!"

When Audrey visited Magnus Stefansson at the L'Anse aux Meadows lab, he was shouting instructions and supervising preparations to ship Thorvald Eiriksson to Iceland for the winter. Since preliminary tests had shown that Audrey, Magnus, and Thorvald shared some DNA markers, the body was being sent to their mutual homeland in hopes of confirming its identity with the comprehensive DNA database there. A permanent resting place for the Viking would be built at L'Anse aux Meadows. "Not quite the travelling companion I was hoping for, but perhaps the easiest to get along with." Magnus laughed. "You are an archeological phenom, Audrey. I only wish I had the balls to be your boyfriend."

"That's quite the compliment!" Audrey laughed, thankful they were conversing in Icelandic. Magnus just shot back a cheeky grin and carried on giving orders in English.

Dr. Ryan Miller shook Audrey's hand vigorously, and vehemently promised to put in a good word for her with the pending Parks Canada search for the Franklin Expedition.

It took quite a bit longer to say good-bye to Dr. Anna Olsen.

"I am still so amused by your blog to the Oxford School of Archaeology!" Dr. Olsen laughed. "I'm glad your scholarship was reinstated, but I can tell you from experience that the British academic establishment will not take kindly to more scolding in the future. Save your battles for bigger victories down the road. I'm sure you will have many more. You share the gift that Anne Stine Ingstad possessed. Use it well!"

Finn and Cody Murphy arrived early at the Views of Vinland Hotel to pick up Audrey for the long drive down the picturesque Viking Trail and beyond to St. John's to catch her plane. "It's the least we could do after you took care of that rimmed blond. We were some scared she'd get us in a right snarl," Finn said.

"I've never met a come-from-away who can work and fight and dance like you can," Cody laughed. "You'd make a good Newfoundlander. That's the best compliment any of us could pay you."

In one of the few silent moments as they drove along the Viking Trail, Audrey noticed evaporation fog suspended over the ocean. "Sea smoke," she mumbled, and smiled to herself.

In the drop-off zone at the St. John's airport, Audrey became alarmed when a uniformed RCMP officer quickly marched up to the truck and began to remove her highly functional, high-end luggage from the truck box. Until she saw who it was.

"Please be gentle with my large suitcase, Sergeant," she called out, as she leapt out of the truck cab with delight. "It's full of cloudberry wine and Aunt Peggy's bakeapple jam."

"Jaysus jumping Moses!" Sergeant Len Anderson groaned, as he lifted the substantial suitcase to the curb. "Did you leave any for the locals? That's gonna cost you a pretty penny to cart 'cross the pond." Then Anderson sent her off with a warning as well as praise. "Just remember those British Bobbies are right sticks in the mud compared to our b'ys. Keep yer head in yer books and yer nose out of their business. And if those tight-arsed professors give you any more grief, you can always come back and be a horseman. We'd be glad to have you."

Audrey pondered all these good wishes and many others as she tried to use a terminal to check her baggage through to Heathrow. A check-in assistant came to her aid when it was clear that flowing tears were obscuring her vision. All she could see was Luc's beaming face when his printout said they were flying first class to Winnipeg.

When she thought she had her emotions under control, she proceeded through security. With mindless efficiency, she placed her carry-on, laptop, jacket, jewellery, phone, and plastic bag of liquid toiletries into bins on the conveyor belt. She cleared the metal detector without incident and awaited the bins, but could see the scanner operator had spotted items of concern in her carry-on. He backed it through the scanner a couple of times, then set it aside to be searched. A security officer opened its zipper with gloved hands and extracted a clear plastic, vacuum-sealed bag with an official document attached.

"This document says the bag contains historical artifacts. What's inside?" the officer asked, as she flipped it over.

Emotionless, Audrey responded, "An Egyptian wig and wedding dress." She picked up her gold chain and cartouche from a tray and fastened them around her neck. "From the Fourth Dynasty."

"And where would that store be located, then?"

Audrey paused and pursed her lips while pondering how to respond. "Cairo," she answered finally.

The officer replaced the bag and pulled out a silver flask. She opened it, sniffed it, and turned it upside down to ensure it was empty.

"Why is this in your carry-on?" she asked.

"It's a family heirloom," Audrey replied, as she fastened the silver chain and romance rune around her neck.

"Be sure to declare it when you get to Heathrow," she warned, as she handed over the carry-on and the flask. "Have a nice flight."

Audrey nodded as she picked up the flask and ran her thumb over its fleur-de-lis crest. Then she repacked her carry-on and headed for the departures lounge for what she hoped would be a perfect non-fat extra dry cappuccino with just a dash of cinnamon.

THE END

Lightning Source UK Ltd.
Milton Keynes UK
UKHW040601021218
333216UK00002B/39/P